Praise for BLACK WOOD

'A fast-paced and chilling psychological thriller from an exciting new talent. If you liked *Broadchurch*, you'll love this.' – Mark Edwards and Louise Voss, authors of *From the Cradle*

'In her atmospheric debut, Holliday effectively and spookily evokes small-town claustrophobia and backbiting. An edgy and authentic new voice in crime fiction.' – Anya Lipska, author of *Where the Devil Can't Go*

'A dark and complex tale about small-town life, *Black Wood* will appeal as much to fans of outsider fiction like *Vernon God Little* as it will seasoned crime readers.' – Nick Quantrill, author of *The Crooked Beat*

'Darkly atmospheric and utterly absorbing.' – Jane Isaac, author of *The Truth Will Out*

'A plot which weaves and twists its way around a tight knit community. . . [where] old sins return to haunt some damaged people and the atmosphere is thick with unspoken dread . . . You won't read a more shocking, or satisfying, thriller this year.' – James Benmore, author of *Dodger*

'A deeply unsettling story of bad deeds, complex loyalties and secrets better left buried, *Black Wood* is a thrilling debut which grips from the very first page and doesn't let go.' – Eva Dolan, author of *Long Way Home*

'Holliday has a knack for creating fascinating, well-observed, and sometimes quirky, characters. *Black Wood* is dark and twisty with a creepy atmosphere that pervades this compelling tale from first page to last. I was gripped. A fantastic new voice on the block.' – Amanda Jennings, author of *The Judas Scar*

'Hugely satisfying twists and great characterisation, creepy and astute.' – Sarah Hilary, author of *Someone Else's Skin*

'A chilling exploration of the darkness that can hide in even the smallest of communities. A superb debut.' – David Jackson, author of *The Helper*

'In *Black Wood*, S.J.I. Holliday has created a small town whose inhabitants are full of dark secrets, rumour, betrayal and murder. A touch of humour, a twist-filled plot and the writer's obvious skill in creating an unsettling and yet all too familiar backdrop, make this a hugely enjoyable page-turner. A must-read for crime fans.' – Steve Cavanagh, author of *The Defence*

'I was drawn into *Black Wood* – drip-fed with intrigue, mystery and menace. It has an absorbing storyline with interesting and engaging characters. An exciting debut novel.' – Mel Sherratt, author of *Watching Over You*

BLACK WOOD

BLACK WOOD

SJI HOLLIDAY

BLACK & WHITE PUBLISHING

First published 2015
by Black & White Publishing Ltd
29 Ocean Drive, Edinburgh EH6 6JL

1 3 5 7 9 10 8 6 4 2   15 16 17 18

ISBN   978 1 84502 953 1

ALBA | CHRUTHACHAIL

Typeset by RefineCatch Limited, Bungay, Suffolk
Printed and bound by Nørhaven, Denmark

To Ali Bali Bee, for letting me read the scary books.

I am a forest, and a night of dark trees: but he who is not afraid of my darkness, will find banks full of roses under my cypresses.

Friedrich Nietzsche

THE WOODS

He spots the two girls through the cracked screen of beech, sycamore and leg-scratching gorse: a flash of red skirt and a unison of giggles.

He waves a hand behind him, silently gesturing for the other boy to stop walking.

They hunker down behind a giant felled oak, and watch. The one with the red skirt sits astride a rusty water pipe that juts out through the hard-packed mud on either side of the burn. Her long, skinny legs dangle like the branches of a weeping willow, her sandalled feet almost skimming the water that bubbles beneath.

'Come on, scaredy-cat!'

Her face is turned in the direction of the far bank, watching the path that runs down the side of the neat little row of square seventies housing where all the *nice* families live with their panel-fenced back gardens and their rabbit hutches and their Swingball sets. Where the other girl stands: shorter, plumper and dressed in denim dungarees and a pair of blue wellingtons.

'I can't. It's too fast.'

The water is high from the rain that has barely stopped for weeks. The ground is soggy, and the boys' footsteps have disturbed the mulch on the floor of the wood, releasing a stink that reminds him of clothes that've been left too long in the washing machine mixed with the tang of fresh grass from the bucket on his dad's lawnmower.

He hears the snap of a twig close behind him and whirls round.

'Ssssh, you idiot. Don't let them hear us.'

The other boy mumbles a sorry.

The girl with the red skirt turns back to face the wood and he holds his breath, desperate not to make a sound. She frowns and shakes her head and dark little curls bob around her face. She is younger than he is. A couple of years. Maybe the same age as the pudgy-faced one in the dungarees, but even from this distance he can tell she's going to be a heart-breaker before long. He stares at the long bare legs straddling the pipe and feels the stirring in his trousers that's becoming increasingly familiar.

The other girl takes a tentative step towards the pipe.

'I'm not going over it like you,' she says haughtily. 'I'll get my dungarees dirty.'

The other girl lets out a dirty little laugh and shuffles over to the end of the pipe, then leans forward and grabs the pro-truding roots of the ancient oak that overhangs the waterway. As she pulls herself up, the front of her baggy T-shirt gapes open and he strains his eyes to see what's concealed beneath. The other one steps onto the pipe and, with arms held out like a tightrope walker, slowly makes her way across, until she is close enough to grab onto her friend's outstretched hand.

He waits until they are both safely away from the bank before he grabs the sleeve of the other boy and they both stand up. The smaller girl sees them first and she lets out a strange little squeak and jumps back, grabbing onto the other girl's T-shirt, revealing a flash of milky-white shoulder.

He grins.

2

1

The routine calmed me. Smoothing an eyebrow upwards, pulling the skin taut, gripping a wiry little hair between sharp metal pincers.

A little nugget of pain. Just for a moment.

Sometimes, if it was a particularly deep-rooted hair, or if I'd dug in just a little too hard, a little bubble of blood would form: a dark, shiny pearl. When that happened, I'd stop for a minute and just stare at it until it sealed itself over before I continued.

I placed the hand mirror and the tweezers by the side of the bed and kicked off the tangled sheets; the movement caused a waft of fetid air to puff out from the bedding. My stink, mixed with Scott's. His imprint burned into the fabric.

Sun was streaming through the blinds; the only sound was the persistent whine of next door's dog. I knelt up on the bed and stared out of the window. Bob the terrier was sporting his usual ridiculous red bow. The barking had always annoyed me, but I knew I was going to miss that silly little dog. I watched him for a moment, running about on the small patch of lawn, sure that he preferred that to being carried in Mrs Goldstone's oversized shopping bag. No animal liked to be trapped.

I glanced around the room, at the piles of clothes and half-packed suitcases. The wine glass by the bed, tinged with red.

The big green numerals on the alarm clock taunted me. Seven fifty-eight . . . -nine. I couldn't put it off any longer.

'Bob, come on, baby – breakfast's ready . . . Bob? Where are you, Bob?'

Her shrill voice penetrated my already banging skull. I slid off the bed and crouched low. I didn't want her spotting me. Bridie Goldstone would have a field day when she found out I'd gone.

Scott would be inundated with offers of home-cooked meals and his washing put on. She'd think it was me who left him. I could hear her now: 'I always thought she was a bit flighty, that one.' She had me all wrong. She had no idea how I felt about Scott. It's just that sometimes I wasn't very good at showing it. I was grateful, though. Grateful that he'd gone and left me to pack up my three years' worth of things with a little bit of dignity.

I plucked jeans and a T-shirt from the floor. The T-shirt looked dark under the armpits, but a quick sniff said I'd get away with it. Just. I smoothed my hair down over my ruined eyebrow, had a quick squirt of body spray. It'd have to do. On the way out of the bedroom I caught a glimpse of my gran's watch, lying on top of a pile of books. It was the only jewellery I wore. I slid the old-fashioned bracelet over my wrist, pressed it against my chest. The clasp clicked weakly into place and I felt that familiar shiver telling me she was close, watching over me. My other hand was occupied with hitting speed dial on my phone.

I was downstairs in the kitchen by the time he answered. The blind was closed, and the sunlight pressing against it gave the dark cabinets a thick marmalade hue. I'd planned to sand and paint them. Yellow, maybe, in attempt to brighten the place up. To brighten us up. Too late now.

4

'It's me. Can you pick me up please? I've got some bags and stuff . . .' My voice came out muffled, as if I had a bad cold.

'Jo? Are you crying?'

Shit. I needed to hold it together. 'No. I've got the flu or something. Can you come and get me?'

'Maybe you should stay in bed. I don't want to be catching anything and . . .'

'Craig! Please . . . I'm . . . I've . . . Look, Scott's kicked me out, OK? I need you to take me to . . .' I hesitated for what I hoped was the right amount of time. 'To Claire's . . .'

I heard the sound of keys jangling and a door being slammed shut. 'I'm on my way,' he said, 'and Jo?'

I sniffed. 'What?'

'You're coming to mine. No arguments.'

I pressed the button to end the call and slid down the dishwasher door onto the kitchen floor. Thank God for that. I was worried that the bluff would backfire and I'd be dropped at Claire's doorstep ready to be greeted by her 'Well I don't really want you to be here but I'm not going to say that' face, having to pretend I couldn't see her parents' disapproving faces peeking out from behind their twitchy curtains in the house next door. I still remembered that day I turned up on their doorstep a month after Claire had come home. We were eleven, and our lives had been turned upside down. We needed each other. So that we could try to make sense of it all.

'I just want to see her,' I'd begged, my voice thick with tears.

'Stay away from her, Joanne. She doesn't need friends like *you*.'

2

I understood unhappiness from a young age. My dad never wanted me. He wanted my mum all to himself. He told me as much when he took me to school on my first day. Instead of being excited about meeting new friends, learning new things, wondering what I was going to get for my lunch . . . instead of all that I felt scared.

Ashamed.

While all the other kids' mums and dads kissed them and handed them their lunch boxes filled with crusts-off sandwiches and chocolate biscuits and own-brand crisps, my dad had pushed me into the playground with the words, 'Pity you can't bloody stay here. I might get to spend some time with your mother for once.' He'd slapped me playfully on the bum, but I could tell by the tone of his voice that he wasn't joking.

My fantasy world had begun before that, though. They say you can't remember anything before the age of three or four, but I can vividly remember being left to play on my own, surrounded by empty cereal boxes and egg cartons that I used to make into castles while I pretended I was a princess. I never really minded. I made up characters in my head and I just assumed it was normal. Why wouldn't I?

I'd already met Claire by then, and I'd hoped she would see me as an ally, both of us starting school together, a bit of history to form a fragile bond. I spotted her on the other side of the playground surrounded by similar girls with similar plaited hair and neat knee-length skirts. My hem was too long, because my mother couldn't be bothered to take it up, and my hair was pulled back into a rough ponytail with an elastic band. I could feel the cheap rubber nipping at the hairs at the nape of my neck. I smiled, but when she caught my eye her cheeks went pink and she turned away. I was confused, but I knew I wasn't welcome.

The only person who didn't seem to be in a group was a small skinny boy with glasses and an eyepatch. His jumper was grey and frayed at the cuffs. Everyone else was wearing navy blue. As I walked towards him, he scuttled backwards like a crab and I could tell straight away that he was just like me.

'I'm Jo,' I said, dropping my gaze a bit. I pulled at the bottom of my jumper, turned my knees outwards until I was standing on the outside edges of my shoes. He stopped, stared at me.

'Um . . . I'm Craig.' His eyes were round with wonder that someone was actually talking to him. He'd no idea that I felt a little flutter in my stomach, because someone was talking to *me* . . .

Maybe it wasn't going to be so bad after all.

How wrong I was.

Craig became my boss, amongst other things. He gave me a job in the shop he managed when I moved back to Banktoun from Edinburgh. I'd had to convince him over several pints of 80/- and packets of plain crisps that I was reliable and that I wasn't going to freak out again and run away. I was OK now, I'd insisted.

And I was.

For a bit.

The shop had become quite a feature on the High Street since the owner had bought the bakery next door and knocked through. It was definitely as big as shops got in Banktoun. Edinburgh was only fifteen miles away, but for some people that was something that involved weeks of planning and a special shopping outfit. For others, it was all about standing in the rain to catch the express bus so you could get to work without taking the scenic route through every town and village along the way. The local council were trying hard to convince people to 'shop local' and for Banktoun Books, at least, it was working.

We made an effort. We had a loyalty scheme. We had book signings, and kids' clubs, where I always had to spend two hours afterwards wiping sticky fingerprints off the hardback picture books and finding the ones that'd been 'hidden' beside travel and cookery or left in haphazard piles under the miniature plastic tables. I enjoyed it, and I couldn't think of any other job I'd rather do.

Even with the worst hangover in the world, there was barely a day when I didn't want to go into work. Not many people could say that. Especially not Scott, who was one of the '7.10 Express Gang'. He detested his job in the bank, but he'd been there since he was seventeen and I couldn't ever see him having the balls to leave the place. One thing I wouldn't miss were his stuck-up colleagues who thought they were special because they spent all their wages on Next 'office wear'. I'd always tried my hardest, but somehow I was never good enough for them.

The more I thought about it, the more I thought he'd done me a favour.

'It's just not working, Jo, is it?' he'd said.

I'd just made the tea, which was a new chicken pasta thing that I'd discovered by flicking though the latest Jamie Oliver during a quiet spell. It'd taken twice as long as it was meant to, and the kitchen looked like the aftermath of a botched burglary. We were having it on trays and *Hollyoaks* was on – one of Scott's guilty pleasures. It wasn't my cup of tea, but I always gave in and let him watch what he wanted.

'Mmm?' I said, through a mouthful of pasta.

'Us. This,' he said, standing up and carrying the tray through to the kitchen.

'Aren't you eating that?' I blurted, shocked at his sudden turn.

I heard him slam the plate into the sink, kick the door of the dishwasher. I went through and found him leaning on the worktop, head in his hands. I'd been ravenous while cooking, but suddenly it felt as if my insides were falling out, like when you drive too fast over a hill.

'Is there someone else?' I said. One of those questions that you don't really want the answer to, but you find yourself asking anyway.

He stood up and rubbed his hands across his face. There was a slight bristling sound as his palms found the five o'clock shadow and I realised that he hadn't even kissed me when he got in. I'd been so busy with the cooking that I'd been oblivious to his awful mood.

'It's not Kirsty, is it?'

I said this nervously, because I was sure I was right. Kirsty was his latest office obsession. There had been a few. Generally, I didn't think he'd done anything apart from sniff around them like next door's dog, but there was something different about Kirsty.

9

'Scott?'

He sighed, stood up straight and put his hands on my shoulders. I stared up at him. My lip started to quiver, because I knew what was coming, even though it had come from nowhere. He hadn't even eaten his tea, which wasn't like him at all. He picked up his keys. 'I'll go to my mum's tonight. Give you some space.'

I let him go without another word. I felt hot tears running down my cheeks. Noticed stringy drips of pasta sauce stuck to the side of the pot, already congealing.

3

Craig pulled into the parking space outside Harrison's Pharmacy and killed the engine.

I frowned.

'Aren't we going to the flat?'

He pulled his keys out of the ignition.

'Nope. Sharon's in the shop on her own. Come on.'

I didn't bother arguing. I glanced over at the back seat, littered with piles of clothes that I didn't have enough bags for. The boot was jammed full of books and CDs and whatever other junk I thought was mine and not Scott's. The last thing I wanted was the humiliation of going back round to collect anything else.

Bridie Goldstone's curtains had twitched the entire time we'd dragged stuff out of the house and bundled it into Craig's clapped-out 'retro' Fiat Panda.

His primary reason for keeping it, despite it breaking down at least once a month, was to wind up his partner. Rob drove a brand-new BMW and refused to set foot in Craig's rust bucket in case he got his shiny suit trousers dirty. They'd met up town one night in the aptly named ManGrove, and despite their apparent opposing personalities they'd been together for nearly six years. I still wasn't sure what Rob thought of me. We seemed to circle around each other like cats defending their territory. Craig was the scratching post in the middle.

We cut through the bollard-ended lane that connects the High Street with Monkton Road, locally known as 'the Back Street', which is the only place you can park in the town centre since they smothered the rest of it in drab block paving. One day, a town planner would come up with a different-coloured brick and there'd be a revolution, but until then we were stuck with ubiquitous orange spattered with dirty grey splurts of discarded chewing gum.

The town clock chimed half nine and the High Street was slowly waking up. Old biddies with wheelie bags on their way to the butchers. Men in dirty jeans, smoking outside the bookies. Later there'd be shuffling kids, nattering mummies with posh prams. The usual small town suspects.

And for the first time in a very long time, I didn't want to go to work. I wanted to curl up on Craig and Rob's massive puffy sofa and drink hot chocolate and watch a load of those TV movies where they always have a happy ending.

A glance through the window revealed nobody in the book-shop, except Sharon, our part-time assistant. Craig had taken her on for the summer, but we both got the distinct impression that she didn't want to leave. She seemed to like working there with us, even though I got the feeling it was more about the social aspect than doing any actual work.

She was standing behind the counter aggressively stabbing buttons on her mobile phone. The bell over the door tinkled as we walked in and she casually dropped her phone and looked up, hands scuffling about the counter as she tried to pretend she'd been tidying up the 'Keep Calm and Carry On' notebooks that were stacked up next to the till. The phrase was getting tired now and we were struggling to shift the things. She tossed a lock of hair as black and shiny as fresh tarmac away from her face. Her purple eyeliner was flicked up in a 'V'; a silver ring stuck out of her right nostril. I preferred yesterday's diamond stud. She had one of those small pin badges stuck to her black shirt. It said 'Bite Me'.

Her eyes flitted from Craig to me.

'Oh, sorry, I . . . Jo! What's happened to your eyebrow?'

She had that way of sounding nosey, shocked and concerned at the same time. It was a common trait in this town, where no one could resist poking about in other people's business. It was something I was used to, having lived here all my life – well, apart from the brief, miserable stint up town – but it was still irritating when you wanted to keep some things private. Oh well. She would find out about Scott and me soon enough. I hastily smoothed my fringe down over my left eye. 'I'm tidying the stockroom today,' I said, scurrying past the counter with my head down so she didn't get the chance for another gawp.

Craig, who saw himself as an amateur psychologist, had told me once that my eyebrow-plucking thing was an indicator that I was about to have one of my *turns*. He used that phrase ironically, trying to laugh off the full extent of what could happen when my mood swung into a downer. I could tell when we were in the car that he was losing patience with me. He didn't have time for this now. He had a wedding to plan.

So I tried to reassure him that I was fine, but I think I was trying to convince myself.

Craig was right, though. I hadn't done the plucking thing in months. Oddly enough, I'd felt happy lately. I should've known it wouldn't last. It'd be less of an issue if I didn't do something quite so noticeable. I stared at myself in the kettle as I waited for it to boil and the convex distortion made me look small and scared.

'Fuck him.'

I spun round. 'Jesus, you made me jump!'

Sharon stood at the door to the stockroom, hand on hip, her mouth curled in disgust. So Craig had told her, then.

'I always thought he was a bit of a knob. Can I have ginger and lemon, please?'

She nodded towards the worktop, where seven kinds of tea were stacked up in little boxes. I only drank Nescafé, but Craig had given in to Sharon's wanky New Age herbal thing, although every time he made his own tea he 'accidentally' used a bag of PG Tips that he kept under the sink. I wasn't sure who he was trying to impress. Certainly not Rob, because he had one of those five-hundred-quid coffee machines that did everything except fly to Costa Rica to pick the stuff.

I dropped teabags into mugs of boiling water. 'You hardly knew him, Shaz.'

She blew air through her nose and counted to three before she replied. It really wound her up when I called her 'Shaz', so she had to go through the breathing ritual before she could speak.

'I knew him enough to know he had bad energy, Jo . . .'

I wanted to slap her. Who was she to tell me things about Scott? Instead I handed her the mug and she blew on it and gave me a patronising smile. Then she picked up Craig's mug and headed back through to the shop.

'Oh,' she said, nodding towards a stack of books piled up behind the door, 'can you bring that top one through, please. Customer's here to collect it . . .'

I picked up the book. *Javascript: The Good Parts*. A website design manual. There was a Post-it on top that said 'Gareth Maloney. Sat AM.' I flipped the book over to read the back and pushed the door open with my foot. I had a mug in one hand, the book in the other. My head was down, so I didn't notice who was in the shop, but I'd sensed that it still wasn't busy.

A man stood bent over the counter, scribbling his details onto the little form for the loyalty card thing. I really didn't pay much attention until he stood up straight and turned to face me.

I froze.

An image from a long time ago flashed in my mind . . . cold, dark eyes. I'd caught only the briefest glimpse that day, but it was him. I was sure of it.

I tried to blink the image away, but it stayed. A sudden wave of nausea washed over me.

'Ah, here she is,' Craig was saying. His voice sounded like it was coming from underwater. 'Jo, Mr Maloney's a web designer. I was just telling him that you're *our* resident design whizz . . .'

He let his sentence tail off.

I started shaking; my hand wobbling so much I was in danger of spilling coffee all over the book. I was only vaguely aware of Sharon at my elbow, lifting the mug out of my hand.

Gareth Maloney. After all these years, I finally had a name . . .

'Jo? Are you OK? Maybe you should sit down—'

Maloney stared at me, his expression unreadable.

You don't remember me, do you? I thought.

But how could either of us ever forget?

15

THE BOY

They wait until darkness falls. The house blanketed in black.

'Will we get in trouble?' the boy says. He already feels the pins and needles. The little bubbles dancing inside his stomach.

'Not if you keep quiet. Stay close to me. Keep your gob shut.'

The boy follows. He wonders why they don't take the car, but he doesn't ask. They walk across fields, keeping tight to the trodden paths that line the edges.

By the time they reach the wood, he is panting slightly.

The man walks fast. He has longer strides than him. The man carries a bag on his shoulder. An old military thing. Soft canvas. Long.

Long enough for the shotgun.

The boy thinks about the other things in the bag. He shivers.

The boy has always been fascinated by the traps.

Strong circles of metal. Big sharp teeth.

He is not allowed to shoot. 'When you're older,' the man says.

Each time they go, he is older than the last. But he is never old enough.

The man lays the bag on the bark-mulch floor. The zip makes a loud noise in the silent wood. The birds are sleeping. The crows, the sparrows, the finches. The noisy, happy birds.

Other birds are awake. The owls. The boy can feel their bright-eyed stares reaching him from their nests in the trees.

A solitary *twhoo* confirms their presence.

They are waiting to see what happens next. There is a scurrying in the undergrowth. Mice, voles. Maybe foxes. Rabbits? The man lifts the torch from the bag, flicks it on. He holds it under his chin.

'Boo,' he whispers.

The boy grins.

The man lifts the shotgun from the bag. Snaps it open. Checks the ammunition.

'Come on then,' he says.

The boy takes his cue. He lifts the traps from the bag. One. Two. Three.

'Now remember . . .'

'I know, I know,' the boy says. He is not stupid. This is not his first time.

He takes the first trap, snaps it open. The man shines the torch and the gleaming metal teeth glow like a monster's snarl in the dark.

He fastens the little clip at the side, careful not to put his fingers anywhere near the gaping maw.

He places the trap on the ground, at the base of a dark, rotting oak. Its drooping, diseased branches hang like tentacles. Ready to grab.

The man walks deeper into the woods. The shotgun cocked. Ready.

The boy lays two more traps.

Then follows.

'How much further?' the boy says. He is tired. The wood is still quiet. The inhabitants can sense the danger. They stay in their holes.

He follows the man deeper into the woods. There is no light. It has been sucked up into the ether. The only thing to guide them is the torch. The boy follows the beam up ahead. Listens to the sounds of their two sets of footsteps crunching on tiny twigs.

Snap. Snap. Like bones.

The man stops. 'Ssh,' he says, 'see that?'

The boy follows the beam of the torch. It ends at shining dark eyes.

He sees the stripe, silhouetted in the spot of light.

A badger! They've never had a badger.

The man hands the torch to him. The shotgun is cocked and ready.

He shoots.

There is a low groan, a whimper. Then a *fluhmp* as the animal drops to the stinking, damp forest floor.

The metallic reek of blood, the smoky tang of fresh shot.

4

Sergeant Davie Gray rolled the centre pages of the *Banktoun Mail and Post* into a ball and launched it overarm towards the metal bin. It bounced off the rim and seemed to hover for a second before it fell to the floor.

'Ooof! Close, but no cigar.' PC Callum Beattie spun across the room on his wheelie chair and picked up the paper, then rolled back and seemed to take an inordinate amount of time to line up his shot.

'Get on with it, man,' Gray said. He was getting bored of the game now. He'd missed three in a row, the third being the only one to touch the bin at all. Beattie, of course, had managed to get all five of his goes bang on target.

The phone rang. Beattie flinched just as he released the paper ball and it went wide, bouncing on the worn navy carpet before coming to a stop. He swore.

Gray picked up the phone and held a quieting finger to his lips.

'Banktoun Station. Sergeant Gray speaking. How can I help you?'

'It's me. Got a job for you. Hope you're not too busy . . .' The voice implied it knew they were anything but. Not for the first time, Gray wondered if his boss had the CCTV feed going direct to his BlackBerry. Luckily Beattie always remembered to reposition the camera that faced the area behind the counter when they were on the skive.

'Oh, er, good morning, sir.' Gray rolled his eyes at Beattie. Beattie stood up and mimed someone swinging a golf club. Inspector Gordon Hamilton jeopardising his Saturday-morning tee-off time to call the station? This must be good.

'I've had a call from Martin about someone making a pest of themselves up at the Track. Nothing's actually happened. Yet. Best go and take a look, though, eh? I said you'd call him. Right. Got to go.' He hung up before Gray could reply.

Gray stared at the phone as if it was a poisonous snake, then placed it back in the cradle and sighed.

Councillor Martin Brotherstone was one of Hamilton's cronies from the Rotary Club. He lived up at the new houses (the ones that Gray liked to call 'Lego Mansions') that bordered the old railway line that the locals called 'the Track'. There'd been no trains on it since the late sixties and now it was all marked trails and bark-mulch paths, the unruly trees and bushes stripped back. It was popular with dog walkers and joggers during the day. At night it was a haven for underage drinkers, the bushes rustling with the low sounds of couples looking for a 'secret' place to shag. It was just him and his son, Pete, who was one of those lads that the older folk liked to call 'slow'. Gray wasn't sure if it was autism or some other thing that affected the boy. It wasn't something that people talked about. Brotherstone's house directly overlooked the railway line and he spent most of his time spying on people who went about their daily business. This was part of his campaign to reinstate the line, arguing that by running trains again he could rid the town of the riff-raff and delinquents who spent their time hanging about at its peripheries, just waiting to cause trouble. The fact that there rarely was any trouble up there was by the by. On a particularly slow evening, Gray would take a drive up there to

20

scare away the underage drinkers, but most of the time he just let them be.

The crime rate in Banktoun was pathetically low.

Their current community objectives included managing antisocial behaviour in the Back Street, keeping an eye on the drug dealers that frequented Garlie Park (both of these, unsurprisingly, only occurred after pub closing time), and, Gray's personal favourite, dishing out warnings to folk who parked for more than the allotted half-hour at the bottom end of the High Street where it led down to the river path. They'd once had a traffic warden to deal with that particular task, but she'd been deemed 'economically non-viable' in the last budget cut. Plus, she'd been a miserable, ticket-happy witch who'd had the cheek to ticket Gray's car when he'd only nipped in to collect his Chinese.

It had been *years* since something of any significance had happened. The usual small town stuff. A missing husband who turned up days later with a stink of some other woman's perfume and his tail between his legs.

There was only ever that one guy who never ever came back.

Gray occasionally wondered if he'd turn up on the other side of the world sometime. Then there was that thing with the kids down by the burn, and the attack in the park – the non-attack, really, as she'd refused to report it formally, despite his best efforts to get her to make a statement. You got the occasional assault, usually between drunken rivals. Nothing very exciting, but, in truth, that was how he liked it. This thing at the Track would be kids mucking about. Nothing more.

He picked up his hat.

'I'm nipping out, Callum. Act sharp, son.'

'Eh? Ach, come on. I'm bored shitless here. Can I come with you?'

'Naw. Lorna's no' coming in. You'll need to stay put, in case the Big Ham phones back. Tell him I'm away up to the Track for a look. See you later.'

Sunlight was bouncing off the windscreen of the squad car parked in front of the station. He glanced up and down the street, at the folk milling about. Taking it easy. There was no rush. Maybe he'd nip down the road for a wander first. A wee circuit. Pop into the bakers. It was the wrong direction, but he could always drop off a sausage roll for Beattie when he walked back up.

He made up his mind.

Beady-Eye Brotherstone could wait.

5

Craig sent me to his flat. I didn't argue, but I knew I wouldn't stay there long. The closeness of their relationship suffocated me. Apparently Rob's fancy law firm had taken him away to some team-building thing in Perth for the weekend. One of those things where you build rafts out of packing crates and pretend to value your colleagues. I couldn't see the point of it myself.

We looked after each other in the shop.

After I'd almost spilled coffee everywhere, Craig had ushered me back through to the stockroom and left Sharon to deal with the open-mouthed Gareth Maloney. The face I'd never thought I'd lay eyes on again.

'Is she all right?' I'd heard him say, the door swinging shut behind us.

Sharon answered in her soothing tone. 'Jo's having a few personal problems at the moment, Mr Maloney. She should really be at home resting, but she's so dedicated to her job, you see . . .'

'Oh, right. It's just that she looked so freaked out there. Like she'd seen . . . like she'd seen a ghost or something. And please, call me Gareth,' he added. 'I'm new here. Well, not new as such. I've been away . . . I thought the bookshop would be a good first port of call, like-minded folk and all that . . . seeing as most of the ones I knew when I was a kid have upped and left . . .'

'Can't say I blame them,' Sharon said. 'I mean, it's a nice enough place to live . . . bit boring, like.'

I zoned them out. What was he doing back here? After all this time?

Craig had made me drink a glass of tap water. It was warm and tasted of old pipes. 'Jo,' he said. 'You need to take a break. This thing with Scott . . . you're not saying much about it, but I know it's going to mess with your head . . . I *know* you, Jo. Are you gonna tell me what happened?'

How could I tell him what happened? *I* had no idea what happened. One minute we were sitting there eating pasta and the next he'd flipped his lid and told me it was over. Thinking about it, he had been a bit quiet lately. Coming home late. Drinking too much. But I just put it down to work stress. Maybe he was just bored with me and didn't know what to do? I don't have a brilliant track record with men, but I'd always thought that Scott was different. That he got me, somehow. Despite my . . . quirks.

But this feeling now . . . this creeping *fear* that had come over me . . . It had nothing to do with Scott. This was something else entirely. A deep wound that I thought had been knitted together had been ripped apart. The neat fissure, slowly widening, ready to reveal the scar tissue deep within. I looked up at Craig and felt my eyes welling up. There was so much I wanted to tell him.

He handed me a bunch of keys.

I rubbed at my eyes, wiping away the tears. 'I'll get a spare one cut,' I said, before slipping out the back door and onto the street via the dark little alleyway that housed the toilet and the bins. A bit of fresh air. Clear my head.

Think.

The street was much the same as before. A few more out

and about, woken by the too-bright sun of a midsummer morning. We were in the midst of a mini-heatwave. A full week already and forecast for more. Most of the town's residents were pink-faced from it already. Far too much flesh on show. Scotland was just asking for a skin cancer epidemic. Sun cream was an expensive commodity, reserved only for the Trades fortnight spent in a Spanish holiday resort.

However, it *was* a perfect day for a walk, so I headed down towards the river. I always felt better down there, watching the swans glide effortlessly under the old stone bridge, excited dogs chasing after sticks. It was idyllic. I almost forgot why I'd walked out of the shop.

But then it came back to me. Gareth Maloney.

The name swam around my skull like a circling shark.

He was taller now, of course, with wide shoulders that said rugby rather than football; the lack of mangled nose or cauliflower ears implied he was lucky, or hadn't played for a while. His hair was muddy brown, styled with gel to look like he hadn't made an effort. He was wearing a pale-blue hoodie with swirly white writing on the front. In that brief encounter, I had taken all this in.

But had he recognised me?

I looked different now too. Taller, but still skinny. Jeans and a T-shirt in place of the little skirts I used to wear when I was a kid. I'd lost the attitude too. Or I'd tried to, at least.

I shoved my hands into my pockets and kept my head down as I walked the length of the pedestrianised street, trying to avoid any opportunity for anyone to speak to me. There was someone I had to talk to, but right now I needed space.

'Hello, Jo.'

I almost walked smack into him, stopping just in time as

his shiny black boots came into view. I looked up and automatically smoothed my fringe over my ruined eyebrow. I wished I'd worn a hat. He pretended he hadn't noticed, but I knew he had. He didn't miss a thing.

'Sergeant Gray,' I said. 'Lovely morning, isn't it?'

'What's with the formalities? Feeling guilty about something?' He winked and I felt my cheeks burn. I looked up at him and smiled.

Davie Gray had the knack of making girls blush. I put him in his late forties, fifty at the most, with a full head of thick, sandy hair, feathered at the sides into as much of a Mod style as he could get away with for work. Somehow he carried it off. His eyes shone like buttons. When he wasn't busy breaking up fights between school kids, he ran the local karate club. I'd heard the teenage girls in the shop talking about his 'perfect fit body'. Not that I'd seen any of it, although he'd tried to recruit me to the club plenty of times. The first time was right after Claire's accident. He'd seemed so much older than me back then, but over the years the gap had shrunk. I definitely felt something for him, but I wasn't sure what it was.

I remembered his kind face in my parents' living room. His follow-up visit after the initial questioning. Trying to cajole me into remembering something else about what happened, when I'd told him I was scared that the boys were going to come back.

'It's not about fighting, Jo,' he'd said. 'It's about making sure you're prepared. Even if you never lay a finger on someone out on the street, or in the woods, or whatever . . . You'll scare them off because you'll know that you can.' He'd turned to my mum then, who'd been sitting on the couch looking bored. I'm sure she was convinced I'd made the whole thing up.

That the boys didn't exist. Because if they did, then why had no one seen hide nor hair of them since? It wasn't that big a town. How could I *not* know who they were? I didn't. I swear I didn't.

'What do you think, Mir—' He stopped himself from saying her name, flipped back to formality. 'Mrs Barker? It'd be great for her confidence too. It's given her a real shake. This thing . . .'

Miranda Barker gave him a girly little laugh. 'It's up to her, PC Gray,' she said. 'I can't make her do anything she doesn't want to.'

He turned back to face me. His annoyance at my mum's flippancy was quickly replaced by concern for me. 'Think about it, Jo. Come down for a trial. Just watch.' He stood up and smoothed the fronts of his trousers, picked up his hat. 'Thanks for the tea, Mrs Barker,' he said. 'I'll let myself out.'

'Oh no! Let me see you to the door.' She'd jumped up and scurried out after him. I heard them whispering in the hallway, but I couldn't make out the words.

I stayed still until the front door had snicked shut. She walked calmly back into the room and sat back down on the couch. 'C'mere, JoJo. Come and give me a cuddle.' She offered her arms to me and I couldn't resist. 'Be careful, Jo,' she continued. 'You don't want to be making a nuisance of yourself with all this silly talk.'

I felt a tear pop out of my eye and slide down my face.

Why can't you just believe me, Mum?

Gray was staring at me now and I snapped back into the present.

I blurted it out. 'I've seen him, Davie. He's back.'

He rubbed a hand over his chin and cocked his head. 'Who's back, Jo?'

27

I felt bile rising up my gullet, burning my throat. I could picture him that day. I could picture all of us.

'The boy from the woods, Davie. His name is Gareth Maloney. It's definitely him. He's older, obviously. But his face is just the same. His eyes. I'll never forget his eyes—'

Gray stepped closer and put his hands on my shoulders. 'Are you talking about one of the boys from the woods? Christ, Jo. That was what, twenty years ago?'

'Twenty-three! Twenty-three years ago this month. Did you think I was ever going to forget? I told you. I told you what he did. If it wasn't for him—'

His phone rang in his pocket and he silenced me with a finger to his lips.

'Gray. What is it? He's what? Right. OK. No, I walked. Yes, I'll come back and get the car. Right. Aye. See you in a minute.'

I was fidgeting, pulling at my fringe. 'What's wrong?' I said.

'I'll need to run, Jo. Something's happened up at the Track . . .' He let the sentence trail off. I could see he was torn. But he had a job to do. And I needed to calm down.

I took a deep breath. 'It's OK. I'll talk to you later maybe.'

He patted my shoulder and took off at a pace.

'Wait!'

He spun back round. 'What? Jo, I need to go . . .'

'I'm scared, Davie . . .' I didn't know where I was going with this, so I just stopped. This wasn't a conversation for the middle of the High Street.

He paused, opened his mouth and closed it again. I'd rendered him speechless, for once. Then he turned away and headed off in the direction of the station.

I watched him for a bit, then I turned back to where I was going. I hurried over the crossroads and down the cobbled lane that led to the river path. I slowed, and lifted my head, and breathed in lungfuls of cool, crisp air. That fresh tang of green leaves. I was going to sort this. With or without his help.

6

The river was Banktoun's main attraction. On one side, the hard-packed mud path snaked its way around the edge of the imposing church of St Christopher and the ancient graveyard where huge, tall oaks swayed gently in the breeze, their leaves whispering like ghosts. On the other bank lay acres of green-grey fields with the occasional block of sharp yellow rape in the distance. More than one developer had attempted to buy the land for housing, despite the river's tendency to burst its banks and flood the ends of the fields. But the landowner wasn't selling.

Past the church, the path grew narrower: narrower still as you headed away from the town centre and past the bubbling foam of the weir, where finally the river shrank away into the trickling burn that flanked the houses of Riverview Gardens, where Claire had lived all her life, moving into the house next door to her parents when it came up for sale. Wanting to leave them, but needing them close.

But I wasn't going there.

I cut back through the graveyard, where a trickle of bowed mourners were heading away from the section of new graves over by the far wall. A fresh mound of earth sat quietly, surrounded by wreaths of ivy and cyclamen, bunches of yellow gerberas, pink roses. A fluorescent-leaved plant in a pot.

Backed up against the other wall, my grandmother's grave lay quieter still. I crouched down to wipe dirt off the cold marble base, pulled up a few weeds that stuck out of the holes in the metal vase. A breeze rippled through the trees and for a moment the sunlight faded as a small dark cloud passed overhead. I traced the outline of the words on the headstone with one finger.

'He's back, Gran,' I said. 'The bad one. The one who hurt Claire.'

Wind whistled through the leaves, swirling past me. Soft fingers brushed the back of my neck. I whirled round, but there was nothing there. The breeze seemed to stutter and fade, until it was still and quiet again. Nothing but the slight sound of the river burbling in the background.

'Are you there, Gran? Can you hear me?'

There was a sudden squawk as a startled crow launched itself off the top of a nearby gravestone, wings fluttering as it made its way skyward. I flinched, fear trickling down my back like ice.

'Jo,' it croaked. 'Jo . . . Jo . . . Jo.'

The wind picked up again, catching my hair and whipping it around my face. I could hear the sound of my heart thumping hard in my chest, blood fizzing in my ears. A swirl of mist seemed to hover above the headstone for a brief moment and I shut my eyes tight, blocking it out.

'Jo . . . Jo . . . Jo.'

I clamped my hands over my ears, willing it all to stop. Then, as quickly as it started, it became quiet once more, as if nothing had happened.

Then a small voice whispered in my ear.

'*Please*,' it begged, 'we'll go away.'

My voice, from a long time ago.

Something snapped inside me then.

That's when it all started.

7

Jenny Brownlee's head felt broken. As if someone had sneaked into her room in the middle of the night and split it open with an axe. She tiptoed down the stairs, trying to block out the racket of the TV blaring out *Saturday Kitchen* in the living room, where clearly no one was watching it, mixed with the raised voices of her dad and Ryan arguing in the kitchen. Ryan had just passed his driving test and he wanted a car.

'It's a classic, Dad,' Ryan was saying. A copy of *Auto Trader* was spread out on the kitchen table, a photo of a red, boxy-looking car taking up half of one page as a featured ad.

Her dad shook his head. 'Son, it's thirty years old! What on earth do you think you know about looking after a car that age? You've never even done an oil change. This thing'll cause you nothing but problems.'

'I thought you'd be interested, Dad. Didn't you have a Ford Escort back in the day? Don't you know how hard it is to get them now?'

Her dad sighed. 'I told you, I'll help you with the money. I'd rather pay for something that's not going to cost us a fortune in mechanic's fees. There's a reason you can't get hold of these things now. Either they're with collectors who know what they're doing, or they're falling-apart heaps that break down every second day. Most of them have probably been scrapped. It's not as if it's an old Jag or something that was built to last. Now, if you wanted one of them—'

32

'Oh, just forget it.' Ryan slammed the magazine shut and it slid across the table and onto the floor.

Jenny made the mistake of bending down to pick it up, and a wave of dizziness almost knocked her off her feet. The noise of the chair scraping on the wooden floor as her dad stood up made her wince.

'Jen? You OK? You look a bit pale, love.'

Ryan looked at her and snorted. 'Hangover, Jenny-Wren? Tut tut.' He shoved her gently on the shoulder and walked out of the kitchen, leaving her to face the wrath of her dad.

His expression had gone from concerned to fuming in nought to sixty seconds.

'Have you been drinking? What did I say last time, Jennifer? You're only bloody fifteen!'

She slumped onto a chair and tried to hold back the acid tang of vomit that was slowly making its way up from her churning stomach. 'No, Dad,' she said weakly. 'I must have a bug or something.'

Her dad bent down and gripped her chin with one of his big hands. 'You better sort yourself out before your mother gets back,' he said. He slammed the kitchen door, making her head rattle.

Jenny considered tea and toast but knew she'd never keep it down. It was all Karen Brown's fault. That bottle of gin she'd nicked from her mum and dad's drinks cabinet had seemed like a good idea at the time. It was typical of Karen to drink a quarter of a bottle and fall asleep. OK, so no one had forced Jenny to drink the rest of it, but compared with their usual cheap wine and alcopops, she'd quite liked the taste. Apparently it was made with juniper berries. Something you wouldn't expect to mix well with Red Kola but, strangely, it did. *At least I didn't do anything stupid*, she thought. *Apart from getting drunk, obviously.* Jenny knew that was pretty stupid, but it wasn't like she did it all the time, and Kenny Long from the fourth year had been there, so she was hardly going to sit there like a stupid little girl. She remembered the feeling of Kenny's lips when he kissed her. Cold and wet and tasting of lager. She wondered if he might like her a bit, after all.

Realising that she was still dressed in last night's clothes, she scanned the pile of shoes at the back door and spotted her trainers. They lay upside down on top of each other from where she'd kicked them off the night before. Then she took a cold can of Coke from the fridge and let herself out. The sun was warm on her face, and after a few gulps of air, her nausea settled. Carefully lifting the latch on the gate, she sneaked out of the back garden before anyone had a chance to notice she was gone.

Jenny's garden was one of several that backed onto Alder's Lane, a cut-through between the rows of houses that bordered the Track.

Jenny spent most Friday nights at the Track with her mates. This morning, it seemed as good a place as any to try to clear her head. She had an essay on *Macbeth* to finish before Monday and there was no way she could write that kind of shit with a fuzzy head.

She hugged in to the side to avoid a sweaty, panting jogger, before passing an old man walking a chocolate Lab that looked almost as old as him. As was usual along the Track, the old man nodded and said 'Morning' and she smiled back. By the time she'd walked under the second bridge, she was starting to feel a bit brighter.

It was peaceful there, at the second bridge. One of her favourite spots. Just far enough out of town to feel like you were really in the country, but actually not far at all if you wanted to get back. There was a worn path up the siding that took you onto the bridge, and from there you could walk back into town through the new estate where everyone in their thirties with their duos of toddlers seemed to live these days.

It was quiet. Just the occasional sound of a small animal or a bird rustling in the bushes. The faint hum of traffic from the bypass at the other side of the estate. She popped open the can of Coke, drank; the cold liquid fizzed as it ran down her chin.

Then another sound.

A twig cracking in the small copse of trees behind her.

She whirled round, and there, right in front of her, separated only by the low undergrowth at the edge of the path, stood a man in a black sports jacket. His face was obscured by a black balaclava, and her first thought was, *No, this is not right. It's July. A hot summer's morning. No need for a hat.*

Definitely no need for a balaclava.

He stepped out of the trees and she felt fear bubbling up inside her, mixing with the remnants of last night's alcohol. She froze, unable to scream.

He took a step towards her. He held something in his hands. A stick?

She couldn't understand what was happening, her brain a useless mush.

'What . . . what are you doing in there?' she stammered. She felt hot bile rise in her throat and gulped hard, swallowing it back.

The figure stared back at her, and although all she could see were slivers of eyes, she could tell he was smiling.

She took a step backwards, her eyes darting frantically from side to side, looking for a way out, somewhere to run to.

The man in the balaclava took a step towards her, and she could see now that it *was* a stick he was holding. He gripped it with both hands and stared straight at her as he snapped it clean in half.

She started to cry then; hot, salty tears ran over her top lip and into a mouth that was seemingly mute, at the only time she really needed it.

Then: another sound.

That panting, huffing she'd heard earlier. Rhythmic footsteps crunching on the bark. She stumbled backwards just as the jogger came to a stop right in front of her. He put his hands on his hips and sucked in air.

'What's wrong?' he said, the words separated with puffs as he tried to catch his breath. 'Are you OK?' She whimpered, raised a limp hand, and finally he realised what was going on. He turned towards the man in the balaclava. 'Oi! What the hell are you doing in there?'

The man turned and fled back through the trees towards the cut-through, branches snapping. A flurry of wings and feathers as he disturbed a flock of watchful birds.

Jenny stared at the jogger through a blur of tears, felt her whole body start to shake. Then she lurched forwards and threw up all over his bright-green trainers.

8

Craig and Rob had bought the top floor flat in a converted maltings that was halfway between the town centre and Claire's house. It had three bedrooms and a roof terrace, and Rob had insisted on getting the whole thing kitted out by a couple of interior designers who'd apparently worked on Ewan McGregor's cousin's place in Glasgow. The result was more New York's Bowery than East Lothian's Banktoun, and Craig had let it slip that the whole renovation had cost them close to a hundred grand. I say 'them', but clearly it'd been bankrolled by the 'I charge five hundred quid just to speak to you' Rob, unless Craig had been concealing a secret lottery win for the past four years.

They hadn't rushed to move in together, which I secretly agreed with, despite the impulsiveness I tended to show when it came to men. I'd moved in with Scott after a month. I thought maybe we could make a go of it. Plus, his flat was nicer than the dingy little house I'd been renting and it was nice to feel like I had an actual home. It'd been a long time since I'd felt like I belonged anywhere.

I passed my old house on the way to Craig's, sitting forlornly in the former car park behind Tesco's garage. As I got closer I realised that the new tenants had taken down my black venetians and decorated the windows with flouncy floral curtains. Brightly coloured pots filled with smiling pansies sat beneath the window ledge.

It looked like a happier place now, without me in it.

Bugger Scott. Where was I going to go now? I couldn't believe his decision to dump me had been so sudden. He must've known he was going to do it. Had he known last week? It wasn't as if I'd done anything that week to annoy him any more than usual. I irritated him, but he was always patient with me. That's why I loved him.

I let myself into Craig and Rob's, kicking my shoes off behind the door. This was one of Rob's requirements. He even provided slippers for guests in a little wicker basket behind the door. I reached into the basket, then changed my mind. My hot feet left sweaty little footprints on the polished walnut floor as I padded through to the kitchen.

I flipped the switch on Rob's ridiculous coffee machine and took a silver pouch of coffee from the door of the fridge. Where did people learn to do things like put coffee in the fridge? All I knew was that you shouldn't keep bananas in there because they go black, and you were supposed to empty leftovers from tins into non-metallic containers so you didn't get aluminium poisoning. Or something like that. As usual it was something I'd read when the shop was quiet. I really was a mine of useless information.

While the machine spattered and bubbled and did its thing, I sat down at the kitchen table – a giant piece of moulded yellow Perspex that looked like it'd been reclaimed from a spaceship – and fired up Craig's laptop. It was silver and paper-thin and ready to go in seconds, unlike my own one (still in Craig's car), which was as thick as a brick and practically needed wound up to get it going. Craig was always on at me to buy a new one, but I didn't see the need. It connected to the Internet and that was pretty much all I used it for.

I'd just filled up a mug with thick, treacly coffee and was

contemplating tipping it straight down the sink when my phone buzzed in my pocket. I wasn't a fan of ringtones.

'Jo? Are you OK? Craig said you've left Scott; what's happened?'

'Oh, Claire . . .' I drew out her name into a long sigh.

'Jo? Will I come round? Or do you want to come round here? I've baked—'

I interrupted her. 'Do you want to come to the pub later? I could do with a drink. I'd ask Craig, but . . .'

A pause. 'I'll see you at seven, OK? I'll get Dad to drive me.'

'Yup.'

I took the phone away from my ear and was about to end the call when I heard her voice again, far away and tinny through the phone. 'And Jo?' Another pause. 'Don't touch your bloody eyebrows.' Click.

I laughed. 'Too late,' I said out loud. My voice echoed around the bare walls. Art was minimalist in the apartment, like everything else.

The laptop emanated a series of beeps and a little balloon popped up to tell me there was a new email. I ran my finger over the track pad, considered opening it.

No.

The temptation to read Craig's emails was strong, but not as strong as the need to do what I was about to do.

I scrolled across the icons on the desktop. Clicked on a green, rounded square – the Banktoun Books logo in a fancy font that I'd designed. The 'Welcome' screen popped up and I entered my username and password for the system.

Then I scrolled down the menu bar at the side until I found the link to the customer database.

Another screen popped up, followed by a cute animation of

a little green book opening and closing. The front cover had a face and a little speech bubble floated out of its open mouth.

Hi! I'm BB! You've got new customers. Click here to edit settings.

I clicked.

A form appeared, with the customers' names, addresses, emails, phone numbers and a series of tick boxes telling us which newsletters they wanted to receive. There were various options: Book News, Author News, Kids, Signings, Special Offers, Reading Group, Events.

There were three new customers since I'd last logged in.

Marion Jones.

Simon McKinness.

Gareth Maloney.

Marion was interested in Reading Groups and Book News. Simon was the same, plus Special Offers. Gareth had ticked all the boxes. Including Kids. He had kids? The thought made me shudder. I supposed he must have a wife too. Maybe a dog. A Volvo. A top-of-the-range Flymo. All that stuff that the thirty-somethings aspire to.

I felt sick.

What are you doing, Jo?

I clicked on 'Edit' and his address came up in full.

Gareth Maloney

Rose Cottage

Burndale Road

Banktoun

EH41 4NX

A lump seemed to have lodged itself in my throat, and I swallowed hard. I knew that cottage. It sat on its own next to the bridge that led down to the woods at the top of the burn. The bit where the water disappeared into a culvert and was hidden below the road. The bit where the drainage pipe crossed over to the banks of Riverview Gardens.

The bit where we met the boys.

THE WOODS

'Well, well. Who've we got here then?' The boy takes a step closer.

The girl in the red skirt stares at them defiantly.

'Who the hell are you then?' she says. 'What's with the stupid-looking masks? A bit early for Halloween is it not?'

The smaller girl clamps a hand over her mouth in shock at her friend's harsh words.

He walks towards them. 'Well, that would be telling, wouldn't it, doll?'

He's right in front of her now. He's only slightly taller than she is. He looks down at her and she looks up. Her mouth curls into a smirk.

'We're not scared of you,' she says.

She turns and takes hold of her friend's hand, and pulls her away from the edge of the water and further into the clearing, where a tyre-swing hangs down from the thick branch of a gnarly, ancient oak.

'No,' says the little girl. 'No. I just want to go home now. Please?'

'In a minute.'

The taller girl pushes her bare legs though the centre of the tyre. Her skirt catches on the edges of the rubber and it is pulled up almost to her waist, revealing more of that smooth, milk-white skin.

She looks over at him and gives him a dirty little smile.

He's mesmerised.

The other boy pulls on his arm. 'Let's go,' he says.

He turns, brought back with a jolt.

'Jesus Christ! What's wrong with you?'

'I don't want to do this.'

'Do what? What're we doing? We're just chatting. We're just watching them, for fuck's sake. What did you think we were going to do?' He holds his hands palms upwards and spreads out his arms. 'We're in a wood. We're just playing.' He turns back to the girls. 'We're just *playing*, aren't we, girls? You don't mind us being here, do you?'

The little one is swinging now. The taller one pushing her. She pushes her higher and higher, the rope creaking ominously. He glances up at the knot that secures the rope around the thick limb of the tree. He tied that rope. He used a sailor's hitch. Secure. Jam-proof. One of the ones his dad taught him, from his years at the docks. Before they moved here. There was no way the rope could come loose, but the height they were swinging at, it might start to fray from the friction as it rubbed against the bark. If it snapped when she was swinging, it'd be a bad fall.

A bone-breaking fall, little girl like that.

He watches the little girl swing.

Back and forth.

Creak. Swish.

Creak. Swish.

He smiles at the thought, feels his erection stir again.

43

9

Beattie was waiting for him outside the station.

'Where've you been? Beady-Eye's doing his nut. I said you were on your way.' He tossed him the car keys and Gray plucked them out of the air. Beattie gave him a low whistle.

'I *am* on my way. Nice throw, by the way. I keep telling you to join that cricket team.'

Beattie snorted. 'Oh aye. Get myself into the nationals, eh?'

'Aye. Another sport this country's no bloody good at.' He jumped into the panda car, a two-year-old Vauxhall Corsa with various scratches along the paintwork, and shot out onto the street. He was tempted to turn on the flashers, just because he'd had no need to for so long that he was starting to miss them. No point drawing undue attention to himself, though. He wanted this nipped in the bud before the jungle drums started banging. Kids. It would just be bloody kids.

He drove up Western Road and onto Burndale. He took it at a leisurely pace, just below thirty, to piss off the bloke in the Merc that was hovering up his arse, desperate for him to turn off so he could give it a few revs. Gray slowed down further until he could see the guy's face in his rear-view mirror. The guy backed off.

He turned right up Alder's Road and noticed a car in the driveway of Rose Cottage at the junction. He wondered who'd finally bought the place. It'd lain empty for the last two

years since Alan McAllister had lost his job and finally suc-
cumbed to the bank's demands. It was a shame to see a place
like that going to waste. The new owner had no doubt got a
bargain at auction. Rumour had it the McAllisters had upped
and left it with half their stuff still in it. Alan, apparently, had
not handled his unemployment well. The wife had gone long
before the repossession had taken place.

Gray turned into the entrance to Alder's Close and was
dismayed to find a small gathering outside Martin
Brotherstone's house. He took in the scene. Two women and
a man. One of the women waving her arms about, the other
with hands on hips and a miserable expression on her face.
The man with arms crossed tightly over his chest.

Brotherstone waddled at an unexpectedly fast pace towards
the car. His fat frame cast a shadow over it; his physical bulk
prevented Gray from getting out.

'Where the hell have you been, Gray? I called Gordon over
an hour ago about this. That constable of yours was a fat lot
of use too. Get lost on the drive up, did you?'

Gray tried not to roll his eyes. Brotherstone was being
his usual officious self, it seemed. Well, two could play that
game.

'Could you step away from the car please, sir.'

Brotherstone's jaw dropped, yet he complied. His face had
turned puce. 'Don't you "sir" me, laddie. This is a serious
matter. I've been saying for *years* that the Track has been cul-
tivating an unsavoury type of behaviour, and what I saw this
morning just confirms that.'

'And what was that, exactly, Mr Brotherstone?' Gray took
his notepad and pen from his pocket. He wrote: *Incident
Report. The Track.* Then the date. He glanced at his watch,
then neatly wrote down the time. He looked at Brotherstone

and had to suppress a smile. He took the phrase 'hopping with rage' to a whole new level.

'Do you find this amusing, Sergeant Gray?' He emphasised the rank, like it was a dirty word.

'Not at all, sir. Maybe we should go inside?'

The small crowd parted as they neared the house, and Gray spotted Brotherstone's son, Pete, hovering in the open doorway. He was a thin streak of a lad, always slumped at the shoulders, trying to make himself disappear. He slunk back inside and vanished into the kitchen. Even if he hadn't been in the house before, Gray would've known it was the kitchen, because all of the houses in the estate shared exactly the same layout. Once you'd been in one, you'd been in them all.

Brotherstone's looked pretty much like it had when he'd bought it from the building firm. Neutral magnolia walls, bog-standard beige carpet. It was definitely lacking a woman's touch. His wife had died not long after they'd moved in.

She'd been a quiet, mousey woman, from what Gray remembered. Even her illness had come and gone without much fanfare. Brotherstone's obnoxiousness and waistline had increased in equal measure since the woman's funeral. Brotherstone seemed to have taken a particular dislike to him after that. Gray suspected it was because the man knew that he understood his grief, but his stubbornness prevented him from accepting any support. Brotherstone didn't want anyone's sympathy. Yet Gray felt sorry for him, despite the slagging they gave him for his community nosiness. It couldn't be easy bringing up a son like Pete with no mother around to help.

Brotherstone ushered him into the living room, which housed a brown leather sofa, a matching recliner and a TV of

46

approximately the same size as Gray's car. A single blown-up photograph hung on the wall behind the sofa: a grinning Mr and Mrs Brotherstone sandwiching a small, scowling boy. The whole room made Gray feel sad.

Gray sat on the sofa. Brotherstone perched on one arm of the recliner. He didn't look comfortable and Gray fully expected the thing to topple over.

'OK then, Mr . . . is it OK if I call you Martin?'

Martin nodded, waved a dismissive hand. He seemed to sag then, like the stuffing had been knocked out of him. 'It was Pete who saw him first. His bedroom faces right out onto the Track. Our room's at the front.' He coughed. 'My room, I mean.'

Gray nodded. 'Can we bring Pete in? I'd like to hear this from him.'

Martin shook his head, a bead of sweat that'd been clinging onto his meaty forehead suddenly losing its grip and catching Gray on the cheek. Gray winced inwardly, letting Martin continue. 'Not just now. He's a bit . . . agitated. I can tell you exactly what he told me.'

Oh aye, Gray thought.

'But you didn't actually see anything yourself?'

'No.'

Gray wrote on his pad: *Son? Unreliable?*

'I can tell you.' Gray turned to find Pete standing in the doorway.

'Petey . . .' Martin said.

Gray shushed him with a wave of his hand.

'What did you see, Pete? You can tell me. I'm going to write it down in this notepad.' He held it up. 'See?'

Pete dropped his head, then spewed out the words without pausing for breath. 'He was wearing a balaclava. Like the

47

SAS. He was tramping about in the bushes. He had something in his hand. I couldn't see what it was. He was too far away. I tried to look in the telescope but then it was too late and he was gone and I didn't see him again after that. Then I told Dad. Then after that I looked again and got the telescope and that's when I saw the girl.'

Gray felt the hairs on the back of his neck stand up. 'The girl? What girl?'

Martin stood up. 'He gets confused sometimes. There was no girl. Was there, Petey?'

'Dad! There was a girl. I told you about the girl. I told you she was—'

The lad was interrupted mid-flow as Gray's phone blared out 'A Town Called Malice', slightly too loud. Pete flinched and ran out of the room. Gray shrugged a sorry, but Martin glared at him anyway and followed his son out of the room.

The ringtone started up again and Gray stabbed at the answer button and shouted 'What?' into the phone.

It was Beattie.

'You need to get round to Alder's Avenue. I've just had Kevin Brownlee on the phone. Apparently his daughter's been approached by some weirdo up at the Track. You there now?'

Gray stared at the phone. 'Was he wearing a balaclava, by any chance?'

'Aye, how'd you know that?'

'You better give us the address.'

10

Gray left Brotherstone to deal with his son and told him he'd be back later. The address that Beattie had given him was only five minutes away by foot, but he took the car anyway. It wouldn't look good for him to turn up on foot for this.

As he drove the short journey to the Brownlee house, he thought about the exchange he'd just witnessed. Why was Brotherstone trying to stop Pete from talking to him, telling him what he'd seen? There *had* been that thing a few years back. The thing with the little girl in the swing park . . . The mother accused Pete Brotherstone of trying to lure the girl away, but Pete's explanation was that the wee girl had been crying and he was trying to take her home . . . The whole thing had been swept under the carpet. By Martin Brotherstone and a wad of cash, Gray suspected. But Gray had always believed the boy's story. He'd go as far as to bet his treasured scooter that Pete Brotherstone wouldn't hurt a fly.

Jenny Brownlee's house was in a cul-de-sac much the same as the one he'd just left. The houses were the same identikit type, only these ones were a bit smaller than the one the councillor lived in. Same generic lack of character. Same beige frontage with random pieces of moulding to make them look like they hadn't come straight from Ikea.

Gray's own house was a 1930s cottage with white pebble-dashed walls and a triangular half-porch that leaked every time it rained, and which somehow Gray never got round to fixing. He told himself it added to the character when, in fact, his cottage was the same as all the others on the terrace.

His front garden was concreted and served as a parking space for his beloved Lambretta. He kept it beneath a custom-made oilskin cover and had it bolted to the house with a heavy metal chain so big it would be easier to cut away the wall of the house than break one of the links.

Didn't stop the little bastards from trying, though.

In contrast, Jenny Brownlee's front garden was a neat square of bright-green turf, separated from its neighbour by a border of neatly pruned yellow roses. Someone was clearly a gardener. The effect was spoiled somewhat by the sight of Jenny's dad, Kevin, standing on the front step wearing a scowl that would sour milk.

Gray parked in the empty driveway and killed the engine. *Here we go then.*

'Morning, sir. Mr Brownlee, is it? Mind if I come in?' Gray nodded his head in the direction of the open front door.

Brownlee nodded and stepped aside to let him in. Gray was about to walk straight through to the lounge but stopped himself just in time.

'Aye, through there,' Brownlee said.

The lounge was an eye-stinging explosion of colour. The complete opposite of the beigey, magnolia'd interior of Brotherstone's house. A huge L-shaped red-fabric sofa took up most of two walls. The majority of the dark laminate floor-ing was obscured by an enormous orange and yellow circular rug. Unsurprisingly, a flat-screen TV hung on the far wall; below it, a modern-design chrome electric fire. Gray noticed the oversized beanbag in the corner of the room and prayed that he wouldn't have to sit on it. He couldn't understand the things. Uncomfortable to sit on, impossible to get back out of, and they made that annoying crunchy noise whenever you moved.

'Here, I'll move.' A tall stringy man in a tight white T-shirt, black lycra tights and bare feet stood up from the sofa and took himself over to the beanbag, where he sat back down with a crunch.

On the other end of the sofa, a girl sat with her legs curled under her, an untouched mug of tea on a small table placed nearby. She looked miserable. Gray suspected there was more than a hint of hangover in the mix.

Gray sat and waited for Kevin Brownlee to come into the room before he spoke.

'So,' Gray said, taking out his notepad and pen. 'Jenny? That's right, isn't it?'

The girl nodded.

'And who's this?' Gray asked, looking towards the man sitting uncomfortably on the beanbag.

'Dave Morriss,' the man replied. 'I—'

'Dave's the one who helped Jenny up at the Track,' Kevin Brownlee butted in. 'I've had to put his shoes and socks in the bloody washing machine.'

Jenny made a small choking sound and Gray turned towards her, hoping for some insight.

'I puked on his shoes,' Jenny said. She pulled a stand of hair across her mouth and sucked on it to try to hide her smirk. 'I got a fright.'

Kevin Brownlee stood up. 'Oh, it's funny now, eh? Wasn't that when Mr Morriss kindly brought you back here while you were bubblin' and greetin' your wee eyes out, eh?'

Gray heard the crunch as Morriss shifted uncomfortably in the beanbag.

'Oh really, it was no trouble, I—'

51

Gray raised a hand. 'Right. OK. Maybe if I can hear from Jenny first, Mr Morriss? Then you can tell me what you saw. Make sure I've got the full picture, eh?' He turned back to Jenny. 'In your own time.'

Jenny sighed. The sigh said I've already told all this to my dad and he's pissed off with me for causing trouble and now I suppose I've got to say it all again to you now, don't I? Gray had heard the sigh before. He called it the 'Teenage Sigh'. It was used regularly by all youths accused of doing something wrong, doing nothing at all, as a first response to a question as innocuous as 'How are you?' Teens, it seemed, viewed all attempts at conversation directed at them by an adult as highly suspicious.

'He was just standing there in the trees.'

'Did he approach you?'

She frowned. 'Kind of. He started walking towards me. He . . . he snapped a stick. It sounds stupid now.' She turned towards Dave Morriss, who was still sitting awkwardly on the beanbag, and smiled. 'He saved me,' she said, pointing at the man, who opened his mouth to say something.

Gray silenced it with a raised hand. *Wait your turn, son.* He scribbled in his notepad. *No physical contact.*

'Did he speak to you? Make any sound at all? Anything you could identify?'

Jenny shook her head again, bit her bottom lip.

Gray changed tack. 'OK. Can you tell me what he looked like? What he was wearing? Height, build, anything like that?'

Jenny sat up straight on the couch. 'Well, he was tall . . . like you. A bit skinnier than you, though. I suppose you'd call him "lanky". He was in jeans and a black fleece. Nothing unusual. No, like, logos or badges or anything . . .'

She paused, and Gray nodded at her to continue.

'I couldn't see any part of his face or his hair. Because of the balaclava, you know? His head must've been boiling.'

The girl seemed more relaxed now, Gray thought. Now that the danger had passed, she was enjoying her moment in the limelight. It wasn't unusual. Unfortunately, though, she wasn't giving him very much to go on.

'Anything else you can tell me, Jenny? No matter how small, anything. Did you see what he had on his feet? Was he carrying anything?'

'No. Sorry.' She bit her lip again, dragging at a piece of skin. 'He just looked normal . . .'

'There *is* something else actually, officer.' There was a rustle of shifting polystyrene beans as the man stuffed into the beanbag finally stood up.

Gray was about to tell him to wait, then thought better of it. The man was desperate to talk. 'Go on.'

Dave Morriss cleared his throat. 'There was something wrong with his face. I saw it as he turned, just before he ran off. Jenny wouldn't have noticed . . .' He glanced across at the girl and gave her a tight smile. 'She was, er, vomiting at the time.'

Gray's ears pricked up. 'Something wrong with his face? I thought he was wearing a balaclava?'

Morriss nodded his head enthusiastically, reminding Gray of one of those little dogs that people put on the back shelves of their cars. 'Yes. Yes, he was. But I could see there was something wrong with him underneath . . . his face looked too big. Bumpy. On his cheeks? I think maybe he had some sort of deformity . . . which is maybe why he was wearing the balaclava?'

Something wrong with his face. Something pinged in Gray's memory. Something he hoped might push itself further towards the surface sooner rather than later. 'Doesn't explain why he was lurking in the bushes, scaring young girls, though, does it?' Gray said. 'Deformity or not.'

'No. I suppose not. Just, well . . . Maybe you could look up some doctors' records or something for the area. Maybe you'll be able to find him like that. He might be registered disabled or something? I'm not trying to tell you how to do your job, or anything, but—'

Gray cut him off. He was rambling now. 'Thank you, Mr Morriss. I'll certainly be exploring that as a possibility. I'm wondering, though – what makes you think he's local?'

Morriss and Jenny exchanged a glance. Jenny spoke. 'Because he ran up through the back of the houses. The cut-through is tiny. No way anyone other than a local could know about that . . .'

Gray flipped his notebook shut. 'Thanks,' he said, 'you've both been very helpful.'

Kevin Brownlee, who'd been listening to the exchange from the doorway, said, 'I'll see you out, Sergeant Gray.'

'I'll be in touch. Oh, and if you think of anything else – either of you – feel free to give me a call.' He handed them both a business card before nodding a goodbye.

He waited until he was back in the panda car before swearing.

He knew exactly which cut-through they were referring to. It came out right next to Martin Brotherstone's back gate.

11

The flat seemed to shrink in on me, stopping me from breathing. I ran downstairs to the car park, leant against the wall.

Breathe in . . . out . . . in . . . out . . .

One of those things that should be obvious. One of those things I sometimes forgot to do.

Eventually, I relaxed.

It was barely four o'clock and the day was still warm, and with nothing to do until I met Claire in the Rowan Tree at seven, I decided to go for another walk. Something was dragging me towards that cottage.

Walking had always been a favourite activity of mine. When I was a kid and everyone else was out on their new bikes – the BMXs, the Grifters, the Raleigh racers, and eventually the chunky-tyred mountain bikes – I'd bucked the trend and stuck with walking as my primary mode of transport. I don't mean rambling or hiking or – God forbid – climbing hills. Just a leisurely pace, through the streets, along the burn. Sometimes through the woods.

Back in the late nineties, everyone used to head down to the beach, which was a good ten miles away from Banktoun. A fairly easy route to get there, mostly downhill. But coming back at the end of the day, fried from the harsh northern sun and stuffed full of greasy fish and chips, was a different story. I'd done it once, borrowing my dad's racer. At the end of it my arse felt like it had been rubbed raw, my thighs cramped tight from the effort. After that, I'd walked, sometimes hitching part of the way on a tractor or getting a lift from some of the older kids like Barry Anderson, who had a Ford Escort Mark II and would pick up anyone as long as they supplied him with fags or let him cop a feel. He'd given me a can of cider one day. Told me I was gorgeous. I lost my virginity to him in the sand dunes on a summer's day in '95. I'd hated the way his hands pawed at me, but I'd let him carry on.

I saw him sometimes, down the pub. Twenty years of hard drinking, fighting and labouring for the local builder had taken its toll on his once boyband-esque features; the deep lines on his cheeks seemed as if they'd been carved from stone. He still liked me, though, and over the years I'd grown to crave the rough feel of his hands against the softness of my skin.

Before I knew where I was, I was at the bus stop on the bridge on Burndale Road.

Across the road, diagonally opposite me, was Rose Cottage.

I examined the timetable at the back of the shelter, as if I was checking the time of the next bus into Edinburgh, then I turned and sat down on the hard plastic seat. From my viewpoint I could see clearly into the wide bay window to the left of the door to the cottage. I didn't know what was in there now, but it had once been a dining room, when the McAllisters had lived there. The smaller window on the other side of the entrance was where their living room had been. A poky room and with far fewer features, but the McAllisters had been more interested in entertaining with food, hence the apparent switch of the rooms.

I'd always thought Polly McAllister was a stuck-up cow, but Claire had met her at gymnastics and seemed to think she was all right. I'd never seen the appeal of star jumps or forward rolls or throwing yourself over a pommel horse, but Claire had been something of a child prodigy so I had to pretend to be interested. Maybe if someone had been bothered enough to encourage me to try it out, I might have felt differently.

It was the Friday of the last day of term and we'd been let out of school early. My parents were away at a trades fair, trying to hawk their horrendous gold-plated jewellery like a couple of cut-price Gerald Ratners, so I was entrusted to Claire's mum and dad until early evening when they got back from Glasgow. We still weren't exactly friends, but she was the closest thing I had to one. I think she liked me more than she made out, but she still liked to disown me in front of her 'proper' pals.

'Polly's invited us for tea and Mum says it's OK, so we're going,' Claire had said, in a tone that beggared no argument. She was stuffing her ridiculous collection of multicoloured dog rubbers into her fluffy pink pencil case.

My bag fell off the desk onto the floor and everything tipped out. Pencils, felt-tip pens, the pack of neat new blue jotters I'd stolen from Miss Reece's cupboard. I felt my cheeks grow hot, terrified that Claire had seen. She would definitely tell on me if she had. We were allowed one jotter per subject, but I liked them in their little shrink-wrapped packs. They were nicer than any of the pads you could buy in the shops. I got a buzz from taking them. Something that prissy Claire would never understand.

'What?' I said. 'Me as well?'

'Yes, you as well. What're you moaning about? Her mum

and dad have got a brand-new stereo and Polly's got *New Kids on the Block*, and anyway, you'd like her if you gave her a chance.'

'She's a hippy bloody vegetarian!' I said.

'So? And don't say bloody. You're not allowed.'

I snorted. 'You just said it. Bloody, bloody, *bloody!*' I said the last one loud, right in her ear and she flinched. I had a bad habit of trying to wind Claire up, just to get a reaction. It always worked.

'You're a . . . you're an idiot, Jo,' she said, and her cheeks flushed crimson. Claire was such a goody-goody. Even *idiot* was a bad word to her back then.

'OK. But I'm going to ask for sausages for tea,' I said. 'I'm not a rabbit.'

Claire rolled her eyes and we picked up our bags and left the classroom. We were the last to leave, and Polly was waiting for us at the main gate with her mum. Her mum had a curled-under fringe like Karen Carpenter and wore a garish, flowing kaftan. Polly had a similar fringe, but her hair was a bit too coarse so it always uncurled at the edges and looked like it was trying to escape off her head. She was wearing a purple hand-knitted dress, even though it was July. Claire blended in, with her dungarees, and I was pleased I'd decided to wear the short red double-frilled skirt that made me look far trendier than both of them.

'Polly tells me you're thinking of playing the trumpet, Joanne,' Polly's mum said.

'Hmm,' I said, trying to buy myself a bit of time. I'd forgotten I'd made that up and I was struggling to think what else I might've lied to Polly about to make myself sound more interesting than her. 'Maybe. Or the double bass.'

Polly looked at me like she'd just scraped me off her shoe.

58

'Ten-year-old girls can't play the double bass,' she said sniffily. 'It's *far* too big!'

Polly and Claire giggled and I felt a little knot of rage in my stomach.

'Can too!' I said. I kicked a stone and it flicked up and hit Polly's mum on the back of the leg. She whirled round, her face full of anger, then the look slid off her face and she was Mrs McAllister the smiling hippy again and I muttered a quiet 'sorry'.

'It's aubergine and sweet-potato pie for tea, Joanne,' she said. 'I hope that's OK.'

'My favourite,' I said, and then we were there, at Rose Cottage, and all I could think about was how soon could we leave and go back to Claire's, where her mum would have a freshly baked chocolate cake to celebrate the first day of the summer holidays.

I was vaguely aware of a change in the light. The sun making its way westwards to start a new day in another world. I was still staring at Rose Cottage when I saw the yellow hue of a lamp being switched on in the bay window, a shadow of a figure, then the curtains being drawn.

I wondered if it was Gareth Maloney.

On the other end of the bench, an old man was singing quietly to himself, and I turned to him with a feeling of mild alarm. I hadn't noticed him sit down. Had he been talking to me?

'Excuse me, have you got the time please?'

He pulled up the sleeve of a threadbare beige cardigan to reveal one of those watches with the elasticated metal strap. It looked about as old as him. 'Ten to, hen,' he said. 'Bus'll be here the now.'

'Ten to six?'

He laughed, and it turned into a cough. I waited for him to recover himself, feeling panic rising in my chest. 'Naw. Ten to seven.'

Had I really been sitting there for over two hours?

'Thanks,' I muttered, already off the seat.

I took off down Burndale Road in the direction of town. Claire hated it when I was late.

12

I nodded at the barman as I walked in. He was slowly drying a pint glass with a blue and white dishcloth.

'She's up the back,' he said. 'You've got one in the tap, I'll bring it over.'

His name was Gary and he'd been the year below me and Claire at school. He was all right now, but he used to be a nasty little shit at school and I hadn't completely forgiven him. I ignored him and walked past a crowd of teenagers who were nursing a pint between them and methodically ripping up the beer mats. Next to them, an elderly couple sat, studiously ignoring each other, him with a half-drunk pint of something dark in front of him, her with a stemmed glass of clear liquid with a sliver of lemon drowning beneath the surface.

'You're late,' she said and squinted up at me, taking in my latest follicular disaster.

'Sorry . . .' I let my voice tail off. 'Was someone with you?'

To the right of her sat an empty pint glass, the foam still mobile on the inside, suggesting that it'd recently been finished. Her own glass had trickles of condensation running down the outside, her sauv blanc still icy cold.

Her eyes flicked to the right and she blinked a couple of times. I could always tell when Claire was about to tell me a lie. We joked about it. Sang the Eagles song about the lying

61

eyes. I didn't feel like singing it then, though; I felt a strange uneasiness.

'Jake was here. You just missed him.'

Who else.

'Hmm. It's almost as if you magic him away when I appear. How *do* you do that, Claire?' I hadn't meant for it to come out nastily, but when I played it back in my head, I realised it sounded bitter. As far as Claire was concerned, I had no interest in Jake, and the feeling was mutual. He was just the boy from across the road who, for some reason, she'd taken a shine to. Or maybe it was the other way round. Claire was good at collecting waifs and strays. Maybe I had more in common with Jake than I thought.

She opened her mouth to say something just as Gary the barman appeared. He slid a Belhaven Best mat towards me and placed my pint of Strongbow on top. Claire smiled at him and he walked off, stopping on his way past the teenagers to scoop up the ripped pile of beer mats they'd left at the edge of the table.

Claire took a sip of her wine.

I sat down. 'What were you going to say?'

She sighed. 'Doesn't matter. How are you, Jo?'

I gazed at her and smiled. She looked lovely, as usual, her blonde hair twisted up neatly at the back of her head. She put her glass back down on her mat and the soft chiffon of her blouse rustled with the movement. I glanced down at my own scruffy outfit and felt grubby. I probably didn't smell too fresh either, compared with Claire and her characteristic floral scent. She stared at me across the table and her eyes shone in that way that they did when she wasn't really there.

When people met Claire for the first time they'd be forgiven for thinking there was nothing wrong with her. It was only occasionally, when it happened like this: when the light changed behind her eyes, like someone had flipped a switch. Then before you knew it, she'd blink, and she'd be back and her eyes would say silently, *Now, where was I?* I rarely noticed it any more.

'So Scott dumped me,' I said.

She blinked. Came back. 'Yeah. God, that's shitty, Jo. I thought things were going well. Didn't you say you'd talked about getting engaged later this year?'

I picked up my pint and downed half of it in one. 'Hmm. Yeah. I really don't know, to be honest. I mean, he'd been a bit odd for a while, now that I think about it.'

'Odd, how?'

'Oh, you know. Distant. Like he had something to tell me but he didn't know how to. I reckon there might be someone else . . .'

'The prick! Who?'

'Well, he didn't actually *say* there was someone else, but . . . I don't know. Really. I mean, what else could it be? I was still giving him BJs . . .'

Claire laughed. 'So oral sex is the gauge of a relationship now, is it? Did you read that in *Cosmo* or something?' She shook her head. 'You're priceless, you know.'

I stared at her. 'I wasn't joking. Don't you do that with Jake? I mean, it's probably one of the easiest things you *can* do, what with—'

She gave me a filthy look and I stopped talking. *Fucking hell, Jo. You do say the most inappropriate things sometimes.*

'I'm going to the toilet,' she said. 'You should get yourself another drink. I'm fine with this one.'

She moved as she spoke, sliding her way along the wooden bench seat. She pulled the wheelchair in closer, then put her hand on the table and levered herself up. I leant forwards to steady her chair, then stopped myself and sat back. She hated it when people tried to help her like that. She hovered, half-standing for a second or two, before flopping into the wheel-chair. She swivelled and spun it out of the alcove, then pro-pelled herself along with her arms towards the ladies'. She rammed the metal kick plate with her footplate and disap-peared inside.

The barman reappeared at the table. 'Same again?' he said. He looked at me pityingly. *Must be hard having a friend like that.*

No, I thought. *It must be hard having a friend like me.*

'Just for me, Gary,' I said and handed him a pile of coins.

He'd brought me the second pint and Claire still hadn't come back. I contemplated going in to see if she was OK, but I knew she wouldn't like it.

I tried to formulate the words in my head into an appropri-ate sentence.

I've seen him, Claire.

Remember the boy from the woods, Claire? As if she could forget.

Claire, I've got something to tell you . . .

I heard the door squeaking open and the sound of her wheels swishing across the carpet. I think if I was her, I'd stay in the chair. Sit at the end of the table. But no. She man-oeuvred herself back onto the bench and slid the wheelchair back into the alcove.

Smiled.

Pretended that everything was all right.

'I saw Bridie earlier,' she said. 'Apparently some girl's been attacked up at the Track . . .'

'Claire, I've got something to tell you.' I downed the rest of my pint. Refused to catch her eye. 'Remember the boy from the woods? I've seen him, Claire. He came into the shop today. Bold as brass. He's living here. He came back. His name's Gareth Maloney. I've told Davie and he's going to help. I—'

'Shut up, Jo.'

'What? I—'

'It was twenty years ago, Jo. You've got to *forget* this now. You've got to let it go. You've got to deal with what's happening to you now. I'm worried about you, Jo. I don't want you getting ill again . . .'

How could she say that? Her of all people. Sat in that chair. Having those blackouts all the time. Ever since it happened, I'd rarely thought of anything else. It had destroyed me as much as it had destroyed her. We had to talk about it. Didn't she even understand *why* I got ill?

'Claire, for Christ's sake! How can you tell me to forget it? Don't you want the police to catch him? To make him pay for what he did to you?'

'Please, Jo. I don't want to talk about this. Forget it. For me. Please.'

But how could I forget it? It wasn't just this. There was so much other stuff she didn't know.

I *had* to tell her. It had been eating away at me for so long, and now . . . now I just wanted to tell someone. I wanted to tell Claire.

She laid a hand on my arm and I blinked back a tear. 'Just leave it, Jo. Call me a taxi, please. I want to go home.'

13

After it first happened, they weren't sure she was going to wake up at all. I stood outside the window of the private room she was in. I think it's called the high-dependency unit now, but back then it was plain old intensive care.

The corridor smelled of bleach and boiled cabbage, with an underlying hint of dirty nappies.

I remember pressing my face up against the glass, trying to see her. A small shape on the bed, wrapped up in white sheets, a pulley attached to her pelvis and legs, trying to keep the bones in place. Hoping they might knit back together again.

Later, I found out that she'd broken two vertebrae at the base of her spine and that the compression had caused a partial severance of her spinal cord close to the base of her neck. She'd also stopped breathing for long enough to cause oxygen starvation to the brain – she was more than likely going to have brain damage.

Back then, they just told me she'd broken her back. At first I imagined her snapped in two like an old rag doll.

'Can't I go in, Mum?' I'd said. The tears had left a sticky, snotty film on my cheeks and I had tried to wipe it off. Someone else's mother might've hugged them, then done that thing where they spit on a tissue and wipe your face. Not mine.

'You've seen her through the window, Jo. What're you

wanting to go in for? She's been in here a week and you've no' wanted to come in to visit her once.'

My mum was drinking coffee from a beige plastic cup. She kept blowing on it and the puffs of steam smelled like burnt mince stuck to the bottom of a pan. I hadn't wanted to see her at first. I was too scared about what I would see. But then, from the window, I could see that they were trying hard to keep her joined together.

I didn't reply, just looked up at her through my eyelashes. My bottom lip quivered.

Mum sighed. 'Five more minutes. I'll meet you outside,' she said. I watched her back as she disappeared down the corridor. Her shoes squeaked on the shiny lino. I wondered if I'd be able to find her again, but then I remembered what the nurse at the desk had said when we'd arrived: 'Follow the blue line for intensive care.'

I'd follow it back towards the car park, where my mum would be standing outside with a Superkings Menthol stuffed in her mouth, sucking like she was trying to get the last dregs from a carton of Ribena.

'Hello, hen. Can I help? Are you lost?' I turned round to see another nurse, this one blonde-haired and fat-faced. She was smiling at me, bent down like she was about to pat me on the head. She was short and dumpy like three marshmallows on a skewer. I took a step back.

'I'm just visiting my friend.' I pointed at the window. 'She's in there . . .' I turned back towards the nurse. 'My name's Jo,' I added.

The nurse's eyebrows shot up into her fringe. She squeezed her lips together like she was snapping her purse shut. I could almost hear the cogs whirring inside her head. She blinked once, then she was all smiles again, as if she'd reset herself. 'Is your mum with you? You shouldn't really be here on your own, hen.' She glanced up and down the corridor, her head turning quickly this way and that like a little bird. 'Wait there.' She scurried off, her feet making fast little squeaks as she went.

I went back to the window and stared in again, cupping my hands round the sides of my face to block out the reflections at either side.

Claire's bed was side-on to the window, so I could see all of her right side. One arm was outside the covers, a little stick and a tube attached to the back of her hand. The tube led up to a metal stand with a big plastic bag full of clear liquid hanging off the side. On top of her was what looked like a metal-legged coffee table without a top. Sticking out of that were her legs, attached to two thick straps.

Her chest moved up and down as if she was being pumped up and deflated. In the background was the faint hiss of the machine that was blowing air into her lungs; over that, the constant *beep beep beep* of the machine that was monitoring her heart.

I'd seen this stuff on TV. I watched *Casualty* in bed every Saturday night. Mum always said it wasn't suitable for ten-year-olds, but she never bothered to check if I was watching it or not. It's not as if she was in the house to check. She and dad went out to the pub most Saturdays, leaving me with a microwaved cheese and tomato pizza, a bottle of cheap cola and a packet of Maltesers. The number for the pub was written on the ripped-off back of a fag packet and stuck onto the fridge under a magnet. I'd only ever had to call them once, when a man had come round the door saying he was collecting for something and I hadn't liked the way he'd looked at me in my short summer nightie.

The reason I wanted to go into Claire's room was that I wanted to talk to her. I'd heard the adults whispering about it when I'd been in the supermarket with Mum, some saying they didn't think she could hear anything. Mum ignoring them.

I reckoned she could hear just fine. I'd seen it on *Casualty*.

Her face looked peaceful, her hair brushed out onto the pillow, like she was sleeping and someone had given her a makeover for when she woke up.

I pressed a hand to the glass.

'Jo! Come away from there, right now. Where is your bloody mother?'

I spun round in the direction of the raised voice, one that I'd heard many times before. Several sets of squeaking footsteps. Claire's raspberry-faced mum striding towards me, flanked by Claire's dad and the fat nurse.

I spotted my own mum in the distance, just round the bend and coming towards us, panting from her hastily stubbed-out fag. 'Linda,' she was saying. 'Leave her . . .'

Claire's mum was at me by then. She grabbed me by the shoulders and shook me hard, all the while spitting in my face: 'Why? Why? Why?'

I tried to wriggle away, but she had a tight grip on me. The nurse and Claire's dad, Mike, were trying to grab at her arms and pull her away from me.

Eventually, her grip loosened and I twisted away, but one of her arms swung back, catching my mum – who had appeared at the back of the commotion and tried to squeeze in at exactly the wrong time – square in the face.

My mum's hands flew to her face, just as a single spurt of bright-red blood shot free from her smashed nose, spraying the window of Claire's room like a streak of wet paint.

Linda started to wail: a long, low sound that reminded me of one of those wild dogs that you see on nature documentaries. The ones that slaughter sheep.

I slid back against the wall and down onto the floor as the scene unfolded in front of me. Mike comforting Linda, the nurse holding a thick white pad up to Mum's nose and getting her to sit down on one of the blue plastic chairs. I shut my eyes and put my hands over my ears, sang quietly to myself until eventually it all stopped.

14

I'd never had a problem sitting in the pub on my own.

I wondered briefly about what Claire had started to tell me about the attack at the Track. Decided it was probably nothing. Maybe I'd ask Gray about it next time I saw him.

Poor Claire.

She thinks I don't know what she really thinks of me, but I do. I always have. But I still think of her as one of my best friends, because in reality who did I have? Craig, of course. But I couldn't spend all my time with him, even if I wanted to.

Claire and me had been pushed together when we were toddlers, when Claire's mum offered to take me back to theirs after nursery because she thought Mum was struggling for childcare. She wasn't. Not with my gran just up the road. But she let me go to Claire's anyway, just to spite her mother. I never knew what my gran was meant to have done that was so bad that my mum hated her, but she did.

Claire's mum was one of those mums who like to be involved in the community. She didn't work, because Claire's dad's job as the manager of the town's biggest bank gave him a high standing and a high salary. Of course he wasn't in such an elevated position now, since the bank had collapsed due to its ridiculous lending policies and had had to get bailed out by the government. After that, his job got moved to the head office. He became obsolete. But forty years' service had given him a pension that would make you sick, and now he spent

71

most of his time propping up the bar in the golf club, talking to all the other unemployed bankers.

Her mum, oblivious to the plight of the people who'd lost their homes in the economic disaster, somehow managed to spin the situation to her advantage and started a support group for the middle-class unemployed, catchily named 'New Beginnings'.

I don't know what I ever did, but Claire's mum took an instant dislike to me as a child.

She tolerated me when my mum and dad were still around, even after the accident, once the dust had settled and Claire was back at home.

Back in the eighties, my parents did her a good deal on jewellery, which she sold at parties in her house that she catered for with vol-au-vents and cheap German plonk. Like Tupperware parties, but with nine-carat gold lockets and charm bracelets and cubic zirconia stud earrings. She never wore the stuff herself, though, after one of her fingers had turned green from a bottom-of-the-range rose-gold dress ring my mum had given her as a 'Client Loyalty Bonus'.

After Claire's accident, she switched to selling nasty nylon and lace lingerie, but she still let me hang round with Claire because she felt sorry for my mum after what happened with the baby.

My brother would be twenty-two now, if he'd lived.

She'd had a perfect pregnancy. Not like with me, she was fond of saying. I'd caused her backache and sickness and headaches for the entire time I lived inside her. Then I came out and I was a girl, and my dad had wanted a boy, so he'd never fallen in love with me. To appease him, my mum decided not to fall in love with me either, although some-times, in secret – she tried.

I was just there. A hindrance that meant they couldn't go down the pub every Friday night like they always had. A screaming, unhappy little runt, driving a wedge between them with every second I continued to breathe.

Thank God my gran didn't feel the same. If it wasn't for her taking care of me, I'm sure I'd have been dumped on someone's doorstep.

The perfect pregnancy that should have brought me my little brother ended abruptly at six months. A rush of blood and a small, unmoving blob. The hospital sent Mum home, but she didn't utter a single word for a fortnight.

After that, she hit me for the first time. A slap on the cheek when I'd cheekily asked for a second slice of bread. Not that hard, but enough to make my cheek sting until I'd skulked off to bed.

It was all my fault. I'd caused her stress. She'd been fine before she got pregnant. Maybe a bit up and down, but mostly she was fine. I knew what to expect from her. Sometimes I drew us together, smiling and happy, and when I showed her the pictures she *was* smiling and happy – for a while. She seemed to resent me after she lost the baby, though. I don't know why.

That's when I started living at Gran's pretty much full time, except the school didn't know officially, so I still had to go round my parents' now and then to make it all look normal: as if we were normal. My gran and my mum spoke in one-word sentences. My dad pretended I wasn't there.

I walked back to Craig and Rob's the same way I came. Up Western Road until it turned into Burndale Road.

Rose Cottage.

There was a light on in the upstairs window, and I hung back against the wall opposite, keeping away from the street

73

light, straining to see if someone was up there in the bedroom. I still didn't know if Maloney had any family. I crouched down behind a cluster of pampas grass so that no one could see me from the road.

A rustling came from somewhere behind me, and I realised I wasn't alone.

The dog's face appeared, followed by a low growl.

Then a familiar voice.

'Bob? Where are you? Come out of those bushes now, d'you hear?'

Mrs Goldstone.

I slid out from behind the bushes and tried to make it look like I was tying my shoelace.

'Hello, Bridie,' I said, casually. Sobering up fast.

'Joanne! What're you doing in there?'

I stood up straight. 'I wasn't *in* there. I was just bending down to tie my lace and Bob appeared. He gave me quite a fright.'

Her eyes flicked down towards my feet and she frowned, and I remembered I was wearing boots with a zip, not laces.

'I—'

'You'll have been up here mooching about the McAllister's old house, eh? Checking out that young man who's moved in. He looks familiar, you know. I'm sure I've seen him before . . . Oh!' Her eyes lit up like someone had flashed their full beam. 'Have you heard about that bother up at the Track? I was telling your friend earlier – ye ken – that *Claire* one . . . So, the Brownlee girl was mugged. Makes me wonder what she was doing along there on her own anyway. That one's a bit of a handful, so I've heard . . .' She tailed off when she realised I wasn't going to give her the reaction she wanted.

74

'Anyway,' she continued, 'you should be getting back down to see your Scott, Joanne. He's really no' himself.'

'Hmm?' I said. I glanced at Bob and saw his ears prick up. He darted into the bushes. Mouse, maybe. Or a vole. Did dogs like catching little animals? I imagined they did. 'How do you mean? He seemed fine last night. I hope he told you he chucked me out on my ear. I haven't even got a place to stay—'

She made a clucking sound in her throat that reminded me of one of my gran's old hens. Cecilia, I'd called her. After the Simon and Garfunkel song.

'I'm sure you'll be fine with your colleague from the bookshop and his *friend*.'

I rolled my eyes. Prejudice was completely normal in this town, certainly for her generation. People of Bridie's age tried to use the correct words when they were talking to the younger generations, like me. But the words were always in implied inverted commas: 'gays', 'blacks', 'Asians'. I'd overheard her talking to her neighbours on the other side, though, more than once. Then the words were different.

Some things never change.

'You know he's not been going to work?' she said. A hint of a goading smile.

I stared at her. 'What do you mean? Of course he has. He gets the 7.10 every day. He leaves the house at seven. Always. He never even has a sickie!'

She smiled properly then. Delighted to have one over on me. 'Oh yes,' she said. 'He leaves the house at seven. But he comes back at ten past nine. After you've left for work.'

15

Claire settled herself on the sofa, mug of hot chocolate and some cheese and crackers on the table beside her. She picked up a cracker and bit into it, then laid it back on the plate, disappointed. It was stale, tasted of cardboard. Or maybe it was just her mouth, dry from the glass of wine in the pub. Or maybe it was her mood, soiled after her meeting with Jo.

Why did she have to bring up the bloody woods again?

Despite the obvious, permanent physical damage, Claire tried hard to keep the whole incident out of her mind. The time in hospital, the recovery . . . the questions. The blame on Jo. Only three people knew what had led them to being in the woods that day: herself, Jo and Polly McAllister. And, funnily enough, Polly hadn't had much time for her after it happened. She clearly didn't want to be friends with a cripple. Claire occasionally wondered what had happened to Polly. Where she'd ended up. No doubt she had a perfectly success-ful and happy life somewhere far away from the cloying com-munity that Claire and Jo had somehow been unable to escape from.

She thought about calling Jake, asking him to come round. But it was late, and he'd said he had things to do. What things, she didn't ask. She never asked. Despite his overprotective nature over the years, she'd never managed to learn as much about him as he knew about her. But she liked it that way.

Actually felt jealous that he had that level of privacy that most people in the town seemed to lack.

She was worried about Jo. Scott had been good for her. Kept her on an even keel, which was no mean feat. Should she call him? Find out what was going on? Maybe if he took her back it would steer her away from this latest obsession, dredging up the past again.

How did she know it was the boy from the woods anyway? She'd always said she hadn't seen their faces. Claire could only agree. She couldn't remember a thing after Jo shoved her through the fence while they tried to get away from the boys . . . Jo always felt guilt for what happened that day, but, in a lot of ways, Claire was to blame for it all. Which is why she preferred to keep it hidden in a box with the lid shut tight.

If only she hadn't joined in with Polly's goading that day . . . but she'd been trying to impress her. She was the best gymnast in the year and Claire wanted to be in *that* gang, not hang about with dropouts like Jo. She felt like such a bitch when she thought about it all, about how she'd treated Jo when they were kids. Sometimes she thought she deserved what had happened to her. She was never meant to be part of Polly's gang . . .

They were in Polly's bedroom, listening to New Kids on the Block. Jo was rifling through Polly's huge collection of CD singles. Polly had whispered something into her ear and Claire had laughed, covering her mouth too late.

Jo whirled round, glaring at them both. 'What's so funny?'

Claire glanced sideways at Polly, who gave Jo one of her butter-wouldn't-melt looks.

'Wouldn't *you* like to know?'

Claire had stifled another giggle.

77

Jo dropped the pile of CDs she'd been holding onto the floor. They landed with a clatter, sprayed out across the carpet. She lifted a foot to stamp on them.

'Hey . . .' Polly started, stopping abruptly when she saw the look on Jo's face. Her eyes were filled with hurt and anger, shining as tears threatened to escape. Jo stepped over the pile of plastic boxes.

'What's so funny, Claire?'

Claire stopped giggling, felt her cheeks grow hot.

'Nothing . . . It's nothing, Jo . . .'

Polly nudged her in the ribs, hissed, '*Tell* her.'

Jo crouched down on the floor so she was level with them both. Polly sitting back against the wardrobe. Claire, cross-legged, in front.

'Tell me what, Claire?'

Claire's bottom lip quivered. 'Maybe it's not true . . .'

Jo was on her knees now, Claire's face close to hers. 'What's not true?'

'About your dad,' Polly shouted, triumphant.

'*Shh*, Polly!' Claire spun round towards Polly, giving her a warning look, before turning back to Jo, whose eyes were as big as dinner plates. Polly's eyes were gleaming, a smile playing at the corners of her lips.

Without warning, Jo grabbed Claire, yanking her forwards by the straps of her dungarees. 'What about him?' she spat.

Claire knew they'd gone too far, but somehow she couldn't stop.

'He . . . he's that policeman . . .'

'Your mum's a slag!' Polly couldn't keep the glee out of her voice.

'I want to go home,' Claire said. She was crying now. Any sense of bravado she'd felt was gone. She felt nasty and sad,

78

and suddenly saw Polly for what she was. Manipulative, controlling. She'd never forget the look of pain in Jo's eyes.

'Me too,' Jo said quietly. 'I think me and you need to have a wee chat . . .'

Polly had tried to protest, but her attempts were weak. Jo stood up, then grabbed Claire by the arm and dragged her out of the room, crunching CD boxes as they went.

Claire heard Polly's words echoing around her head as Jo dragged her out of the house.

'She's a *bastard*, Claire. Her dad's that policeman! Her mum had *sex* with him when he was really young . . . No wonder her mum's such a nutcase!'

Claire hadn't asked Polly how she knew this. Didn't bother to check whether it was true or not.

Jo seemed to read her mind. 'It's not true, Claire. I've heard the rumours too. I overhead that old bag Bridie talking about it in the butcher's one day. My mum told her to shut her mouth or she would shut it for her . . .'

Claire nodded, still sobbing. 'Where are we going, Jo? I just want to go home . . .'

'We're going home, Claire. But first we're going for a wee walk in the woods . . . You're going to walk over that pipe.'

Claire spun round to protest, but Jo just grinned.

What could she do? She deserved it.

16

After Bridie and Bob had shuffled off, I sat at the bus stop, not really caring if anyone saw me. What the hell was Scott playing at?

I couldn't think about that now.

The upstairs light went off and my eyes dropped to the room below. The faint flickering light of a TV. *Are you in there alone, Gareth?* I thought. *What're you watching?*

I went through a stage in my teens of refusing to watch TV. I associated it with the hours spent alone while my mum did anything other than interact with me. When I first started school and we got time for free play, I'd sit in the corner of the classroom, my eyes fixed on a spot on the wall. I imagined I was watching *The Flintstones*. *Scooby-Doo*. Or my favourite, *The Wind in the Willows*. I wanted to be Mole. I wanted friends like Ratty and Toad. Miss Wallace let me away with it for the first week. Then I was made to go and play with the others, although by then they'd formed their little cliques. I could still picture Claire's face as she walked over to get me. Reluctantly. Even at five, she knew how to roll her eyes. What it meant. *I know what she's like.* 'I'll look after her,' she'd said. Poor Claire. Stuck with me ever since.

I willed Gareth to sense me out there. To come to the window.

I wanted him to see me.

80

A bus pulled up in front of me, air brakes deflating and the folding doors squeaking open. The driver looked out at me with a bored expression. I was surprised he'd even stopped. It was a request stop and they liked to ignore those who didn't bother to stand up and stick their arm out. I shook my head and the doors folded closed again. By the time the bus had pulled away, Rose Cottage was in darkness. I watched, just a little while longer. Then I jumped over the wall and walked carefully down the sloping path into the woods.

It was a stupid way to walk home in the dark. I was only assuming that Gareth Maloney was tucked up in bed. What if he'd seen me and used the time that the bus was obscuring my view of his house to sneak out and hide? He could be waiting for me in the woods. Ready to pick up where he'd left off.

There was no way he hadn't recognised me in the shop. Was he waiting for me to make the first move? Ask him outright?

I'd never been in the woods in the dark, but I could still make out the winding path through the trees, from memory more than any hint of light. I could hear the faint burbling of the burn to my left. The occasional rustle. Things scurrying around in the undergrowth. Somewhere nearby, the sound of a back door being pulled shut and locked. The faintest hint of tobacco smoke drifting through the trees. My skin prickled. Was someone there?

As I came out from the thickest part of the trees, the light changed. The burn was illuminated by the street lights from the path on the other side that ran along the back of the houses. Riverview Gardens. I could practically see Claire's bedroom.

The pipe was still there, exactly as it was. Smaller, though.

Or maybe I was bigger. I remembered Claire, too scared to cross.

If only I hadn't made her do it.

A light snapped on at a window in one of the nearby houses and something made me stop walking. I held my breath, listening. More rustling, followed by the unmistakable sound of a branch snapping behind me.

Close behind me.

'Who's there?' I said, quietly. Not turning round. My heart started to thump hard in my chest.

Nothing. Just the slightest sound of leaves blowing on the trees.

'I *said*, who's there? Come out you fucking coward. I'm not scared of you.' Once I was, a long time ago. But not now.

I caught another hint of smoke drifting softly on the breeze.

My mind flashed back to that day: to my defiance, despite being scared out of my wits. I thought I was braver now, but the eerie silence was weakening my resolve. Slowly, I turned, expecting to see him standing right behind me.

But there was no one there.

My shoulders sagged with relief. 'What's the point of this? Come out. Talk to me, for fuck's sake . . .'

Another snap, more rustling, then a dark-clad figure darted out of the shadows of the trees and made off in the direction of the bridge.

I bolted across the pipe in two steps, my heart threatening to burst out of my chest. I ran along the path, in touching distance of Claire's back fence, didn't slow down until I was back at Craig's flat. Chest heaving, my breaths coming out in sharp bursts, I rammed the key into the lock and slammed the door behind me.

I took the stairs slowly, tried to let my breathing return to normal. I hesitated outside the door to the flat, hoping that Craig was asleep. I was in no mood to talk.

Inside, Rob was sitting on the couch, alone. A bottle of wine sat next to his left foot. He held a glass in his hand. With nothing but the small table lamp lighting the room, the liquid in his glass looked black.

'I thought you were in Perth?' I said, panting. I tried to keep the surprise out of my voice.

'Came back early.'

I looked at the piles of stuff that Craig had brought up from his car. My clothes spilling out of bags. A small stack of boxes. A mound of shoes.

'Sorry about the mess. I was going to sort it, I—'

He shook his head, then bent forwards to pick up the bottle. Refilled his glass. 'Want a drink?' he said. 'You look like you could do with one.'

His friendly tone threw me. What was he after?

I tried to hide my shock. I thought he'd have been fuming about the mess. About me being there. 'Thanks,' I said, and walked through to the kitchen area to get myself a glass.

'There's another bottle in the rack,' he said. Then: 'Craig said you've split up with Scott . . .'

What else did Craig say? I wondered. I hadn't even had a chance to talk to him about Maloney yet. I decided to play it safe. 'Yeah. I suppose it wasn't really working out.' I took a glass from the corner cabinet and slid out a bottle of wine from the rack. The label was creamy coloured, the writing dark and swirly. Châteauneuf-du-Pape. Even I knew that was a good one.

I sat down, and he took the bottle and the glass from my hands. Balancing the glass between his knees, he took a bottle opener from the side table and opened the bottle with a swipe of a knife, two twists. The cork popped out. The wine glugged as he poured it into the glass; then he turned to me, glass in hand. Said: 'So who's this Gareth Maloney, then?'

I got it now. Scott was trying to use Rob to wheedle information out of me. To see if I was losing the plot or not.

He stared at me as I took the glass. I nodded a thanks before downing the contents and holding it out towards him for a refill.

'How much do you know?' I said.

He took a sip from his glass. 'Nothing.'

I didn't believe him. 'Probably best that way,' I said, knocking back the second glass of wine. I placed the glass on the floor and stood up. His eyes followed me, expecting more. He wasn't getting it.

'I'm going to bed,' I said. 'Thanks for the drink.'

THE BOY

The boy wonders how long he has to wait.

The woman has been crying for too many days. He has been trapped inside the house. The other boy too. But they haven't spoken about it.

Not about the man, or the crying woman. Or anything else.

The woman's mother comes round every day. Makes them all food. Fish fingers and beans and chips. Sometimes other things too. The woman doesn't eat.

Her face is wrinkling up.

'You have to eat something,' her mother says, 'for the boys.'

The boys are fine. They stay in their separate rooms. Sometimes, at night, he hears the woman talking to the other boy. Murmuring things to him. Soothing him. Then she goes back to her own room and cries and sniffs.

She turns up the sound on the TV. Some late-night American crap she watches. But he can still hear her, underneath.

The man has been gone for twenty-five days.

The crying started when it was obvious he wasn't coming back.

The boy needs to know when it is safe for him to go to the Place. To see if the bag is there. The guns. The traps.

The collection of *things*.

Every night, he peers out of the window – hoping to see the beam of the torch.

Somewhere.

He waits until thirty days have passed. The police have stopped coming round. They last came on day twenty-eight.

'There's nothing else we can do. He's an adult. Maybe he doesn't want to be found.'

'But he wouldn't leave us. I know he wouldn't.' The woman cries and the female police officer hugs her.

The boy watches through a gap in the stairwell from the upstairs hall. He sees the policewoman's eyes. She thinks the man has run off. She thinks, *I don't blame him.*

The woman looks ugly now. Her face shrunken and lined like one of those witch doctor's heads. Her clothes hang off her like rags.

She is broken.

Now she only has the boys.

The one she wanted, and the one she didn't.

The Place feels cold without the man. Empty.

The bag is gone, and the boy feels a moment's hope. He has run away. He has had enough. But he is not dead. He can't be dead.

But then he sees the other bag. The one they always hide deeper in the hole.

The Collection.

He would never leave it there for someone to find.

The boy feels his heart seem to grow bigger in his chest. The *thud thud thud* threatens to choke him.

The man would never have left him. The other boy, yes. The woman . . . maybe.

But not him. The man loved him.

The man is dead.

The boy hears a terrified wail of fear, and realises it is his.

17

Sunday morning.

Traditionally, I'd stay in bed until at least ten. Scott would bring me tea and a bacon sandwich in bed. He'd stick the TV on, but I wouldn't pay much attention. I'd read. I'd been in the middle of rereading Stephen King's *Carrie*. I'd always had an affinity with the main character, Carrie White. She had friends who didn't really like her and a screaming nutjob for a mother too. It was really no wonder she chose to massacre the lot of them. I realised I'd left it at the side of the bed. Scott's bed.

Damn.

I really didn't want to go back round there.

What Bridie had told me about Scott not going to work had left me with an odd heavy feeling in my stomach. Something wasn't right, but I wasn't sure I really wanted to know why.

I headed towards town, taking my usual route. It was early, still before ten, but clearly Maloney was an early riser too. All the curtains were open. A silver Volkswagen Golf was parked in the driveway. His, presumably. It'd been there every other time I'd looked. Yet, something. A feeling. The house had an emptiness to it and, despite the car suggesting otherwise, I sensed that no one was in.

A flash: that day I'd gone to Polly McAllister's for tea . . .

her mum taking a key from under an ornamental stone hedgehog near the back door. Could it still be there? I jogged across the road to his house and felt bile rising in my throat. Last night's wine. I swallowed, and my mouth felt dry and stale.

I hadn't ventured over this side since I'd found out he lived in the cottage. Although part of me wanted him to come out, the other part was terrified that he would.

The downstairs windows reflected the trees from the other side of the road. That empty feeling again. Definitely no one in. I walked up the little lane that led round the back and felt a trickle of fear. Anticipation. Same old gate, slightly ajar because it was out of alignment with the post. He hadn't bothered to fix it, believing like everyone else that Banktoun was a safe place. No one would creep round the back of his house, would they? I lifted the gate gently to prevent the wood scraping on the path. If by chance he was in the house, he'd definitely hear me.

I crept round the back.

The garden looked the same as I remembered it. A thicket of overgrown magnolia. A haphazard rockery. Up near the back wall, a rusty iron bench sat under a saggy-looking tree. On a small patch of lacklustre grass, a wooden bird house, tilted and rotten from years of rain and woodworm. Scattered around the back door were a few chipped ceramic pots of parched lavender.

And there it was, almost obscured by a clutch of stringy marsh grass.

The hedgehog.

Once it'd been smooth grey stone, the spikes somehow moulded to look realistic. Now it looked weathered, the spikes eroded into bumps. If you didn't know what it was supposed to be, you'd never think it was a hedgehog. I lifted it up and a family of furious beetles skittered away.

The key.

Wedged deep into the soil; dark brown from rust so ingrained I expected it to fall apart in my hands.

I stared at the door. Turned the key over in my hands, leaving a dusty metallic residue.

I dropped the key into my pocket.

Carefully, I replaced the hedgehog and crept back round the side of the house, lifting the gate behind me again as I went and letting the latch slot back into place.

No one would know I'd ever been there.

The supermarket café was packed. It was the only place open on a Sunday morning and it did a five-item breakfast for three pounds fifty. People queued outside from when it opened at nine and then there was a mad scrabble for seats. People shared tables with strangers. People stood glaring at other people who were taking too long to eat. There was no lingering allowed during the Sunday Special. Every other day of the week was much less frenetic, but that was because there were three other cafés in the town: Landucci's, the family-run Italian place, which was always good as long as you didn't mind waiting and weren't too fussy about your clothes reeking of grease afterwards; Betty Brown's, which was the favourite of the twinset-and-pearls crowd, with its floral tablecloths and homemade scones; then there was the newest place, Farley's, with its fancy coffee machine and its selection of French pastries. I'd never been in it, actually. It was hard to get in the door past the oversized buggies. The 'real' locals were yet to be convinced that two pounds fifty was a reasonable price to pay for a cup of 'milky coffee'.

My tray was still wet from the dishwasher, and as I discreetly tipped the water onto the floor, I scanned the tables. The worst thing about the people who live in small towns is that, on some level, you know them; and there's usually a reason why you don't speak. Normally I wouldn't dare share a table, but I needed to eat. My stomach felt hollow, and I realised I'd eaten nothing but two packets of crisps in the pub with Claire since the failed pasta disaster at Scott's. The smell of frying bacon was making me ravenous.

'Tomato or beans?'

I turned back to the counter. 'Can I have mushrooms please?'

That was met with a sigh. My plate held a wrinkled sausage, a rasher of bacon with a crust of thick, gelatinous fat, a shiny fried egg and a triangle of bread that had soaked up so much lard I felt my arteries clogging just looking at it. The woman behind the counter never once caught my gaze as she dolloped a pile of slimy mushrooms on top of the egg. I remembered too late that I detested tinned mushrooms. Should've gone for another sausage.

'Tea or coffee?' Another voice, but with the same weary tone.

'Coffee. Can I have hot milk please?'

Another sigh. 'There's cartons of milk next to the cutlery.' She turned to the next in the queue. 'Coffee or tea?'

Then the first voice again: 'Tomato or beans?'

Christ, what a life.

I slid my tray along towards the till, collecting a slice of toast and a pat of butter on the way.

'Toast's extra,' the cashier said. 'Fifty pee.'

I handed her a fiver and she dropped a pound coin on my tray and gave me a weak smile. I recognised her from school. Mary something. She had a smattering of spots on one cheek that she'd tried to cover up with foundation that was too dark for her pasty complexion. It looked like she'd dipped half of her face in sand.

I scanned the tables again. Since I'd been in the queue, a couple of extra spaces had opened up. Window seat on a table of four, facing away from the counter. The inhabitants were an elderly couple on their last triangles of toast and a young lad in a hooded top who appeared to be attempting a new world record in speed bean-eating. The other available seat was next to a stressed-looking young dad with two little kids who were gleefully spreading tomato sauce all over the table while he sipped his tea and pretended he couldn't see them.

I chose Option 1.

'Is this seat free?'

'Aye, hen. We're nearly done anyway.'

The young lad ignored me.

I put my tray down on the table and tried to press myself as far as possible against the window, leaving the maximum gap between me and the lad. Not that he was doing anything wrong, but the way he was shovelling the beans into his mouth, I was in danger of puking.

I ate the sausage first. Then the bacon. I balled the mushrooms up inside a napkin and wiped their brown sludge off the egg. I was trying to decide whether to put the egg on top of the fried bread or to dip the toast in the yolk when I realised that the couple had been replaced by a much younger version and the young lad in the hoodie had gone.

'Excuse me, is this seat free?'

I turned in the direction of the voice, ready to say, 'Of

course, help yourself,' but the words stuck in my throat and all I managed was a little squeak.

He was two tables away. Must've come in after me.

He put down his knife and fork and picked up his napkin, wiped his mouth. Took a sip of his tea.

I stared.

Felt the bacon fat sticking at the back of my throat.

The man standing next to me must've sensed something was wrong, and he muttered something before turning and heading off to take a seat in the other corner of the room. As far away from me as possible.

I stared over at Gareth Maloney, and after what seemed like an age, he lifted his head.

He looked confused, then realisation washed over his face, and he smiled at me.

I felt myself smile back.

18

The summer that my parents died, after one of my infrequent trips home, I'd been packed off to Black Wood Cottage again. I remembered the short journey in the car, my dad driving. Me in the back, surrounded by plastic bags stuffed full of shorts and T-shirts. Sandals. Thin cotton nighties. Piles of books.

He didn't say a word the whole way.

I stared out of the window at the fields, the church spire shrinking away as we drove further from the town. I hadn't realised then that it was only a few miles away from home, because when I was there it was like being in another world.

I was another me. After what had happened to Claire, I needed the comfort of being with someone who cared.

Gran was waiting at the front door as we pulled up the bumpy pot-holed driveway. She gave me a little wave. My face was pressed up against the window, grinning.

My dad pulled on the handbrake and left the engine running. He turned to face me. 'You be good for your gran now, you hear? No funny business. I don't want any bloody phone calls this time. OK?'

'OK,' I said.

I'd already pushed open the back door and my legs were dangling out of the car. I was clutching as many bags as I could carry. Gran walked towards us, her plain grey dress flapping around her ankles, her heavy work boots crunching on the gravel. She leant beside me and picked up the rest of my bags, and as she pulled back out, she touched her cheek against mine. Her skin felt like brushed cotton sheets. I slid off the seat, dropping my bags onto the ground. She slammed the door shut and I heard my dad sigh through the partially rolled-down window.

She folded her arms and took a step closer to the car, bending slightly to meet him at eye level. She craned her neck to peer deeper into the car. 'Jim,' she said, sounding disappointed. 'Miranda not with you?'

There was a gentle squeaking sound as he wound the window down further. 'She's got one of her headaches,' he said. He handed her a fat brown envelope. 'Here. This should do you.' The window squeaked upwards again until only an inch of a gap remained. He'd already turned away and I heard the crunch as he fumbled with the gears.

He was rubbish in mum's car. The Citroen 2CV was a clunker, but she loved it. 'Don't thrash it,' she always said, and he always ignored her. He didn't like to drive his own car, a much newer Saab, up the path to Gran's in case it got flicked with mud. I hated his car. It reeked of Magic Tree air freshener and stale B&H, and it always made a horrible screech when he stepped on the brakes.

Gran held the envelope in front of her for a moment as if wondering what to do with it, then slipped it into the pocket of her apron.

He drove off without another word.

I felt that little wobble in my legs that I got sometimes. That lump that popped up in my throat like I'd swallowed too big a bite of apple. 'Bye,' I said, not loud enough for anyone to hear. I had a feeling then, a prickling, like pins and needles. I knew then. I was never going to see him again.

19

The fried breakfast lay like a lump of stone at the bottom of my stomach.

I'd smiled at him. What the fuck was I thinking?

'Oh, hello. Jo, isn't it?' he said. 'Nice to see you again.'

Clever, I thought. *Playing it cool*. After all, no one knew what he'd done but me. I swallowed, trying to hold back the breakfast that was threatening to make a reappearance. For once I was lost for words.

'Are you all right now? You had a wee turn when I came into the shop . . .'

He stopped talking, suddenly self-conscious that he was the only one having a conversation. Everyone else was shoving food into their mouths, gulping tea. All eyes and ears were on him.

Who's the newcomer? What's he doing talking to her?

'I'm fine. Thanks. I hadn't eaten. Low blood sugar or something. I hope I didn't spill coffee on your book . . .' I was babbling. 'So, what brings you back to Banktoun?' I could play it cool too.

He gave me a broad smile, showing neat white teeth. Not a smoker. Not much of a coffee or red wine drinker either. I wondered if they were all real. Most rugby players would've lost at least one, I thought. Scott had lost two. I still had every single one of my own teeth, which was pretty good, considering.

'It would've been my dad's 60th birthday this weekend . . . Mum said I was daft, but I wanted to come back here. Mark it somehow. I've been renting that cottage up at the top of the town . . . Do you fancy another coffee?'

He gestured to the seat opposite him, which had become free since he'd started talking to me. He was still smiling and it hit me then, how good-looking he was. I hadn't noticed before. All I'd noticed were the eyes, and how the smile didn't quite reach them. I thought about what he'd said about his dad, that it *would've been* his birthday . . . A memory flickered like a half-lit cigarette.

'I—'

'Jo! Oh thank God you're here. I called Craig, but there was no answer. Is your mobile switched off?'

I spun round at the familiar voice and felt annoyed yet relieved at the interruption. I was about to do something I'd regret. Like sit down and have a civil conversation with Maloney. That wasn't part of the plan.

Not yet.

'Scott,' I said. I spoke quietly and tried to keep my voice level. I didn't want to have a scene in the middle of the café. Not another one. People had only just begun to get bored of my first exchange and now here was Scott, with his hair sticking up in tufts and his usual smell of Boss aftershave replaced by stale BO. 'What do you want?'

'I need to talk to you. Can we go home?'

'You chucked me out, remember?'

I heard shuffling in seats as the earwiggers picked up on more juicy gossip. I turned back to Maloney, who looked crestfallen. 'Sorry.' I shrugged.

'Another time,' he said. That grin again.

I grabbed Scott by the elbow and ushered him out of the café and into the car park.

'What is it?'

'Please, Jo. Come back to the house. There's something you need to know.'

I sighed. I couldn't deal with it. So he'd cheated on me with the girl from work. Kirsty. Whatever. It didn't matter any more. I had bigger things on my mind.

'Not now, Scott,' I said. 'I'll pop round tomorrow. On my lunch break, maybe.'

His face fell. He looked pathetic, like a kicked puppy. He didn't seem to care that I knew he'd be in at lunchtime on a Monday when he was supposed to be fifteen miles away, in Edinburgh. Popping out for an M&S sandwich or a cheeky lunchtime pint with the 'lads' from the office.

I felt bad, almost contemplated going round . . . but then I heard a voice behind me, spun round.

'Jo – you dropped this . . .'

I stared at Maloney's outstretched hand. In it, my watch. I hadn't even noticed it falling off.

'Thanks,' I said, 'I really must get that clasp fixed . . .'

'Are you sure you don't want that coffee?'

I bit the corner of my lip. It might be the right thing to do . . . get it over with . . . but no. Not yet.

'Another time,' I said, and when I turned away, hoping to find Scott waiting, I was disappointed to find out that he was gone.

20

When I got back to the flat, Craig and Rob were gone. A note was propped up against a vase on the kitchen table.

Gone suit shopping! Eeek!
See you tonight for pizza and beers,
C & R xx

Craig had been preoccupied with the wedding plans for months now, but I was perplexed as to how much arranging they actually needed to do. Rob seemed to be behind most of it, of course, with Craig just tagging along and pretending he wasn't terrified by the whole idea of the civil partnership and what it really meant.

The last time we'd slept together was three years ago, just before I'd started going out with Scott. Rob had been away in London for a week.

Craig had rolled over onto his side straight afterwards, so that I couldn't see him crying. 'This is the last time, Jo,' he said, 'I promise . . .'

I pulled the sheets up to my neck and sat up. The sex with Craig was always frantic and guilt-ridden, but there was love in there, somewhere. I felt it and I knew he did too. 'Craig,' I laid a hand on his shoulder, 'you need to decide what it is that you want . . . I get that you're confused . . .'

He jumped out of the bed and grabbed a pair of pants off

the floor, hastily pulling them on. 'I'm not confused, Jo. I told you. I love Rob. He makes me feel . . . complete . . . I know that sounds naff.'

'And what about me? What do I make you feel?'

He sniffed. 'You make me feel dirty, Jo.'

I opened my mouth to protest, but then he was on top of me again, laughing, smothering me, kissing me. Eventually he pulled away. 'It's complicated. You know that. But I just feel like I need to be with Rob. This is not real.' He rocked back onto his knees, cupped my chin with one hand. '*We're* not real.'

I pushed him off. 'It always feels real to me.'

His voice went cold and he turned his back on me. 'You'd better go, Jo. Rob's back tonight. I need to tidy up. Change the sheets . . .'

I slid out from under him and started to pick up my clothes. Wondered again what it was I needed to do to make him want *me*. Then I met Scott in the pub and leapt in without another thought for Craig. Our relationship had been damaged after that, and I knew there was nothing I could do to fix it.

I don't think he'd actually told Rob about us, but I think Rob suspected – which is why he seemed to blow hot and cold with me. There was no way I could stay trapped in that flat with the two of them, eating pizza and pretending I was happy to see Craig affirming the sexuality that I knew was a lie. So despite the voice in my head telling me that it was a terrible idea, I decided I had to go back to the only place that I could still call home. So I packed my stuff back up and called a taxi.

I was going to Black Wood.

*

As I walked up the path, rough gravel crunching underfoot, I got that familiar feeling of small fluttering wings in the pit of my stomach.

It reminded me of the times I used to spend in the pet shop in the High Street. I went in to look at the rabbits, even though my mum had stated more than once that there was 'no bloody chance' I was getting a rabbit and if I stopped whinging about it I might be allowed a goldfish. I'd mooched around the cages for a bit. Staring in at the mice as they wrinkled their noses and wiggled their whiskers.

The woman in the shop was nice to me.

After I'd been in there a couple of times, she used to let me top up the water bottles that were stuck on to the side of the cages. Let me post slices of carrot through the bars. It was on my third visit that I'd spotted the containers of live food they kept for reptiles. Clear plastic boxes of chirping, skittering crickets and locusts, confused and desperate to escape from their plastic prisons before they either ran out of air or got fed to the snakes.

I was fascinated and repulsed at the same time.

Ever since then, the feeling that people describe as 'having butterflies' made me relive that terrible fascination with the insects. That first encounter with the concept of survival of the fittest.

Life and death.

The taxi driver dropped my various bags and boxes in the porch, huffing and puffing with each one. 'Are you sure you don't want me to take these inside, hen?'

I shook my head. 'No thanks, this is fine. I need to sort it out first, and I don't think it's going to rain . . .'

'Right then, that's the last of it. That'll be a tenner then.'

I gave him a fiver tip for his exertions and he wheezed a

101

thanks as he climbed back into his car. I stood there watching him drive off, waited until he'd gone.

I crouched down at the front door and carefully removed a loose brick from the left-side wall of the porch.

The key was in its usual hiding place. A big brass thing on a ring.

It was risky of me to leave the key there, but most people thought the place was abandoned. Yet, oddly, no one had tried to break in. Not once. The house seemed to serve as its own protection, what with all the rumours about the 'witch' who used to live there. Gran and I had laughed about that at the time.

I placed the brick back into position and turned the key in the lock. The heavy wooden door swung open with a creak, and instantly the atmosphere changed. The fresh, mulchy air of the surrounding woodland was instantly replaced with a cloud of stale, airless fog. It was like climbing in between the covers of an ancient, musty library book that no one had opened for decades.

Stepping inside, I pulled the key back out, then slid it into place on the other side of the door.

It'd only been a couple of months since I'd last been there, but because of the cottage's position in the shade of the trees and the fact that I couldn't leave any of the windows open to air the place, it always maintained that damp, heavy air.

If I was to tell anyone about Black Wood, they'd ask why I didn't do it up and live there. That's what any normal person would do if they'd inherited a perfectly good cottage on the outskirts of town. The place was probably worth a fortune.

But selling it just wasn't an option, and up until now I'd never imagined myself living there. But things were different now. I had to adapt.

I carried in a few of the bags, dumping them on the kitchen table. In my mind's eye I saw rabbits being skinned and chopped up for the pot. I saw blood and guts, the remnants still visible in the form of faded brown stains. I shook it away. There was nothing to be scared of.

But then something made me turn round. I looked out the open doorway to the woods beyond, and there was a strange shimmer of light, my vision suddenly distorted like I was looking at an old film. I saw my gran, covered in blood and dirt. A mound of earth in the distance.

I heard my own voice, barely a whisper, 'What's happened, Gran? What was that noise?'

And then I heard it, so faint I almost missed it. Another voice, calling to me. Not in the past. In the present. Was it real?

Welcome home, JoJo.

The front door banged shut with a sound like shotgun-fire, and I screamed. Then I watched, quivering, the only sound my own heavy breathing, as the key turned slowly in the lock.

But when I blinked, I was sure that it hadn't moved at all.

THE BOY

He has never been on the hunt alone. He wants to carry on, though. Keep adding things to the Collection. The man might come back. He won't be happy if the boy has been lazy. Caught nothing.

He has no gun, though. Or traps. Both were in the man's hunting bag, and now that's gone. Just like the man.

Vanished without a trace.

He waits until he knows the woman and the other boy are asleep, and he climbs out of the window – the way he always did before.

The boy knows that the woman knew about the hunting. Knew the man went at night.

'It's called poaching, son,' the man had told him. 'If we get caught, we'll get in a lot of trouble.'

The boy wasn't scared.

They always took back something. Rabbits, usually. The woman would make them into stew or pies and say to the man, 'Why? What's the fascination? We can buy rabbits in the butchers, you know.' She'd laugh, and the man would laugh back.

'Makes me feel manly . . . like a real hunter gatherer.' He'd beat his chest and howl.

The woman doesn't laugh any more.

She doesn't know about the Collection.

'Our little secret,' the man said.

He makes a new trap from ropes and sticks. He learned how to tie knots years ago, in the other place.

He used to wish he was still there. Until the man came into his bedroom one night, said: 'Do you want to see something, son?'

The boy shrinks. Pulls the covers over his head. He's heard it before. In the first place, in the last place. He didn't expect it in this place.

The man senses his mistake. 'No. Oh Christ, no. I'm sorry, son. That's not what I meant . . .'

The boy pokes his head out.

Stares.

Waits.

The man is clutching a holdall.

'Look,' he says, shaking it towards him, 'look at my collection . . .'

The boy peers inside. Four sets of shining dead eyes stare back.

The makeshift traps work better than he expected.

The animal is in the hole. The twigs surround its small, quivering body.

Just a rabbit. He considers letting it go.

What would the man do?

The boy stares at the rabbit for some time. It has stopped

struggling inside its twig cage. It waits, patiently. Its eyes shine under the torchlight.

The boy reaches into the cage with both hands and with a single deft move snaps the animal's neck.

Crick.

Another sound in the woods. A twig snaps behind him.

He can just make out the dark figure at the edge of the trees. Close to the creepy cottage. The one where the Witch lives.

He scurries away on all fours, rabbit in hand.

The figure doesn't move.

It will be safer to take the Collection home.

21

Monday morning and I had barely slept a wink. Being back at Black Wood felt right, but I couldn't get rid of that sense of unease that the house was trying to tell me something, that my gran was somehow *there* – pushing me to remember something that I'd kept buried for a long, long time. Stupid, I know. I didn't believe in ghosts.

I went into work, even though it was the last place I felt like going. Funny, that. Last week I'd have said there was never a single day I didn't want to go in. But now my head was full of whatever it was that Scott was up to. Not to mention what I was going to do about the return of Gareth Maloney.

I considered spending the morning in the stockroom again, but then I realised that from the time it had taken me to come in, dump my jacket through the back, make a coffee and make my way back to the counter, Craig was standing at the door.

Denim jacket draped over one arm, Spiderman-printed messenger bag slung over one shoulder.

'That's me off then.' He looked at me hopefully and I stared at him for a bit, wondering what it was he wanted me to say. Then I remembered. *Shit.*

'Er, good luck – do you need luck . . . ?'

He shook his head. 'It's just a few forms. I wouldn't really expect you to be as excited as Rob and me . . .'

'Yeah, well, don't forget – you still need a bridesmaid, eh?'

He rolled his eyes. 'Sharon's in at twelve. Don't leave her on her own all day, though. Please?' He turned to go, then stopped, remembering something. 'Oh, and Jo . . . you know you didn't need to take off like that yesterday. You should've waited. We could have helped you with your stuff . . .'

I shook my head, smoothed my hair over my eyebrow. 'Go,' I said, and pushed him out the door. I thought about flipping the sign over from 'Open' to 'Closed' but decided I needed something to distract me, and even though Mondays tended to be quiet, there was always the slight hope that someone interesting might pop in. In the meantime, I decided to reorganise some of the shelves.

I'll admit to being a bit of a True Crime nut.

There was only a small section at the back of the shop, but there was enough on there to keep most serial-killer fanatics happy. I was fascinated by what made people like that tick. What has to happen to you in your life to make you want to murder others, especially kids, in brutal, unimaginable ways? I'd been reading a lot on Fred and Rose West and come to the conclusion that she was the driving force behind it all. Female killers might be in the minority, but when they did it, they didn't pull any punches. I'd just piled up all the books on the floor, ready to sort them into 'types', when the bell tinkled above the door. Typical.

'Hello, Jo. Sorry I had to run off on you the other day. You OK?'

I stood up too quickly and whirled round too fast, and as a result I stumbled, knocking the entire pile of books all over the floor.

Then he was there, at my side. 'What's this? Killer Jenga?' Gray laughed and bent down to pick up a scree of books. He stood as I turned, and I found myself looking straight into his eyes. He raised an eyebrow. 'Fred and Rose?' he said. 'Sounds like a kids' TV show from the eighties.'

He was standing too close to me. I could smell his after-shave. Something lemony. Clean. I felt myself blush.

'If only,' I said, turning away so he couldn't see my flaming cheeks. I took the book from his outstretched hand. 'Killer Jenga, though? I like that. Only I'd get them to make it with body parts rather than books. Fingers would be quite easy to stack up.'

He chuckled. 'What're we gonnae do with you, eh, Jo?'

'Fancy a cuppa?' I said. I didn't wait for a response. 'Watch the shop for a minute, will you?'

I flicked on the kettle and put out two mugs. I already had a coffee on the counter, but I wasn't going back out to get it. *What's wrong with me?* Davie Gray had a peculiar effect on me. I don't think I fancied him, as such. Yeah, he was prob-ably too old anyway, but that wasn't the point. Something about him. Something about the way he was with me. Like he cared about me, and it wasn't just for show.

I took the cups out the front and was relieved to see that he was still alone in the shop. I needed to talk to him and I wasn't really in the mood for customers.

He took the cup and gave me a small nod, eyes flicking to a place just above mine. 'See you've been at it with the eye-brow again. Want to talk about it?'

Davie Gray was one of the few people who ever mentioned my eyebrows. He was far from the only one to notice, of course. But after he'd seen me the first time I ever did it, I suppose it must've stuck in his mind. He was a policeman, after all. It was his job to notice things.

I sighed. 'I've split up with Scott . . . and apparently he's up to no good, according to Bridie Goldstone . . .'

He blew onto the top of his mug before taking a tentative sip. 'You know better than to listen to gossip, Jo. Why don't you just talk to Scott? You two seemed happy enough. Can you no' sort it out?'

'I dunno. Anyway, it's not just that, is it? I told you on Saturday. I told you about—'

Gray turned towards the doorway as the tinkling of the bell interrupted me mid-flow. Damn that bloody bell! I was sorely tempted to yank it off the sodding doorframe.

I thought I'd had enough shocks for one week, but here was another one smirking in my face.

'What the hell do you want?'

Jake shrugged. 'We're having lunch in Farley's. Claire asked me to pop in and see if you wanted to join us.' He waited until Gray turned away again, then he puffed out his lips and blew me a kiss.

Sharp, acidic rage bubbled in my stomach.

'Since when do you and me get to have lunch together, eh? Thought that was Claire's idea of hell?'

She'd always kept us separate. The two of us rubbed at each other like tinder sticks and Claire couldn't stand the tension. You can't get on with everyone. I knew that better than most.

'I better be off. Cheers for the tea,' Gray said, his expression unreadable. No doubt he was wondering what the hell was going on. We'd never talked about Jake before. There were too many other things on the 'why is Jo so fucked up?' list to deal with.

'Everything all right? Bit of a party, is it? Listen – have you heard about what's been happening up at the Track? I just bumped into Bridie, and I . . .' She stopped talking when she realised we were all staring at her.

Thank God for Sharon. Jake had left the door ajar so we hadn't been alerted to her presence by the annoying little bell.

'Oh good, you're here. I just need to pop out for a bit. I won't be long.'

I dragged a startled Gray by the elbow and walked out.

22

Gray gently lifted my hand off his elbow, placed his hands on my shoulders and turned me around to face him.

'What're you playing at, Jo? You're lucky the shop was quiet or I'd have had to make more of a fuss there, you know. Manhandling a police officer is an offence, young lady.'

I'd been staring down at his feet, wondering what he was going to say, trying to work out how he got his boots so shiny. I lifted my head as the tone of his speech changed. Manhandling? Young lady? He had a smirk on his face now and I frowned. This wasn't funny. None of it was funny.

'Sorry,' I managed, before pulling down at my fringe again, fully aware I was acting like a sulky teen.

Gray sighed. 'I don't know what it is with you, Jo. You're a nice lassie. You just seem to be so angry about everything. With everyone. What is it that you hate so much about Jake? I saw the look you gave him when he asked you to go for lunch. Mind, I saw the look he gave you back . . . What is it? Bit of jealousy there? Fine line between love and hate, eh?'

'Oh, just shut up,' I said, immediately regretting it. I didn't have many allies, and here I was pushing away yet another one.

Gray stiffened, adjusted his hat. 'I need to get back now. Give us a shout if you want to talk.'

He turned and I stood there staring at his retreating back.

I dug my nails into the palms of my hands until I felt the flesh break.

I couldn't face going back to the shop. I'd made a fool of myself with Jake. With Gray. I needed to go somewhere where none of that would matter for a while.

Scott's house was a ten-minute walk from the shop. I walked fast, head down. Avoiding all eye contact with passers-by. God forbid someone might actually want to be nice to me. I was panting by the time I reached the top of the hill. The midday sun was beating hard on my back and I felt a trickle of sweat running down between my shoulder blades. Another stinking-hot day. I preferred the cold. Preferred wrapping myself up and sitting in front of a roaring fire with a hot chocolate and a tot of rum, and a Jackie Collins novel to transport me away. Not this harsh northern heat that left everyone pink and sweating like newborn pigs. Bad things happened in the summer.

Too many bad things.

I heard the low clang of the town hall bell strike one o'clock. Scott's curtains were still closed. I shuffled about on the doorstep, debating whether to knock or just go in. If he was in there, it'd probably be unlocked. He'd always been crap with security. I'd always been the one to lock the windows and double-bolt the doors from the inside. It might be a small town, but you never knew who might want to try their luck. I leant up against the door, straining to hear sounds from within. The low murmur of the TV, voices chatting. What crap was on at this time of the day? That panel show with the annoying middle-aged women. If Scott was watching that, he'd stooped to new lows. I decided on a knock and a simultaneous push on the handle. It opened.

'Scott? It's me . . .'

The house smelled different already. I'd only been away a couple of days, and the familiar scent of my citrus body spray that usually hung in the air had been replaced with the stink of dirty dishes and unwashed skin. I stepped into the hall. My winter coat was still hanging on the row of pegs on the wall in front. My black biker boots still in the rack below. A couple of letters lay on the mat and I bent down to pick them up, suddenly feeling sick. The aching familiarity of the flat mixed with regret that I couldn't hold on to the most decent man I'd met in years. The pain of my failings stabbed me in the gut. When I stood up, I felt a single itchy tear inching down my cheek and hastily wiped it away.

He was standing in the entrance to the living room, hair mussed and sexy. The look partially ruined by the washing-machine-stretched greying T-shirt and the ancient tracksuit bottoms he was wearing. His face was pale beneath the smattering of stubble. His eyes rimmed red. When I'd seen him in the supermarket the day before he'd looked rough, but today he'd taken it to a whole new level.

'Babe,' he said, lifting an arm to greet me in a sort of half wave. In his other he held a can of own-brand lager, blue with a white swirly logo. Pikey Pilsner, we used to call it. Now here it was in his hand at one o'clock on a Monday, and the worst part was it didn't look like it was his first of the day.

What the hell was going on here? Thoughts of Jake and Gray and Gareth Maloney disappeared from my brain as I followed Scott through into the tip that used to be our living room. Plastic bags dotted across the carpet, empty cans thrown half-heartedly on top. An overflowing ashtray sat on

114

the edge of the coffee table, resting precariously. A pizza box, lying open with a couple of curling triangles and a pile of crusts. A polystyrene chip box on the couch beside him. He shoved it onto the floor.

'Take a seat.' He wobbled slightly, then fell backwards onto the couch, can still in hand.

I surveyed the carnage. Stared at him in disgust.

'Jesus Christ. What the fuck happened in here? Have you started organising coffee mornings for tramps now?'

He snorted and took a swig from the can. 'Stand then. Whatever you want. Fuck it.' He crushed the can and threw it onto the floor, and then he sagged forward and dropped his head into his hands. He started to sob.

This . . . this was not what I'd been expecting at all.

I couldn't decide whether to go to him or leave him to it. I'd never seen him cry before. I'd certainly never seen him crack up. That was my job. I'd held the monopoly on meltdowns for a long time. Seeing someone else hit the skids was a new one on me. Eventually, I decided just to let him cry it out. I bent down and picked up an empty carrier bag and started to fill it with rubbish. I was on the third carrier bag of beer cans and pizza boxes when my mobile buzzed in my pocket.

I stared at the screen.

Scott and his problems would have to wait.

23

Claire's primary reason for choosing Farley's over Landucci's was because they had a wheelchair ramp. She used to hate doing things solely because it made life easier, but as she'd gotten older it'd become more and more pointless to keep fighting the fact that she was actually disabled and really couldn't do everything for herself.

It hadn't come easy, though.

The day she'd woken up from the coma, she'd known. Even before the doctors said one single word. She knew her life was never going to be what she'd hoped it would be. It might've been more than twenty years ago, but it was as fresh in her mind as if it had happened yesterday. She picked up the laminated menu and stared at it, feeling herself float off as the words became a jumbled blur of swirly font and pictures of cakes . . .

'Claire? Claire? Oh God – I think she just opened her eyes! Doctor – come quickly! I think she just opened her eyes!'

Her mum's voice had sounded weird, thick and squeaky. Like she'd been crying. She'd felt her eyelids flicker, and she'd tried hard to do it again, but it felt like they'd been stuck down with glue. Then the light had changed from dull to bright to an intense prickly feeling, like when you get shampoo in them in the bath. Then the light dimmed and she heard a small click. A torch. The doctor had been shining a torch in her eyes. Then she felt a slight tickly fuzzy feeling as someone dragged something across her eyelids.

'What's that? Is that going to hurt her? What're you doing? She's trying to open her bloody eyes!'

The doctor's voice was calm but with an undercurrent of annoyance. 'It's only a cotton bud, Mrs Millar. We're just trying to soften the build-up around the lids to make it easier for her. Looks like she might've developed a bit of conjunctivitis or something. We'll get her some antibiotic drops and it'll make her more comfortable. That's probably what's causing the flickering. As I told you earlier, Mrs Millar . . . Linda . . . there's still no change in her vitals. She's still at grade two on the Glasgow Coma Scale. No voluntary movements. I hate to keep saying this, but they don't often wake up from this sort of thing without some lasting damage. If they wake up at all . . .'

But I can hear you! she'd screamed. But it was only in her head, because her mouth refused to comply. She lay there listening to the sounds of her mum's frantic gibberish and the doc saying the same things he'd been saying for the last two weeks. They had no idea she could hear them. The first person she'd heard hadn't been the doctor, though.

Nor her mum.

It'd been Jake.

'Earth to Claire – anybody home?'

Her head flipped up at the sound of his voice and the menu that she'd been staring at for the last ten minutes fell out of

117

her hands and slid across the table. 'God, sorry. I was miles away . . .'

'I could see that . . .'

Jake bent down to pick up the menu and kissed her hard on the lips. She felt that familiar stirring down below her stomach. She loved that he could still make her feel like that, after all these years. Something Jo would never understand.

'Is she coming?'

Jake snorted. 'Of course she's not! I won't tell you what she said to me, but I'm sure you can imagine. That copper that's always sniffing around was in the shop. Should've seen the look on his face when she told me where to go.'

Claire sighed. 'Right, well that's the last time. I've tried, Jake. You know I have. I really don't know what it is that makes her hate you so much.'

'She's pretty good at hating, Claire. I'm surprised that mug Scott stuck with her as long as he did. Did you find out what happened yet? Better offer? Someone with a heart come along, eh?'

Claire picked up the menu again and pretended to study it. She didn't even need to look at it. She always had the same thing: cheese and pickle sandwich on white bread and whatever soup they had that day. She kept her gaze directed at the menu, though, so Jake couldn't see her eyes. She knew she couldn't lie, but she didn't want to mention what Jo had told her in the pub. Jake didn't like it when she mentioned her accident. Whenever she thought about it, she felt angry with herself for not being able to remember. Whenever she talked about it, she got herself into a state. Jake hated to see her upset, so it was easier not to mention it.

'She didn't say. Says she suspected he'd been seeing a girl at work but that he hadn't actually admitted it. According to

Jo, things hadn't been great for a while. Which came as a shock to me cos she was singing his praises last time I saw her. Then again, I'm never entirely sure when she's bullshitting me.'

Jake pulled out a chair and sat down, nodding to the waitress as he shrugged off his denim jacket.

Claire stole a glance at him as he had his head down towards the menu. He seemed content enough. Clearly she must've sounded convincing. By the time they'd ordered their lunches, talk had shifted to other things. But Claire's mind was still half on what Jo had said about bumping into the boy from the woods. The one who – according to Jo's version of events – had sparked the chain of events that had changed the course of Claire's life. Not to mention Jo's.

The waitress set a pot of tea and two cups and saucers on the table, and Claire smiled up at her and said, 'Thanks, Carol.'

As she watched Jake lift the lid of the teapot and stir the contents with his teaspoon, she felt her mind slipping out of focus again. The blackouts had been more frequent recently. She really needed to make an appointment with the doctor. Maybe she'd do what he suggested last time too. What she'd been shying away from for years. Maybe she'd make that appointment for hypnosis. See if someone couldn't help her remember what had happened on that day.

Problem was, she didn't want to.

24

Gray left Jo standing outside the bookshop, her face battling embarrassment, anger and something else that he couldn't quite place.

He was usually good with tells. The way people tried to hide them. Purposely stopping their eyes from flicking to the left when they were lying but not realising they were giving it away by the way they were wringing their hands or pushing a hair behind an ear. Jo was usually easy to read. It wasn't as if she ever tried to hide how she felt about things.

He knew she believed that this man who'd come into the shop was the one that'd caused Claire's accident all those years ago. They'd investigated it as much as they could, at the time. Gray had been a young PC, desperate to find something out. But there was no trace of the boys. No witnesses. Just Jo's statement and what Claire remembered after – which wasn't much.

Gray had always stood by the girl. He'd felt sorry for her, apart from anything else. He only wished he could get through to her and get her to drop this thing. What was it, twenty-odd years ago?

But Gray had made a promise. To someone special.

Jo's mother.

He remembered that night. It was imprinted on his brain. *Bang. Bang. Bang.* The alarm clock beside the bed: 11.45.

She was at the front door, hair mussed up. Eyes wild. Why the hell didn't he invite her in?

'Please,' she says, 'look after her . . .'

He wasn't someone to go back on his word.

A white transit van was parked outside the newsagent's, the engine idling. The back doors were wide open and Gray couldn't resist having a look inside. Piles of multicoloured things in packets; cheap plastic robots. Stacks of colouring and puzzle books. He peered over at an open box and found it full of fancy-dress outfits. He was reaching for what looked like a Spiderman costume when a voice in his ear made him jump back guiltily.

'See anything you like, Davie? I've got a Wonder Woman at the bottom if you fancy that. Adult-sized . . .'

Gray turned round to find a man in tight black jeans and a burgundy polo shirt with a blue stripe around the collar, face pulled into a smirk beneath neatly Brylcreemed hair.

'All right, Ian? Bit early for Halloween is it not?'

Ian grinned. 'You're behind the times there, man. Kids are into fancy dress all year round these days. Only yesterday morning I bumped into a young Luke Skywalker in Tesco's, howling the odds at his ma when he wasn't allowed three boxes of Coco Pops and a carton of Ben and Jerry's for breakfast. Thought I better get in on the action before anyone else thinks of it.'

'Don't they sell this stuff in Tesco's then?' Gray said, picking up another outfit, turning it over in his hands and squinting at the packet.

Ian took the packet from his hands and flattened it out. 'Dracula,' he said. As if it should've been obvious. 'Aye, they do sell it in Tesco's, just like everything else I bloody sell here. I've practically stopped doing cards now. I can't compete when they sell them for a quid. But if I stop trying, what do I do?'

Gray nodded. He felt for him. A few years ago, Ian Watson's shop was the only place in town to buy papers. Now there was Tesco, and combining it with picking up the bread and the milk and something for the tea, Ian was struggling. Gray changed the subject. 'How's Anne?'

Ian threw the costume back into the box, then leant into the van and scooped the box up in his arms. 'Come and ask her yourself,' he said, 'and don't come empty-handed.'

Gray picked up a stack of robots and followed him into the shop. It was one of those Aladdin's caves of a place. Anything and everything.

Anne was standing behind the counter. Her face looked pale, but there were two high spots of red at the top of her cheeks. She had some sort of elaborate scarf wrapped around her head, blonde hair cascading from beneath. She was handing over a brown paper bag to the customer in front of her. She noticed Gray looking and gave him a wide smile.

'Hello, Davie,' she said.

The customer snatched the bag and turned quickly, almost walking straight into him in his hurry to escape the policeman's gaze.

'Ah, Pete, it's yourself. I'm glad I bumped into you . . . I was hoping we could have a wee chat later, on your own?'

Pete Brotherstone scuttled towards the door of the shop without looking up. Bag clutched to his chest. 'Can't talk to you. I need to go home now. Dad's waiting,' he said in his usual rapid-fire monotone.

122

Anne smiled at the lad, but it didn't quite reach her eyes. 'Bye, Petey, see you again.'

She turned back to Gray, patted the side of her head. 'Made it myself. What do you think?'

'I think you look beautiful, Anne. As always.'

'Idiot,' she said, but the smile she gave him was like a flood-light being switched on. He liked Anne. She'd been in his class all the way through primary school and he'd thought about asking her out but never did. He took defeat graciously when she chose Ian instead. Ian and Gray bought their first scooters together. They'd attended all the meets together, pogoed to The Jam together on Glasgow Green. He loved them both.

Something felt off, though.

Gray frowned. 'Does Pete come in here a lot, Anne? I'm surprised to see him without his dad . . . Thought he kept him wrapped up in cotton wool 24-7?'

Anne gave him a strange look. Like she was mentally battling with what to say. 'This is about the only place he's allowed to go on his own. He feels safe here, even if . . .' Her eyes dropped, and when she looked at him again Gray was sure he could see tears forming in the corners. 'Martin came in and had a wee chat with me one day. Said the laddie had a crush on me – as if it wasn't obvious . . .' She paused, took a deep breath. 'He's no bother really. He buys his card and glue and string . . . and his other bits and bobs for his models. Actually, I'm not really sure what it is he makes. I keep expecting him to turn up with one of his creations sometime . . .'

'Hmm,' Gray said. He was only half listening. He was still thinking about Pete, but mostly he was musing about Anne. He still couldn't understand why she wouldn't tell him who it was who had grabbed her in the park. The cut on her face from tripping up as she ran away hadn't been seen to. She'd patched it up herself and the scar was a jagged streak of pearl down the side of her otherwise perfect face: a constant reminder of that night.

He wondered, vaguely, if it was connected to the thing up at the Track now. But it didn't quite fit. There had been no contact – so far – up at the Track. He had a feeling that Anne knew her attacker. That she was protecting him. Why, though, he had no idea. The Track thing was different. In his gut he still thought it was down to kids mucking about.

'Listen – I need to get back, but how about we sort out that curry sometime soon, eh?'

'That'd be nice,' Anne said. 'Actually, we were thinking of doing something on Thursday . . .' She paused. 'I was going to ask Marie.' She winked then, and Gray's heart sank. He wasn't up for match-making. His heart had been broken a long time ago and he could never quite muster the enthusiasm for a relationship. Marie was lovely, though. Maybe it was time to take a chance. After all, he wasn't getting any younger.

'OK,' he said, before he could stop himself. 'I'll probably regret this . . . but why not, eh?'

Anne already had her phone in her hand, fingers texting furiously. 'See you at seven, then . . . or you can come earlier and watch *Eggheads* with Ian, if you like.'

Gray laughed. 'Done,' he said. He turned towards the door just as Ian appeared carrying a pile of masks that'd fallen out of the box. The top one was black and bumpy, small white ears at the top. He lifted it off and held it up. With the eyeholes, it looked sinister. Definitely not something he'd want his kids to be playing with. If he had any.

'What's this meant to be?'

'Black sheep. There's white ones underneath, I think.'

Gray stared at the mask. The strange bumpy surface that was meant to look like curly wool but actually just looked creepy. The bumpy face was freaking him out. It was triggering a memory of something bubbling under the surface. Something that'd been niggling at him since he'd spoken to Jenny Brownlee about her encounter at the tracks.

His face looked weird. Sort of bumpy.

'Ian, can I borrow this one? I'll bring it back.'

Ian looked bemused. 'Have it. It's only a quid.'

Gray was already out of the door.

A mask. A bloody mask. Under the balaclava. It made perfect sense. And hadn't Ian said you could buy them in Tesco's? Anyone could've bought one. That, with a cheap balaclava from McCurdie's Outdoors at the bottom of the street. But that wasn't the only thing he'd remembered.

It was something Jo had said, a long time ago. The reason she'd never been able to properly identify the boys. They'd been wearing masks.

THE BOY

He has the perfect place.

They gave him the room at the back of the house, with the window looking out onto the garden. The gate that leads to the fields beyond. Further, the woods.

He has a small bed. Action Man bed covers. A small bedside table. A lamp.

At the far end, a deep built-in wardrobe. Although he has little to store in there, it is a place he likes to sit sometimes. Close the doors.

He has a small torch. A penknife. He keeps them on him at all times.

At the end of his bed is a heavy wooden trunk.

'For your toys,' the woman told him, with a smile that didn't quite reach her eyes.

The man came in later. 'Here,' he said, 'some things for you.'

Books, comics. Some Action Men. The one with the eyes that move back and forwards from the little switch on the back of his head.

Eagle eyes.

The boy is not interested in these toys. He puts them in an old shoebox in the back of the wardrobe.

In the toybox, he keeps the Collection.

He lines the things up neatly on the bottom, another layer. Another.

He wonders if the other boy would like to see them.
Decides that he wouldn't understand.
The Collection is his now.

He underestimates the other boy. Never imagines for a second that the other boy would dare go into his room.

The other boy's room is stuffed full of all the things that boys like.

Footballs, cricket bats. Books, music. More Action Men. Even a tank.

He has nothing to offer.

He has gone to his room after dinner. Fish fingers again. The woman drank a cup of coffee with them at the table and smiled.

'I'm still here for you both,' she said.

It wasn't the same. Wasn't enough.

He has the lid of the toybox open, organising the things. He is digging deep inside.

A rabbit's pelt. The small skull of a vole. Three whole mice.

The animals feel different now. Their fur rough. Their bodies hard.

Their eyes dull without the shining light of life behind them.

In the heat of the house, some of them are beginning to rot.

He barely notices the smell.

It's when he takes out the head of the badger – the last

thing he collected with the man – that he notices that the doors of his wardrobe are open slightly.

He never leaves them open.

He hears the intake of breath.

Sees one bright eye peering out at him, open wide.

He has two options. He has to be careful. It could all backfire on him now. He can pretend he hasn't seen. Or he can invite the other boy to play.

He feels a fluttering in his chest as he makes his decision.

'Come out,' he whispers. 'I'll show you.'

He waits.

After a few moments, the wardrobe doors open and the other boy creeps out from his hiding place, eyes blinking from being in the dark.

'She'll go mad if she sees these,' the other boy hisses. 'They stink.'

'It's just nature,' the boy replies. 'Nothing to be scared of.'

He offers up one of the mice in cupped hands, and the other boy, shaking, takes it.

25

Lydia McKenzie hated maths. She hated English too, and French. Come to think of it, she wasn't that keen on geography, history or modern studies either. God knows why she'd chosen any of them. She'd tried telling her dad she wanted to be a children's book illustrator, but he'd just laughed.

'So you go to art college for that, do you?' he'd said. 'Hang out with your pot-smoking mates, sitting drinking black coffee and talking about Monet all day, eh?'

For an intelligent man, he really was a first-rate arsehole. He'd blackmailed her into taking a load of subjects she wasn't interested in, saying he'd pay her two hundred quid for an 'A', a hundred for a 'B'. There was nothing for a 'C' and if she failed anything she was getting kicked out and disinherited. Prick.

Lydia wasn't interested in his money, but it didn't stop him throwing it at her. It was his way of trying to look after her, he said. Now that it was just the two of them. The two of them plus that gold-digging bitch Louisa who called herself his girlfriend. Poor mum'd be turning in her bloody grave.

She took her mobile phone out of her bag and stared at it. Still nothing. Where the hell was Fraser? Quarter past two at the Track, he'd said, on the note he'd aeroplaned across at her halfway through Baldy Baldwin's monotonous drone about uniquely shaped rock formations caused by thousands of years of volcanic eruptions. What was that wide one called again? Gorge? Gulley? Something like that. She could do with finding one of them now and flinging herself down it.

She knew she wasn't supposed to be going near the Track – what with the thing that had happened to Jenny Brownlee. But, really . . . what *had* happened? Nothing, by all accounts. Jenny had always been a drama queen and Lydia wouldn't put it past her to make up something like that, although there *had* been a witness, that jogger Dave Morriss. There'd been some rumours about him a while back too. What was it again? Something to do with one of last year's sixth formers and a pub up town. Not that it was *illegal* or anything, but still, he was a few years older . . . Ruth Colgan would know. She'd have to ask her.

She was positive that Fraser had shagged Lynne Daniels at Ruth's party at the weekend. The way they'd both mysteriously appeared in the kitchen after she'd hunted the whole house for him for nearly an hour, bumping into Lynne's boyfriend more than once and finding out he was doing the same. They'd looked at each other, both suddenly getting it, but neither of them had wanted to voice the pain. If you don't say it, then it's not true, right? Lynne's pink flushed cheeks were a dead giveaway. Not to mention the little smirk when she thought no one had sussed them. Bitch. Fraser was a bloody prick as well. What was it with blokes? The only reason she hadn't dumped him yet was because they were meant to be going to see Foster the People together at the O2 Academy and there was no way that Lynne flippin' Daniels was taking her place for that!

She was nearly at the second bridge when her phone finally beeped.

Sorry, running late. Wait for me! XOXO

Lydia frowned. Yet again, she had no choice. She could turn and walk back. Slink back into the school with a well-worn excuse. Nobody would give that much of a shit. Or she could wait, and eventually he'd turn up and he'd probably have a flask of hot chocolate and a stack of cheese sandwiches wrapped in foil – which to some people wasn't worth skipping school for, but for her it was the only time she could have a proper homely treat without someone nagging at her about fat and carbs and the glycaemic bloody index. Oh yeah – not only was her dad a control freak when it came to her grades and what he wanted her to be when she left school, he was also obsessed with her staying a size ten and wearing the right clothes and seeing the right people. In fact, Fraser was a top choice, as he planned to study law at St Andrews and that was as good enough a reason as any to dump him before he humiliated her any further.

He did make good hot chocolate, though.

OK, she decided. Ten more minutes. Fifteen, max. Then she was going home and fuck it if her dad or Louisa were in. She'd say she had a headache. Period pain or something. Louisa would turn her nose up at that. The woman didn't have an ounce of motherly love inside her fully inflated chest. At least she would leave her alone.

She sat on the concrete blocks at the base of the bridge and took out her phone again. No more messages. She thought about texting Sarah, but she knew her friend wouldn't be happy at the interruption. For some unfathomable reason, Sarah actually liked maths and was considering becoming a teacher. Lydia often wondered if they'd manage to stay friends if they both went to different universities. She didn't have many close friends, and Sarah had been there for her

131

when her mum had got ill. No one else seemed to know what to say.

As she scrolled through the messages on her phone, hoping for something to cheer her up, she zoned out. Didn't hear the footsteps crunching carefully down the siding from the bridge above. A small pile of loose stones and mud skittered down the slope, and finally she turned round, a frown on her face, fully expecting to see Fraser standing there, rucksack slung over one shoulder, sheepish, irresistible smile on his face.

A man stood in front of her. He was dressed from head to toe in black, his face obscured by a balaclava. She gasped, but the pang of fear was soon replaced by a sharp bark of laughter.

'Nice try, you arse. You shouldn't be doing that, you know . . . What if there *is* a nutter up here, eh?'

She took a step forward, hand outstretched, ready to pull off the stupid hat.

He took a step to meet her, and that's when she realised it was all wrong. He was too tall. Too skinny. He didn't smell like Fraser, and there was something . . . something wrong with the shape of his head.

Lydia screamed loudly, right into his face, like she'd been taught by her dad – one of the only decent things he *had* taught her.

The man stumbled backwards, before lurching forwards, making a grab for her bag, catching the strap and pulling her towards him. She let him pull it off her shoulder, but it caught on her elbow as he yanked, and she skidded on the gravel, her legs flying out from under her.

She screamed again, and he dropped the bag at his feet.

Lydia sensed his confusion and took the opportunity to launch herself forwards, kicking out at him. She caught him on the knee and he yelped, retreating like an injured puppy,

132

before finally getting his bearings and fleeing back up the embankment, the way he'd come.

Leaving her panting on the ground, wondering what the hell it was that had just happened.

26

Gray was stopped twice as he walked back to the station. The first time was Harry Stevens, asking when he was sending someone round to investigate his missing onions. Gray told him they were looking into it.

He'd been to the station three times in the last week.

'I need to report a crime,' he'd said to Beattie, who was standing behind the desk looking bored. 'Some little bastard has stolen my onions again. Giant Whites, they were. I was growing them for the county show . . .'

Gray had clocked Beattie's eye-roll and decided to deal with it himself. 'Hello, Harry. Do you want to come through? We can have a cuppa in the interview room and you can tell me all about it.'

The old man had looked at him like he had two heads. 'I've no time to be sitting about drinking tea, son. I've work to go to. The bus'll be there now.' He'd turned and walked back out, muttering something about time-wasters as he went.

Gray smiled inwardly at the irony and picked up the phone. 'Sheila? Davie Gray. Aye, no problem. He's just left. No. No. Don't be daft, Sheila. OK then. Right then. Bye.' He put the phone back in its cradle and shook his head sadly.

'I don't know how you've got the patience,' Beattie said. 'That's the third time this week.'

'Let's just hope you never have to deal with old age, eh?

Happens to us all, Callum. You need to stop thinking you're invincible.'

Beattie looked suddenly pained. 'Sorry, boss. I wasn't thinking.'

Gray had waved the conversation away with his hand, like he was fanning away the cloying heat that seemed to have seeped into the station when Harry had left the door open. Beattie was young. He wasn't being malicious. Gray couldn't expect him to know how it felt to lose a loved one to dementia. His mother had died last year after six years of it, and if he was honest, it was a blessing for everyone who knew her. She was never herself after the day his dad had dropped dead on the way to buy a paper, five years before her mind started to fall apart, like an old photograph slowly fading in the sun.

The second person to stop him, just as he was crossing over from the bank, was Marie Bloomfield.

'Hello, Davie,' she'd said, looking up at him through dark mascara'd eyelashes. 'Anne says you're joining us for dinner on Thursday?'

Gray felt himself shrinking into a slouch to get closer to her. It was automatic. Marie, at five foot three in her immaculately polished burgundy Doc Martens, was nearly a foot shorter than him. She was pushing forty but could pass for twenty-five with her clean, unlined skin. Her hair was like it had been when he first met her, twenty-odd years ago: shaved except for fringe and tails. She was wearing her usual attire, which was a tailored pinstripe suit jacket and neat black pencil skirt. They'd gone on two dates about ten years ago, but she hadn't asked for a third. She'd taken his awkwardness for disinterest, and he hadn't had the heart to put her right. Maybe it was time to fix that.

135

'News travels fast, eh, Marie? I'm looking forward to it, actually. Be nice to get out. Not to mention have someone cook my tea.'

Marie beamed, then a thought seemed to strike her and her face fell. 'I heard about the attack up at the Track, Davie. Terrible thing . . .' She let her sentence trail off when he didn't react. Realising that he wasn't going to say anything else, she stood up on tiptoes and kissed him on the cheek. Her lips felt like velvet. 'See you on Thursday.'

She took off at a pace, leaving Gray standing at the edge of the pavement, wondering what had happened. The kiss on the cheek had felt nice. But he was concerned by what she had said. So it was an attack now? This town and its Chinese bloody whispers.

By the time he got back to the station, he felt flat. Like someone had punctured his football and stamped on it until it sunk.

So he wasn't really expecting the scene that greeted him as he walked inside.

Martin Brotherstone had hold of his son, Pete, by the hood of his Iron Man sweatshirt. He was almost chest to chest with the Big Ham, who had clearly decided to grace them with his presence for a few hours.

'Talk to him yourself, Hamilton – he'll tell you – he didn't see anything else . . .' He paused briefly to pull on the hood, causing the lad to cry out. 'Did you, Pete? Tell the inspector . . .'

On the other side of the counter, Beattie and Lorna the analyst were studiously ignoring the fracas. Lorna was banging on the keyboard so hard that Gray expected to see a fountain of little black boxes spray out from behind the screen where she was, ineffectively, trying to hide. Beattie was standing by her side, inspecting his nails as if he'd grown a new microbiological specimen underneath.

Between the two scenes, a girl with mascara-streaked cheeks was sitting on one of the plastic seats looking like she wished she hadn't bothered to come in. Gray took it all in. Sucked in a deep breath. It was something he'd learned from his martial-arts training.

Assess the situation.

Take a breath.

Prioritise the threats.

Strike.

He started with the girl. 'Has anyone seen to you?'

She stared up at him and he looked back into eyes that were red raw from tears. 'Not yet. They said they couldn't take my details cos the computer's bust. But I just wanted to tell them before it was too late cos I was worried that maybe he might still be there . . .'

Gray flinched, like someone had just dropped an ice cube down the back of his shirt.

'Who might still be there?'

'The man at the Track.'

Brotherstone and the Big Ham fell silent. Brotherstone let go of his son's hood, giving Pete the opportunity to say, 'See, Dad, that's what I was trying to tell you . . . I did see someone . . . I saw him again today.'

Gray noticed that the boy was shaking. Possibly from just being mildly choked, possibly from more than that. Gray stored this in his memory for discussion later. For now, he had to talk to the terrified, tearful girl.

'Right. Lorna, what's the status with the computer? Have you been on to HQ?' To Beattie, he said under his breath, 'Could you not have taken the details on your notepad,

Constable? You can clearly see this girl is in distress . . .'
Then he turned to Brotherstone and Hamilton and said,
'Maybe we can continue this later? I'd like to talk to Pete
myself' – he turned to face Hamilton – 'if that's OK with
you, sir?'

'Yes, yes. I'm off now anyway, Sergeant Gray. I'll leave
things in your capable hands.'

Gray watched as the Big Ham ushered his crony and his
son out of the station, then sucked in another deep breath.

'OK,' he said to the girl, 'sorry about that. You caught us at
a bad time. If you'll just come through to the interview room,
we can have a chat.'

The girl stood up, clutching a schoolbag awkwardly in
front of her. 'I was skiving school,' she said, her voice
wavering.

'Never mind that now,' Gray said gently. He turned back
towards the desk. 'Lorna, if the PC's still on the blink, would
you mind bringing us some tea and biscuits through please?'

'We've no' got any, Sarge . . .'

Gray lost his last crumb of patience. 'Well away out and get
some then!'

27

The girl was called Lydia McKenzie and, as she'd stated from the beginning, she'd been skiving off school. Gray wasn't particularly concerned about that part. She didn't look like a serial offender. More like someone who was a bit bored and fancied meeting up with her boyfriend during the day. Young love. He missed that feeling.

She'd wanted to talk to Gray without her parents present, and as it was only an informal chat, Gray had agreed. He'd have to pop round to see her at home later, though. Get her to sign a statement.

She didn't really say much until Lorna appeared with a tray of tea and biscuits. The three chocolate digestives she ate had the useful side effect of loosening her tongue. Or, more likely, after the shock she'd had, the sugar was re-firing her brain.

'So, tell me again, just so we're clear . . .' Gray had been scribbling frantically in his notebook and was worried that the scrawl might be indecipherable, even to his own trained eye.

Lydia sighed and took a slurp of her tea. 'Tall. Thin. Black fleece. Balaclava.' Another slurp. 'Is this Tetley? I like Tetley. We never have it now, though. Dad doesn't drink tea, so Katia – that's our housekeeper – just buys whatever's cheap and that's usually PG Tips, and I find that a bit bitter. I do like Monkey, though.'

Gray tapped his pen on the table, trying to penetrate her adrenalin-fuelled ramble. 'Anything else? You say he was quite close to you . . . Did you catch his scent? Was he clean? Smelly?'

Lydia looked confused. 'Actually, come to think of it . . . he smelled of soap. Not many people use soap now. Dries out your skin. I recognised the smell though, cos Katia likes to put it in the downstairs loo. I think she thinks it's posh or something . . .'

Gray coughed. 'Don't suppose you recognised the brand, did you?'

'Funnily enough – yes . . . It was Dove. Very distinctive. I think it's on three-for-two in Tesco's at the moment . . . Katia thinks three-for-two is the most exciting thing anyone's ever seen. I suppose they might not have things like that in her country . . .'

'OK. Dove. Right.' Gray scribbled it down. Could be important. You never know.

'Can I go now?'

Gray hmm'd and flicked back through the pages of his notebook. 'Yes. Hang on, though. You mentioned something about his face?'

Lydia sighed. 'Yes. Something weird. Like it was too big for his head. I know that doesn't make sense, but it was under a balaclava and I could still see there was something wrong with it. Oh, and he'll probably have a bruised knee. I kicked back pretty hard, and I'm wearing these, see?' She uncrossed her legs and lifted her foot up to show Gray. Sturdy-looking shoes with a hard block heel.

'Bit warm in this weather, eh? Would you not be better in sandals?'

'Huh,' she said, 'my toenails are a mess. Haven't had time

140

to paint them. I'd rather suffer the heat than display chipped nails!'

Fair enough, Gray thought, *and hopefully you did some damage to the prick's leg with those clodhoppers too.*

He flipped the notebook shut. 'OK, thanks Lydia. I'll be round later to talk to you again with your parents . . .'

'It's just my dad, actually, and I'm sure you don't need to tell him . . .'

'Sorry, it's just procedure. Off you go now. Lorna will see you out.'

When he stepped back out into the waiting area, the station was calm at last. Lorna was typing less aggressively on the keyboard. Beattie was busy with a pile of old files that he'd started sorting through a week ago and never got round to finishing.

This was how it was supposed to be. Calm, ordered. On the whole, crime-free. He hoped he wasn't going to have to involve the big boys from the CID. Since the Scottish police forces had merged into one big gang, there were new rules and regulations and plans. Total pain in the arse.

They weren't even sure that the station would survive. Cutbacks, restructuring. The Big Ham knew that his days were numbered. Technically they were now run by the new divisional commander in Dalkeith. The First Minister's great plan had been to cut costs by cutting the number of chiefs, streamlining the force. Gray wasn't so sure he liked the idea, nor many of the others being brought in by the SNP. He was pleased with the result of the referendum. Glad that the country had a new leader, not that he imagined it'd make much difference. He'd always thought of the First Minister as a Wizard of Oz type of character. All mouth, no trousers. Hiding behind a . . .

Christ!

In all the commotion, he'd forgotten what he'd picked up from Ian's paper shop. He'd left it on the chair.

'Lorna. You busy?'

'Well, I'm . . .'

'Right, I need you to look something up for me. I need you to search for any attacks, or attempted attacks, flashers, anything like that . . . Anyone who was wearing a mask.'

'What kind of mask? Like a kids' mask, or . . .'

He held up the sheep mask from Ian's shop, slid it across the counter. 'Any mask. We don't know what he had on under that balaclava, but I've got a funny feeling about this. It's not a deformity. I think he's wearing a mask.'

'But why? You can't see his face anyway,' Beattie said.

'I ken that, Callum. He's got a reason for it, though. We just need to work out what it might be . . . Call me if you find anything. I'm away up to the Track to see if our weirdo has left any traces.'

'Should we not call Dalkeith? They'll be fuming if—'

'No' yet, Callum. Come on. When did we last get anything interesting to investigate around here? See yous later.'

28

It wasn't until the rattle of the letterbox woke me up that I realised I'd drifted off. I checked my phone. Had I really been asleep all afternoon? Or had I just tuned out for a bit? I only vaguely remembered sitting down. I reread the text that had come in when I arrived. Scott was curled up on the couch, fast asleep and snoring beer-scented fumes. I paused on my way out, to pick up the free ads paper that had landed on the mat. I would've stayed. Waited until he woke up, soberer, ready to tell me whatever it was that was so bloody important to him.

To be honest, though, I didn't really care any more.

Once he'd told me it was over, I didn't see much point in trying to flog a dead horse. It wasn't as if we'd been best friends. Both of us were settling. Me trying to forget about Craig, him thinking I was a great catch because I was good in bed, even though all his friends tried to tell him I was a nutter. It had worked for a while. Until it didn't. God knows, he was never my type. That over-styled hair, the 'going out' shirts. I'd never really known what it was he saw in me, with my tendency to forget to shower and my tomboy wardrobe.

We didn't even have music in common. Scott was into mainstream crap like Coldplay and James bloody Blunt. He thought U2 were edgy. I was much more of an alternative sort of girl. Indie before everything became Indie. The Pixies before anyone in Banktoun knew who they were. I was into the sweaty, tortured rocker look. In hindsight, it was incredible we'd lasted so long. I think it was our completely opposing personalities that kept us together. Which is why it was pretty ironic that I was round there clearing up his mess while he slobbed about oblivious.

I ran back down to the bookshop, just in time to find Sharon fretting over the alarm. A skinny boy was leaning on the wall outside.

'Oh thank fuck you're back. I can't remember the bloody code. I thought I was going to be here all night.' She thrust the keys into my hand. 'Oh, and cheers, by the way. Cheers for leaving me all afternoon. I nearly went insane in there with those bloody kids.'

Kids? What the . . . Oh shit!

'Monday Club! Oh God, Shaz, I am *so* sorry. Honestly. I'd never have left you alone with that . . . It's just, I had to . . . it went clean out of my head—'

'Yeah. Whatever.' She pushed past me and out of the door.

I was about to say sorry again when she turned back round and said, 'And you can do my shift on Saturday morning,' before flouncing off along the pavement, her DMs squeaking gently as she walked.

I sighed. Great. Another fuck-up from me. Another Saturday morning ruined. I needed to get my shit together. Decide what I was going to do about Maloney. Try to convince Claire to listen to me.

Now, though, I had somewhere I needed to be.

I typed in the alarm code and waited for the three beeps to confirm that it was set, then I locked up and left.

The best thing about Scottish summers was rarely the weather – the heatwave we'd been having for the last week would end soon, and we'd be left with the usual white-cloud

144

mugginess, only broken by the window-rattling storm that was sure to be on its way. No, the best thing was the fact that it stayed light until nearly 10 p.m. People were different in the summer. More free. Not constrained by the dark and the rain that kept them indoors from October to March.

It was nearly six o'clock and the sky was still a bright turquoise blue, the air still warm. A perfect night.

I checked the text again. *See you at seven* was all it said.

After I left the shop, I stopped off at Tesco's. As I walked past the café I had a sudden flashback to the breakfast. Bumping into *him*. Feeling myself getting sucked in by his charm. Did he even know what he was doing? I walked down the aisles, tossing things into my basket as I went. Nibbly stuff. Cheese, a packet of crackers. Houmous. A bag of pre-chopped veg sticks. I remembered Maloney's smile and I still couldn't work it out. *Did* he remember me? Was this all a game to him? I tossed a packet of tortilla chips into the basket, then headed to the wine aisle.

'All right, Jo. Having a party? I didn't think you had any mates.' Sharon's voice dripped sarcasm. She was hand in hand with the skinny boy from outside the shop. He had a shaved head and big brown eyes and long eyelashes like a cow. He wore a Metallica T-shirt and had those freaky ear spacers in both ears. The holes were already as big as ten pees.

'If you take them out, do your ears grow back?' I said, ignoring Sharon and nodding my head towards the boy's ears.

His face flushed and he blinked. Like most of Sharon's boys, he looked scary but had the personality of weak tea.

'Um, I don't know,' he said. 'Maybe?'

I snorted. 'If they don't, you can always stitch them up

145

with black thread and start a new trend,' I said, and laughed. Sharon scowled at me and the boy just looked redder. Must be annoying, blushing like that. I was about to comment on it, but Sharon got in first.

'Well, make sure and enjoy yourself, whatever it is you're doing. See you tomorrow.' She took the boy by the elbow and he gave me a half smile before he got dragged off by the fuming Sharon.

I stared down at my basket and felt a bit bad for being such a cow.

I just couldn't help myself.

Sand-face from the café served me at the checkouts. She had her name badge on this time. 'Melanie'. Then I remembered her at school. She'd been friends with a fat blonde girl who stank of onion BO and always wore a skirt that was too short for her footballer's legs. Mandy? Mindy? She'd tried to nick my lunch money once and I'd poked her in the eye with a six-inch ruler. She ignored me after that, and Melanie always looked terrified. She must've forgotten about it now, though. She barely glanced at me as she scanned through my items and I had to bite my tongue to stop myself asking about her friend.

By the time I'd walked through the town, across the bridge and along the side of the fields, the carrier bags were cutting into my hands and I had to set them down for a minute to let my hands recover. Dark-red weals had formed on my palms and the skin was burning. It wasn't a long walk. Half an hour or so. I'd always walked everywhere so it was nothing to me, but I remembered Scott not being too happy when I'd once brought him up here. Once, because he complained so much I never did it again. And also because when I got there I decided I didn't want to let him into the cottage. Thinking

146

back, that might've been the first sign that things weren't going to work out between us after all.

I worked out a way to pull my sleeves down under my hands to cushion myself from the handles of the plastic bags, which had become tight and sharp like cheesewire. Only five more minutes and I'd be there. I could already make out the outline of the cottage through the trees as I approached the edge of the field, lush green with an abundance of barley, the evening sun glistening across the tops of the plants.

Across the road, the woods were dimmed, trees casting long shadows across the dirt-track lane at the side. In the clearing, the cottage loomed ahead. Grey brick walls, blackened from damp in the corners. Windows curtainless, unlit, like black holes reflecting back the branches of the swaying oaks outside.

Light and dark.

I crossed over the road towards the cottage, feeling a smile play on my lips.

I was looking forward to this.

29

I'd always loved spending time in Gran's kitchen. It had a warm, homely feel, in contrast to some of the rooms upstairs, which always felt a bit dark and cold, like there was never enough going on in them to bring them to life. Around the edges of the kitchen were a series of high cupboards, the doors once painted a sunny yellow, now cracked and discoloured. I took out plates, cream with a brown floral edge. Plates that were about the same age as me but that had fared significantly better.

I arranged the crackers on the plates, unwrapped the cheese. I hesitated for only a brief moment before pulling open the drawer under the sink and taking out a knife. Not just any knife. My gran's favourite, and also the one I used when I helped her skin the rabbits. Ingrained in the small wooden handle were years of trapped blood.

I sliced the cheese and laid it on the plates. Then I wiped the knife on my jeans and dropped it back into the drawer. As I pushed the drawer back in, a piece of paper slid down the back, falling out on the floor beneath the sink. I bent to pick it up. It was a newspaper cutting, yellowing and fading like the cupboards that surrounded me. I unfolded it carefully, curious as to why it was in there. At first I thought it was a segment ripped from a sheet she had used to line the drawer, but it was too neatly cut to be that. My head swam as I read the words printed on there:

MISSING LOCAL MAN:
FAMILY FEAR FOR HIS SAFETY

My hands shook as I folded it back up, placed it neatly back in the drawer.

Not now, Jo.

Shoving the drawer closed again, I tried to shake the memory away.

I thought about Claire then, and I knew I had to talk to her soon. There was so much I had to say, but I had to be careful . . .

Pushing the dark thoughts from my mind, I laid a tray with the plates, cutlery, napkins. Added the wine and two glasses.

I was just about to carry it upstairs to the bedroom when I heard a sharp rap on the door. I paused, waiting. Another single rap, then a break, then two in quick succession.

Morse code. Something that he had taught me.

I pulled my phone out of my pocket to check the time. 6.58.

He was early.

30

Gray headed back to the Track for the second time in as many days. Rumours were starting to spread around the town now. The would-be attacker had turned into a flasher . . . Next he would be seven feet tall. He needed to sort this out before it went any further. At this point, he still wasn't ruling out an idiot and some sick prank.

He parked near the kids' playground and was glad to see a few mums out with buggies, toddlers climbing like monkeys up the complicated-looking frames. They weren't like that when he was young. They had a single metal-poled cube-shaped thing with concrete at the bottom. None of this 'safety flooring', the dull-red spongy stuff that seemed to be everywhere now. Funnily enough, though, he'd never known anyone to fall off one of the old-style ones and do themselves any damage. Maybe they were just more wimpish now.

Or maybe the opposite: one of the toddlers had already leapt off from the top of the slide and landed in a heap. It was no wonder the mothers were so neurotic.

He cut down the narrow alley, past Brotherstone's house. Thought about popping in.

The son, Pete – he definitely knew more than he was letting on. It was obvious to think that he might be the one scaring the girls. His build was right, and the way his dad was trying his hardest to shield him from any sort of questioning

. . . The boy's innocence was a difficult thing to work out. Clearly he was desperate to talk to Gray. Clearly Brotherstone was desperate for him not to.

He could understand, to an extent. Brotherstone had a reputation to protect. Pillar of the community and all that. Plus, it wasn't the first time that Pete had been accused of something like this.

But he wasn't guilty then, and Gray's gut said he wasn't guilty now.

Gray's gut was usually pretty accurate.

It told him to not even bother to drink strong coffee, because it would reject it instantly with sharp muscle spasms. It told him there was no point thinking about the past, because there was nothing he could do to change it, and it was telling him now that Pete knew something, but he wasn't behind it.

If Pete had frightened those girls – even for some warped kind of fun – he'd never be able to keep quiet about it. His speech was strictly one speed. He wondered what his dad had said or done to him in the station to shut him up.

He passed through the stile that separated the alley from the Track: something that he had never quite understood, assuming that stiles were only supposed to stop animals from straying out of their safety zones – and he was pretty sure there were no animals on the Track. Well, not of the four-legged variety anyway.

When he reached the other side, he turned round and faced Brotherstone's house, just in time to see a figure retreat from the top window. Martin? Or Pete? Either way, what Martin had said earlier was right – the room had a clear view of the Track and, it seemed, the alleyway.

He walked along to the bridge that Lydia had mentioned. It was a five-minute brisk stroll, and he was slippery with sweat by the time he got there. He could've parked on the bridge, walked down the embankment – but he wanted to see it from this angle first.

At the section where Lydia said she was waiting for her boyfriend, there was no sign of any disturbance. It was hard to tell with the bark-mulch path covering. If anyone had walked over it since, it'd be disturbed anyway.

Nothing looked out of place.

He turned back on himself, walked back out into the sunshine. It was oddly quiet, for the time of day – nearly seven on a warm summer's evening. There should've been plenty of people around. Dog walkers, joggers. Old men. Teens heading to their hangout places.

Even the birds seemed subdued. Upset at someone tainting their habitat.

A rustling behind him made Gray almost leap out of his skin. He whirled round to see a small grey and white rabbit sitting on the path behind him. The colour surprised him. He'd never seen a wild rabbit with white patches.

'Hello, boy,' he said, bending down towards it. The rabbit didn't move. Odd, as they normally ran a mile when you tried to get close to them. He took a step closer, saw a dark-red stain on one of its feet.

'Are you hurt, boy? Let me see . . . I can try to help you?' He felt a bit mad talking to the rabbit, but he could see that it was injured. He wondered what he was supposed to do in these situations. Call the RSPCA? Try to catch it and take it to a vet?

In the end it didn't give him a choice.

A sudden breeze whipped up the bushes that lined the Track and the rabbit's ears cocked.

Then it bolted up the embankment.

Gray whipped round, followed the rabbit's path. Watched as something seemed to fall off behind it as it ran. For a horrible fleeting moment, Gray thought it was its tail.

The rabbit was gone, but clearly it was OK.

The thing it had dropped, though – that was something else. Gray picked up a stick and poked at the white, blood-stained blob and realised he was looking at a tissue.

Lydia said she'd kicked him hard, that he might have a bruised knee.

Maybe not bruised. Definitely bleeding.

Gray pulled a small plastic bag from his pocket – some-thing he always carried, just in case – picked up the tissue on the end of the stick and dropped it in.

Might be nothing.

Might be everything.

He was about to turn back in the direction of Brotherstone's house when he saw the footprint.

He had to stop himself from laughing. Two potential bits of evidence right at his feet, thanks to that daft wee rabbit.

Pity he didn't have a suspect to check them against.

If he sent the tissue to the lab for analysis, he'd have to inform the CID boys about what was going on, and in they'd come, stamping their size 9s over the whole thing. This was his town. He wanted to find this prick himself.

He took his phone out of his pocket and bent down to take photographs of the footprint. It was clean. An exact shape of a foot, with distinctive ridges across the ball. He made sure to take one with his own foot next to it, so that it could be sized against his own size 11s. It looked like a 10 to him. A size 10 trainer.

Not exactly unique.

It'd be something, though.

Once he found the bastard.

31

I let him wait. Not for long. Long enough for him to consider whether he should knock again. I could sense him standing there on the other side of the door. Wondered if he felt that same frisson of excitement I did. It felt like my heart was doing somersaults inside my chest. I counted slowly to sixty before walking down the stairs and unlocking the door.

He smiled at me. His eyes shone, and I wondered how much he'd had to drink already. Then he held out a plastic bag, bottles chinking together inside. I took it.

'I wasn't sure you'd be here,' he said. He stepped in. I moved back and he pulled the door closed behind him.

I didn't answer straight away. We just looked at each other. Stared into each other's eyes. Sometimes we never said a word to each other the whole night, but he'd gone and spoiled it now.

Broken the spell.

'Where else would I be?' was all I said. I frowned. But before I could say or do anything else, he pushed me onto the table.

I slid backwards across the surface, pushing packets of crisps and crackers and tubs of olives and hearing them drop on the floor. He took the bag with the wine in it back out of my hand and set it on the worktop next to the sink. I started to unbutton my jeans, but he'd already grabbed them by the ankles and then slid them off over the top of my boots in one easy move, like one of those sleight-of-hand magicians yanking out a tablecloth from under a table full of crockery. Then he was on top of me. The only sounds were the clanging of his belt buckle as he freed himself, the rasps of my breath mixing with his. Hard. Heavy.

He crushed my mouth under his. His lips dry, chapped. He tasted of beer and fags and something else deeper inside. Coffee, maybe. Slightly stale. Underneath it all, that familiar scent of him that I craved.

It was quick, anxious. My thighs burned from the friction of his jeans against my skin.

He grabbed hold of my hair as he came. Tugging it slightly too hard. I had to bite his shoulder to stop myself from crying out. *No*, I wanted to shout. *Not yet*. He left me lying there as he zipped and buckled himself back up. Both of us still panting.

He stared down at me.

Then he pulled me forwards by my ankles and pushed my knees far apart and his face disappeared into the space between my legs. I thought I might dissolve into the wood of the table. Felt like there would be nothing left of me except a faint, unidentifiable stain.

Afterwards, we sat in the lounge. The wine hadn't lasted long. My picnic lay mostly untouched.

He passed me a squashed packet of Marlboro Red, one cigarette poking out from the top. He did this with an effortless shake of the pack that I could never replicate. I only ever smoked with him.

'Why tonight?' I said eventually.

He lit another cigarette from the butt of the last. Sucked hard, releasing perfect smoke rings towards the ceiling.

'You know why,' he said.

I sighed. It was always like this. The passion was like nothing I'd ever felt before, but afterwards it was always the same. Cold. Empty. I was scared to ask him how he felt, because I was terrified of hearing the truth from him. About how he felt. About why he came to me, like this. Our secret thing that definitely wasn't love.

'He's back, you know.'

He nodded as if he already knew this.

'He's staying at Rose Cottage.' I stared at him, waiting for a reaction. He took another long drag on his cigarette and pushed a slow stream of smoke out from the corner of his mouth. 'I've got a key,' I continued. 'You could go round there?'

He turned to face me, his mouth bent into a sneer. 'What would I want to do that for?'

I felt panic rising in my chest, my heart speeding up, fluttering. 'To help . . . to help me. And to help—'

'You should drop this shit, you know.' He ground his cigarette into the ashtray with such force I almost expected it to burn through the glass. He leant back in the armchair and closed his eyes.

End of discussion.

I left him there, sitting on the sofa in the fading light.

I slept in Gran's old bedroom, the soft sheets still carrying a hint of his scent from the last time we'd been there together, when he'd wanted me more.

*

157

I woke up early, to birdsong and the morning sunlight streaming through dirty windows. I turned over towards him, flung my arm over his body, to the space where it should've been. I needed him close. But he wasn't there. He'd never been there. I'd woken up briefly during the night at the sound of the front door closing.

I sat up, pulling the duvet up over my naked body, hugging it around myself, trying to generate some warmth. Even in the height of summer, the cottage was cold. Stone floors, old-fashioned windows. There was no central heating or anything luxurious like that. The hot water came from a coal-fired boiler connected to the fire in the kitchen, so if I wanted a hot wash I was going to have to put the fire on. I wasn't sure there was any coal and I wasn't about to start chopping wood at the crack of dawn. I'd left my phone on the floor at the side of the bed, and as I leant over to check the time, all the blood rushed to my head. It wasn't even six o'clock. I felt sick.

Then I remembered the night before. The scene on the kitchen table coming back to me in little stabs of light, as if I was watching under a strobe light.

His hands on me. The weight of his body.

Maybe a cold bath was the answer, after all.

I walked through to the bathroom, felt the cold air poking through the gaps in the floorboards beneath my feet. I turned on the bath taps, those old-style ones with the cross-handled tops. They squealed in protest and the water came out in a juddering grey spurt. The pipes whined like fighting tomcats. Finally the water flowed, the colour changing to a milky-white, then finally running clear. As it started to fill the bath, I wandered out into the hall to the big built-in cupboard where Gran kept the towels. I'd never bought new ones. I'd never bought new anything. The cottage was my secret. To

158

most people it was uninhabited. Practically a ruin. If I'd had any business sense I'd have sold the land by now, but I couldn't.

Not until I'd worked up the courage to find out who was buried out there.

As I leant into the cupboard to pull out a greying, threadbare towel, I felt a weight, like a hand. It pressed hard on my shoulder and I took a step back, dropping the towel at my feet.

A gust of wind whipped at my ankles and I felt every hair on my body stand up.

A door banged shut. I held my breath.

Froze, waiting.

Nothing.

I crept to the top of the stairs and peered down, conscious of my nakedness. I wished I'd kept the duvet wrapped around me until I'd got in the bath.

'Hello?' I called. 'Who's there?'

Nothing. The breeze that had come from nowhere had stopped. There was silence.

That's when I realised I couldn't even hear the sound of water running into the bath.

Someone had turned off the taps.

Turn off the taps, JoJo . . . you're a wee water-waster . . .

I had no memory of going back through to the bathroom and turning them off, but I must've. Or else they had turned themselves off because they were old and creaky and the thread on the handles was gone . . . or . . .

When I finally worked up the nerve to walk back into Gran's bedroom, I found the wardrobe doors flung open wide. Piles of clothes lay scattered across the bed.

Had I done this?

Lying at the bottom of the bed was an open shoebox.

Inside were my sketchbooks.

Each one containing the very things I'd tried to push out of my mind.

THE WOODS

He walks over to the swing and grabs hold of the rope, bringing it to a jerky stop.

'Oi,' says the girl in the red skirt. '*We're* playing on the swing.'

The smaller girl stays where she is. He doesn't look at her, but he can hear the soft blubbering of her tears. He picks up the tyre, twists it, then smacks it like he's trying to get the last out of a bottle of ketchup, and the girl plops out onto the dirty mulch floor. Her crying becomes louder and she curls into a ball, wailing.

'I want to go home! Please!'

'Oi,' says the girl in the red skirt. She marches over and pokes a finger into his chest. 'What the fuck did you do that for? You're a big fat bully.' She pokes him again and he grabs hold of her hand.

'Brave, eh?' He twists her wrist until he has her in a position that's impossible for her to wriggle out of. 'Let's see how brave you really are, you wee slut.'

He's aware that the other boy has gone to tend to the little girl who lies curled up under the tyre, which is still swinging gently above her. It has not yet come to a complete stop, and there is a faint creak as the rope pivots on the loop that holds it secure on the branch. He hears him muttering something to her. He ignores them. He's not interested in either of them. He's got the one he wanted.

Weirdly, she doesn't scream. Doesn't say a word. He drags her over by one arm towards the fallen oak. She doesn't struggle. He wants to throw her down onto the floor, but as soon as he releases his grip, she slides away from him and sits down. She leans back and fans away dead leaves with her arms, sliding them back and forth to leave an imprint like an angel's wings.

'D'you want to kiss me then?' She whispers it, gives him a little smile.

He steps back.

Fuck. This is not what he wanted. In his head, he was holding her down by the throat, pumping himself into her as she bucked and cried, tears mixing with snot smeared across her terrified face. He looks at her with disgust. Little tramp. He probably wouldn't even have been her first.

'Fuck off,' he says. 'Just fuck off.'

He kicks a pile of leaves at her and she pulls her legs together and pushes herself up with her arms until she's sitting. The smirk back on her face.

'What's wrong?' she says. 'Can't get it up?'

She jumps to her feet before he can react. She runs across to the swing and drags her friend up by the arm. 'Come on,' she says.

Then they're running. Out of the woods and into the field.

He hears her laugh as it fades away in the breeze.

He looks down at the other boy, who is still crouched down next to the swing, his face a mixture of bewilderment and fear.

'Can we go home now?' he says.

'No. We're going after them.'

32

Claire had been working for the local paper – the *Banktoun Mail and Post* – since she'd finished university. It was a decent enough job, especially in a place like Banktoun. But on a quiet Tuesday afternoon, it wasn't exactly exciting.

She'd studied a joint MA in English and Journalism with thoughts of working for one of the glossy fashion mags. *Marie Claire* or something. But the four years at Glasgow University had taken their toll. There were plenty of facilities, plenty of help for people like her. She'd lived in the student halls for the whole four years. That was one of the things that made her realise she was never going to cut it out in the real world. While all her mates moved into trendy West End tenements after the first year, she was left with no option but to stay where she was. You don't see too many tenements with lifts. Maybe some of the swanky ones that've been converted by builders into luxury apartments.

Not the ones off the Byres Road above the kebab shops where the students lived.

Even going round to visit her friends was a chore. She had to be practically dragged up the several storeys of worn stone steps, and even though no one ever said anything, she could tell what they were thinking.

She'd overheard a couple of girls talking one day, discussing the end-of-term piss-up in someone's flat. Someone who just happened to live on the top floor.

'Don't invite Claire. It's just too much hassle.'

The girl who said it had been someone that Claire had trusted. Someone she thought was a good friend.

She withdrew after that.

She seemed to have gone full circle: when she was young, she was a mouse. Wouldn't say boo to a goose. The gymnastics had gone some way to alleviating that, though, and for a while, she did well.

'Come on, Claire, remember your landing. Feet together, arms raised . . .' Miss Albert's voice haunted her dreams. That clipped Morningside tone. 'Chop chop, girls. Run along.'

Claire had hung back after the class one day to talk to her. 'Er, Miss?'

The woman spun round, seemingly unaware that there was someone left in the gym. 'Yes?'

'I was wondering if I could get some extra practice sometime. My mum said maybe she could pay, and—'

'Why yes! Of course.' The woman's face softened. 'I think you might do rather well with a wee bit of help, you know, Claire. You'll maybe need to work on your fitness a bit, though. Working with the beams and the rings can take its toll. How about you talk to Mrs McCreedie to see about some sports coaching too? Jogging maybe? Hmm? What do you think?'

Claire hesitated. *What have I done? I hate jogging! Mrs McCreedie thinks I'm a fat waste of space . . .* A sudden determination came over her. *But she's wrong.* 'OK, if you think it'll help . . .'

Miss Albert clapped her hands. 'Excellent! I'll talk to your mother. Is she waiting outside?'

'Yes, um . . .'

'Come on then, girl! Chop chop!'

Miss Albert was one of the first people she remembered seeing after the accident. She was sitting on a plastic chair at the side of her bed, on what was maybe only the second or third time she'd woken up 'normally' in the morning after a six-month extended sleep that most people didn't expect her to wake up from.

Everyone asked her the same thing.

'How're you feeling, Claire? Do you remember what happened?'

It made her want to scream.

But she had no energy for that.

If there was one benefit to her six-month liquid electrolyte diet, it was getting rid of her puppy fat. She hadn't had to jog a centimetre. Pity her chances of becoming a champion gymnast were as good as her suddenly having the ability to speak Russian.

She knew she was taking the easy route. Letting her parents buy her the house next door to her childhood home. Converting it with low kitchen units, handrails in the bath. An emergency fucking pull-cord in case she slipped. Her dad had wanted to put CCTV in, 'just in case'. Luckily her mum had vetoed that. 'She's an adult, Mike,' she'd said. 'She doesn't want us spying on her the whole time.'

She'd told Jake about it one day, expecting him to laugh.

'What the fuck did he want to do that for, eh?' His tone was hard, bitter.

Claire had backtracked immediately. 'He was only joking. He's just a bit overprotective, that's all . . .'

'I don't like it. *I'm* here to look after you now, Claire. Not . . . him.'

She'd been shocked by his tone and immediately changed the subject. She didn't mention her parents to him again.

He kept asking to move in full-time, but something was stopping her and she couldn't quite put her finger on what it was. He *was* lovely to her.

They'd been going out properly since she was sixteen. She'd been flattered that someone could still find her attractive despite the chair.

'But you know I love looking after you, Claire,' he said, whenever she complained.

She was sure her mum and dad would've said something about him. Disapproved. But they were too politically correct to comment on his background, and they couldn't deny he was good to their daughter.

So they just channelled their negative energy into hating Jo instead. But Jo, being Jo, clung on like a limpet, refusing to give in. Forever trying to repent for taking Claire into the woods that day.

Claire knew *why* they went into the woods. It was just what happened when they got there that was a mystery. And when she saw Jo's scared face whenever she mentioned it, she knew it was better to keep the memories locked up.

She was browsing some fancy fonts on the Internet, trying to finalise an order of wedding invites. She needed to have them prepped for printing in the morning. The local paper survived on advertising, and its secondary business of printing brochures, business cards, flyers . . . all that stuff. At least designing them was interesting when there wasn't much news copy to deal with. She was engrossed, and when the door opened she didn't even bother to look up.

'Hello, Claire. How're you doing?'

'Ah, Sergeant Gray . . . not seen you around for a while. What can I do for you?'

She'd had to stop herself from saying 'business or pleasure?' He cut a fine figure in his uniform and she'd often found herself hoping that he might see her as more than just that wee girl from the woods. She wondered what her mum and dad would think if she ended up with him rather than Jake. *Dream on, Claire . . .*

He took off his hat. 'Er . . . have I missed the deadline for tomorrow's adverts?'

Claire laughed. 'Technically, yes. By two full days . . .' She smiled at him, and he smiled back, raising an eyebrow. *Don't do that, Davie, I can't bear it . . .* 'But seeing as it's you . . . if you've got it ready I can fire it in right now. They don't start printing until eight tomorrow morning.'

'Oh, is that right? I'll remember that next time I need to advertise my latest bike-part rejects in the Buy-and-Sell . . .'

'Ha . . . no . . . I'm guessing it's something a wee bit more urgent than that?'

She'd had Bridie Goldstone in earlier, ostensibly to check the line prices for an advert for her granddaughter's birthday. In actuality, she was there to tell Claire about Scott chucking out Jo and apparently losing his job. Claire had nodded, pretending she hadn't known about the break-up. She had to remind herself to ask Jo about the job thing, though. She hadn't made any reference to that. Maybe he was skint and would have to sell his flat? That'd explain why he'd chucked Jo out without explanation. Too embarrassed to tell her the truth.

If that was true then the man was pathetic. As if Jo cared about stuff like that.

Davie coughed, alerting her to his presence. 'Well, yes it is, actually. I suppose you've heard about the girls up at the Track?'

Claire nodded. 'Of course. Sorry . . . I was thinking about something else.' Bridie had told her about that too, and it *had* been a scoop. God knows where the woman gleaned her information from, but Claire was considering offering the old biddie a job. Unfortunately, half the stuff she passed on was embellished and the other half was outright lies.

Claire swung her chair round and positioned herself back behind the desk. Davie slid a piece of lined paper towards her.

'"Emergency Self-Defence Class for Girls",' she read out loud, '"Wednesday, 7 p.m. at the Church Hall. Free." It's that last bit that'll get their attention,' Claire said. 'Do you think enough people will see it in time for the class? The paper only comes out at four . . . How about I jig it round? Free Self-Defence Class . . . Do you really just want to say it's for girls? There might be some boys who'd be interested too, you know . . .'

'Haven't really got the space for the whole school turning up, Claire. I think there'll be enough interest, even at short notice. You know what people are like. Everyone's in a panic already. Anyway, I'll see how this one goes. Might get a few recruits for the usual class. I could do with more boys, actually. Laura's scared most of them off.'

Claire laughed, 'She's good, Laura, isn't she? I watched her do that demo at the summer fair last year. She's a bright girl too. Quiet. You'd hardly believe she was related to Bridie . . .'

'Ah, Bridie's all right. She's my unpaid eyes and ears of the town!'

'Funnily enough, I was thinking of offering her a job . . .'

168

'Christ, I wouldn't go that far . . .'

Claire typed the advert into the desktop publishing system while Gray waited.

'Actually,' he said, 'while I'm here . . . do you think you could look up something in the archives for me?'

Claire glanced up at the clock. She still had to finish the invites. It was Davie, though. She'd work late if she had to.

'Sure,' she said, flashing him her best smile. 'What is it you need?'

It wasn't that strange a request. But as soon as she heard it, she had a sudden urge to throw up.

Masks.

He was asking her something about masks.

Claire had pieced together what happened that day in the woods from what Jo had told her, and from small pieces of memory that resurfaced at will, like splinters of a broken glass that keep turning up no matter how many times you sweep the floor clean.

But when she tried to put it all together, it never made sense.

'I've a feeling that Jo mentioned something about them in her statement. I've got Lorna checking the files back at the station, but I was just wondering if there was anything actually printed . . . It's so long ago that despite Jo's constant need to remember it I'm slightly hazy on the details . . .'

Claire nodded and clicked on the icon to open up the archive search facility. She was only half listening. She'd felt herself zone out when he'd first asked the question; somehow she'd managed to avoid Gray noticing. He was distracted, that was obvious.

'Do you think that these things are linked, Davie? Seems a bit far-fetched. You had no idea who the boys were back then,

169

why do you think they'd do nothing for twenty-three years then suddenly decide it was time to come back? I mean, they're not even boys now, they're older than me and Jo . . .'

'I'm not sure they ever went away, Claire . . . One of them, both of them. I don't know. They managed to avoid being caught after what happened to you, but I think they've been watching. Waiting for another time to strike. There've been a few other things, mind. This is a small town, Claire. Would you rather we had two loonies or a whole pack?'

Claire forced a laugh. 'You're being a bit flippant, Davie . . .'

He shook his head. 'Quite the opposite. I'm trying to find a link. Trying to find something to go on. If I don't nail this soon, the big boys will be down from HQ, wondering why we haven't called them sooner . . .'

'Why haven't you? Are you meant to? Are you going to get in trouble?' She bit her lip.

'Don't worry about me, Claire. I'm taking advantage of the current situation to do something interesting before we get shut down and relocated. Or offered voluntary redundancy . . .'

'Is that going to happen?'

'Probably. I don't think the station's viable under the new structure. I mean, it's not like we've much to do, most of the time. They'll station a couple of beat bobbies here on secondment from area command. Make them commute. It's hardly far.'

'But what if anything happens at night? It'll take them longer to get here . . .'

Gray snorted. 'You've clearly never needed our services or you'd know that the station shuts at six – there's a phone or the wall outside for you to call HQ. If you call 999, the dispatcher sends out whoever's nearest. I'm starting to think we're just there as an ornament.'

'Don't you think if there was no station, it might cause more folk to start acting up?'

'Good on them if they do. Like I said, the lads from CID will be here in a flash . . .'

'You sound bitter, Davie. I never thought that of you.'

Gray took a deep breath, blew it out. 'I do. I'm sorry, Claire. You know I'm not. I'm just frustrated that things are going to change. I kind of like them as they are . . .'

Claire stared at him. She'd never heard him like this before. She had a feeling there was more to his little outburst than being pissed off about the restructuring of Police Scotland, as it was called now. No. This had something to do with the weirdo at the Track. And it definitely had something to do with Jo.

What was it that Jo had that seemed to create such a hold over men? She was useless with them, yet they all wanted to protect her. Claire couldn't help but feel jealous.

The results of the search popped up and she clicked it open. Ten hits.

The first one from 1990.

She scrolled down and noted that the others weren't actually in Banktoun. The paper covered the whole county, and some of these had happened elsewhere. Not far, though. Maybe they were still linked somehow. She clicked on the icon to print them out in full.

While the printer sputtered and began the print job – forty pages' worth, the whole articles coming out just in case the summaries didn't give the full context – she clicked open the first entry.

171

1st July 1990

Girl badly injured after
attack in Riverview Woods

Police are searching for two boys,
aged approximately 13 years old, who
were involved in an attack that has
left one girl in a coma . . .

She felt her hand start to shake as she scrolled down with the mouse.

It was the first time she'd managed to read past the headline.

'Are you OK, Claire? You've gone white as a sheet . . .'

'I . . . I don't like to read this stuff, Davie. I keep it as far down inside me as it'll stay. I'm too scared to remember it. I don't want to picture those boys . . . It's too much . . . my head . . . I still get headaches, you know?'

Gray went behind the counter and swivelled her chair round slowly to face him. 'Listen to me, Claire. I've never stopped thinking about what happened to you and Jo. Never. I want to find those boys as much as she does. I want justice for you, and I want closure for her. But she goes off half-cocked. I've no idea if this Maloney has got anything to do with it. But I will find out. I promise you that. Now. Is there anything you need to do here right now that can't wait until tomorrow?'

Claire sighed. 'The wedding invites. But . . . well, I suppose. They use a different printer for these. They could be done later tomorrow and they'd still be ready for the customer to collect at five . . .'

172

'Right then. That's settled. I'm taking you home. OK?'

'OK,' Claire said. She waited until he had turned his back before she rubbed at her eyes and gently shook her head, trying to disperse the fog that was threatening to send her off into another blackout.

THE BOY

He enjoys the woods during the day even more than he enjoys them at night.

Different sounds. Different animals. Sometimes he wears a mask. The woman bought them for them both at Halloween, although they are too old for them now. He has kept them safe, in the dark of the wardrobe.

Witch. Wizard. Skeleton.

Devil.

Just a bit of fun . . . But the other boy likes them too.

He has a new hunting partner.

Someone just like him, he thinks.

Until the other boy decides that animals are not enough. Until the other boy decides to hunt the girls.

The other boy doesn't tell her about the Collection, but they both know that the woman knows.

She is scared of him now. Starts to cry again. He wants to tell her that it's OK. That it's just for fun. But she wouldn't understand.

She emptied the toybox while he was at school. Now, at the end of the bed, there is just a rectangular indentation in the pale-grey carpet from where it used to sit.

*

In the brightly lit office, the lady doctor asks him questions:

'How long have you been collecting the animals?'

'Whose idea was it to cut them up?'

'Have you ever wanted to hurt a person?'

'Have you ever wanted to hurt yourself?'

'Has anyone ever hurt *you*?'

Yes.

He answers only in his head, and apparently his cooperation is 'unsatisfactory'.

He wonders if he will ever see the other boy again.

He wonders what the other boy might become.

Before they send him to his next home, he goes into the woods once more.

The Black Wood.

The sun never seems to make it through the blanket of trees, and the trees look scorched and dead, hence the name. He knows that the story about the Witch isn't true. Just a tale, to scare boys away from the cottage.

But he is not scared.

He creeps as close as he dares. No, he is not scared.

He knows she's not a real witch.

If only the little girl would come out to play. He's seen her before, with the rabbits. He wonders if she has a Collection of her own.

33

I didn't feel like working, but Wednesdays were usually OK and it was probably good to take my mind off things. I'd spent the whole of Tuesday cooped up in the cottage, avoiding phone calls, trying not to think about Maloney. It was a waste of a day off. I'd have been better going in to work. I realised I was glad to be out of the cottage now; it was suffocating me. Finding those sketchbooks had given me a jolt. Not to mention the bath taps and the wind that came from nowhere and disappeared. Just like the day at Gran's grave. It felt like she was all around me, trying to warn me about something . . . just an eerie feeling I couldn't seem to shake off.

Scott was waiting for me outside the shop. He'd managed a half-hearted attempt to clean himself up and put on fresh clothes. There was a stain down the front of his pale-blue polo shirt and his hair had that fuzziness as if he'd dipped it under the tap rather than giving it a proper shampoo. I felt confused and recoiled slightly at his scent.

'Jo,' he said. His breath smelt of old beer with a hint of toothpaste; his teeth looked grimy, small bits of food stuck to his gum line, as if he'd wiped them with a finger rather than scrubbed them with a brush.

'What is it, Scott? I'm already late.' I could see Craig inside the shop. He was standing next to the counter, peering outside. Taking us in.

'There's something I have to tell you,' Scott persisted. He put a hand on my arm and I felt myself flinch. Only a few days ago I was sharing a bed with this man. Sharing a life. Yet now I wanted to be as far away from him as possible. I wasn't sure what it was, but something in him had changed. Discoloured. Like a bitten apple left in the sun.

I frowned. 'Five minutes,' I said. I held a hand up to the shop window, my fingers splayed apart. Craig shrugged and turned away. Pretended he was busy.

'Can I buy you a coffee?' Scott said. He gestured towards Farley's. *Fuck it*, I thought. A quick hot chocolate and a croissant might give me a lift. I'd been feeling light-headed since I'd left the cottage. The walk across the fields had blown away the cobwebs, blasted the remnants of last night's wine from my head. But I still felt like shit. Waking up to a dent in the pillow wasn't enough for me any more.

I walked into the coffee shop behind Scott, staring at the back of his head. Remembering the feel of his skull. That little bump halfway up the back that always got caught in the hair clippers.

A sudden feeling of nausea washed over me and I had to stop to catch my breath.

Did he know?

Had I done this to him?

He turned back round to face me and he must've seen the panic in my expression because suddenly it was him frowning. Looking confused.

'Jo? Are you OK?'

'Fine. I'm just late.' I scanned the tables, let my eyes settle on an empty one at the back. It was still littered with dirty cups, a plate with a half-eaten pastry and a screwed-up red napkin. 'I'll have a croissant,' I said. I contemplated the thought of a hot chocolate, then decided it might make me feel worse. 'And a Coke. Please.' I sat down and started piling up the dirty cups and plates, but before I could finish the waitress appeared and scooped it all onto a tray with a practised effortlessness.

I was busy straightening the napkins into their little clipholder when Scott turned up with a tray. He'd brought me what I'd asked for, plus a black coffee for himself . . . he looked like he needed it. Plus a hot chocolate in a tall glass mug. It had cream on top.

I sighed, and started spooning the cream into my mouth. He knew me better than I realised.

He took a sip of coffee and made a face. Either it was too strong or too bitter, or both. Then I remembered he didn't even like coffee. I opened my mouth to say so, but he silenced me with a raised hand.

'Look . . . This is not going to be easy, so I'm just going to blurt it out. You don't need to say anything . . .'

I nodded. My raised eyebrows saying 'go ahead'. I took a bite out of the croissant and the flakes of pastry fell down all over the front of my black top like dandruff.

'I've been sacked . . .' He paused, searching for my reaction. I ripped off a piece of croissant and dipped it in the chocolate. This was what French kids did for breakfast, apparently. So they told us in the textbooks at school anyway. Except they had oversized teacups like bowls. Not these stupid long glasses with a handle at the bottom that if you actually used you'd tip the whole thing over. I'd have loved to know who designed those things, with their complete ergonomic disastrousness.

'Go on . . .'

He blinked once, then carried on. 'I, uhm . . . we . . .'

Another pause. This time I just stared at him. That creeping feeling of bile burning its way up my throat.

I ripped off a piece of croissant. ' "We"?'

'Me and Kirsty . . .'

He pulled a face.

'I fucking *knew* it. Get caught in the stationery cupboard, did you?'

'Something like that . . . I'm sorry, Jo. It was one of those stupid things. She was all over me. She never bloody stopped. To be honest, I don't care about that – I care about my job – getting sacked – I'd been there nearly fifteen years, Jo. I was looking at a massive pension. My career is ruined now. What the hell am I going to do?'

I swallowed, and felt the croissant sticking to the back of my throat. I stared hard at Scott. 'I don't fucking *believe* you,' I said.

He downed his coffee and shuddered. 'What?'

He sounded pathetic, like a kicked puppy. I wasn't sure how to react. How he wanted me to react.

My face must've given me away.

He started to cry. 'What the hell am I going to do, Jo?'

'To be honest, Scott,' I said, 'I couldn't care less.'

All this melodrama about a bloody job? He hardly seemed to care that he had cheated, but then I couldn't really be outraged about that, given my own situation. I was just pissed off that he'd tried to turn this all round to be about him, when all I had really wanted was someone I could trust.

He was just another one to strike off my list.

I stood up to leave. 'Out of interest, Scott – where have you been going every day when you've been pretending to go to work?'

179

His expression was strange and I couldn't decide if it was guilt, confusion or something in between. 'I just go walking, Jo. Along the Track . . .'

34

Making a mental note to tell Gray that Scott had been spending his days hanging about at the Track, I left him there with his empty coffee cup and went to work. It felt like I hadn't actually done any work in days. With everything that had been going on, I wasn't really with it. Craig's face told me I was pushing our friendship too far, but, being who he was, he soon perked up and tried to pretend everything was all right.

'Could you sort out the travel section today, Jo? There's two boxes full of new stuff through the back. I was thinking we could get rid of some of the old stuff in a wee sale? What do you think?'

'S'pose so,' I said. I walked over to the current sale table, which was looking a bit bare and boring and picked up the pile of 'How To' books that sat there. We'd managed to offload a few, but it seemed that there really was no one who was interested in *How To Make Your Own Vitamins*. 'Bargain bucket then?' I said, gesturing to the dog-eared stragglers.

'Whatever you think,' Craig said. He disappeared behind the counter, presumably to start replacing the 'Last Minuters' – the small, supposedly quirky or funny books we left next to the till for that moment when you're ringing up the pile of purchases and the customer suddenly decides that they'd like one. The current bestseller was *18th-Century Tips for Husbands*, unsurprisingly bought by women.

I stacked up the last of the sale books and tossed them into the bargain bin – everything a pound. There wasn't a book we hadn't managed to sell at that price, even if they inevitably ended up in someone's recycling bin or the Sue Ryder shop a few days later. The bargain bin was a large plastic tub, and sometimes people treated it like a lucky dip, deciding they'd buy whatever they pulled out. I decided to give it a shake to shuffle up the contents. I didn't think having all of the How To's on the top was likely to pique anyone's interest.

There was no one in the shop, but as soon as I tipped the contents of the bargain bin onto the floor (it was too heavy to actually shake), the bell above the door pinged and a rabble of school kids shoved their way in. I glanced up at the clock behind the till: 12.30. Jesus. I was losing track of time.

The kids liked to hunt in packs, even in the bookshop. They huddled in small groups around the YA fiction – the girls were still interested in sexy vampires, although I couldn't see the appeal myself. The boys were starting to get into the more adult thrillers. Spies, espionage, running across rooftops with their tops off fighting kung fu warriors. That kind of thing. I liked to keep an eye on their interests. Listen to what they said. Always trying to find them the 'next big thing'. That was the best part of my job, and the girls in particular loved to talk to me about books – I could even convincingly tell them whether I was pro-vampire or pro-wolf. God, they were gullible. I'd never read books like that. I was much more of a realist when it came to fiction. Gritty, character-led dramas that reassured me that there were people with worse fucked-up lives than mine – even if they were only fictional. I'd particularly enjoyed the trend in Scandinavian crime – brutal, straight-talking stuff set in bleak landscapes. Complete escapism, despite the authenticity of it all.

'Jo?'

It was one of the fifth years, Katie Williams. Her mum worked in the bakers next door. She was one of a trio. The three of them like triplets, with their willowy figures and flipped-over dark-blonde hair. Skinny legs poking out of too-short skirts, rolled up at the waistbands after they left their homes every morning. Eyeliner and lipgloss hastily applied using a hand mirror round the corner from the school gates. I've made them sound awful, but actually they were all right. They seemed to like me, anyway, which was always nice.

I stood up from the scattered books. 'Yes, ladies?' I always called them that. They always giggled.

'Lindsey was wondering if you still had *Fifty Shades of Grey* . . .' Giggles.

I looked from Katie's face to the other two. One of them had a spot of pink at the tops of her cheeks. The other was looking down, but her shoulders were shaking slightly and I could see she was trying hard not to laugh. Katie had managed to maintain a look of wild-eyed innocence and I worried for her future. She was going to be a nightmare.

'Oh, it's for *Lindsey*, is it? You two have already read it then, I presume? Can't you just lend her one of your copies?'

'I got mine from the library,' Katie said, deadpan.

'Me too,' the other one said, smirking.

I had a feeling there was a wind-up going on here. A bet maybe. I wasn't in the mood. I marched over to the corner, where we still had a small display of modern 'erotica', even though its time seemed to have come and gone, so to speak, and picked up the book, along with the other two in the trilogy. I handed them to Lindsey and she took them. Her cheeks shone like Christmas baubles.

'Um, thanks,' she muttered.

The other two looked at me questioningly. They'd wanted a bit of banter. They'd wanted me to tease the girl as to why she hadn't read them. I wanted to know why they were in the shop pissing about when there was some nutcase getting ready to attack one of their friends up at the Track.

'Craig will serve you,' I said, turning back towards the books strewn across the floor.

The three girls shuffled over to the till. Their giggles had gone.

'Oh, and girls?' I raised my voice slightly, just enough so the boys in the corner pawing over the latest Lee Child could hear. Their heads lifted in unison, like meerkats. 'If you need any help working out what to do with a vibrating cock ring, I'm sure one of that lot will be more than happy to help you out.'

The boys dissolved into laughter. All three girls had gone the colour of ketchup.

Craig's eyes widened, but he didn't say anything until they'd all left, a few minutes later. The boys were still laughing, making lewd comments at the girls' backs as they left. Katie threw me a glance over her shoulder and I rolled my eyes back at her.

'That was a bit *mean*, Jo. You know those girls like you.'

'They were trying to embarrass their friend. Two against one. That's a bit mean, isn't it?'

'You didn't have to humiliate them, though! Those boys will tell their mates . . . They'll make their life hell.'

'They have to learn. Besides, it'll be over before you know it. One-day wonder.'

Craig shook his head. 'Have you forgotten what it was like at school? That Lindsey – she looked nervous enough as it

184

was. She won't forget that in a hurry. They're only kids, for Christ's sake!'

'They're old enough to read that book, they're old enough to learn.' I threw the pile of books into the bargain bin and the vibration almost knocked over the flimsy fold-up wooden table next to it – the one I was meant to be putting the travel books on. I hadn't got very far.

'Right,' Craig shouted. He never shouted. I took a step back as he marched out from behind the counter to the door, turned the lock, flipped the closed sign over to open. An old woman outside gave him a questioning face and he held up his hand, fingers splayed wide.

She nodded and walked off.

He turned back to me. 'Right, Jo. I've had enough of this. I can't keep carrying you. Either you talk to me properly, or . . . I don't know. Fuck! You were worse than useless on Saturday, you buggered off early on Monday and left Sharon with the bloody kids' club on her own . . . Today you come in an hour late and then proceed to go for a coffee for another hour, before you come in, do fuck all, then upset the kids who probably buy more books from us during the week than . . . Jo? Where the fuck do you think you're going now?'

I turned the lock on the door, yanked it open, walked out without another word. Those girls had to learn. They had to learn that men are only after one thing.

Sooner they learned that, the better.

35

There are things that I haven't told anyone. I've wanted to, but somehow the time has never been right. I wanted to tell Craig, but I wasn't sure our fragile friendship could stand it. With Claire, though, it was different. It had always been a love/hate thing. She was one of those friends that you stick with no matter what happens, although I do often wonder if we hadn't been bonded by what happened to her, would we still be friends now?

I left the bookshop and walked round to Claire's work. I saw her behind the desk, sitting there alone, face lit up from the glare of her computer screen, and I realised that there was never going to be a good time. I had to get it off my chest.

She lifted her head and smiled when I walked in. I think she was expecting a customer, though, because her mouth twisted into a frown when she realised it was me.

'What're you doing here? Aren't you supposed to be at work?'

'Craig been on the phone crying about me, has he? He's being a right dick at the moment.'

'Christ, Jo. You've been a mess since you left Scott's. He's worried about you. I am too.'

I sat down on the window ledge. Looked out to see if anything exciting was happening on the street.

'Jo? Are you listening to me?'

I turned back to face her. 'Look, Claire. This is not abou

Scott. I need to tell you something. A few things, actually. I've been waiting for the right time, but it seems like there's never a right time . . . and what with Scott and me splitting up, I dunno . . . It's made me want to wipe the slate clean or something. Confess my sins . . .'

'Don't you need a priest for that?' she quipped.

I ignored her. 'Remember when you were away at uni and I moved up town for a bit?'

She took in a breath, let it slowly back out. 'Of course . . .'

'Well, you know I ended up in hospital . . . after I . . .'

'You don't need to say it.'

'I do. After I tried to kill myself in the bath . . . and Lisa found me. I wonder what happened to Lisa? I never went back to that flat after the hospital. I came straight back to Banktoun, thought I'd be able to make it work, living here again . . .'

'Jo . . .' she warned, urging me to get on with it. 'Why don't you just spit it out?'

'I never told anyone why I did it.'

'I know that.'

'I tried. I did. I tried to tell Craig, but . . . well.'

She nodded. 'He's happy with Rob, Jo. You should leave him be.'

'He's not. I know he's not. Anyway . . . I did it because of my gran.'

'Grief is a terrible thing, Jo. No one blames you for reacting like that. You have to understand, people just want to help you. You could've told me this before, you know. I mean, I guessed that anyway. First there was . . . well, there was what happened to me . . . And then your parents died, and God, that was just so horrible, Jo . . . And then finally you seemed to be on track and then your gran died. You know what, if I could go back to uni now, I'd do science and go and work in a lab and find the cure for bloody cancer, because seriously, that is the most—'

I cut her off. 'She didn't die from cancer, Claire.'

'What?' She'd been knocked off her stride, so sure she knew all the pieces of the jigsaw – then I just waded in there with my sledgehammer and smashed the whole thing to pieces.

'What did she die from then, Jo? Was it a secondary illness? Did she have a heart attack? Did she—'

'Shut up, Claire.'

She flinched, and I knew what was coming. But I kept going. My voice loud in the small office. 'Come on, Claire. Do I have to fucking spell it out for you?'

I could see her eyes starting to glaze over. She was going to bloody fade out, right at this crucial point. Right at the point of my confession.

'It was *me*, Claire. I killed her.'

THE BOY

The new house is much smaller than the last. Poky rooms, plain walls. One of the posh-looking ones near the river. He never expected to find himself here. He misses the old farm-house. He even misses the other boy. It was the first time he'd felt like he had a brother, of sorts.

This is his fifth home in fifteen years.

One more to go before he's on his own.

It started with the shoebox on the steps of the hospital, although he doesn't remember that one, of course. He wonders if they ever tracked down his mother. He imagined her on a dirty mattress in a stinking flat full of junkies. He'd seen it in that film *Trainspotting* that he and the other boy had sneaked into the cinema to see.

After living in the hospital for a year (although he didn't really count that as a home), the next was with a young couple who were desperate for a little boy. He only lasted a year. The withdrawal from the smack addiction he'd been born with caused too many problems. Screaming, shitting little rag that he was.

'But he's clean from it now,' he imagined the nurses telling the petrified, red-eyed wretches who'd tried to be his parents.

He'd learned all this much later, of course. From the

miserable bitch in the third home – the woman he called 'mother' for the sole reason that he'd been brought up by her since he could barely walk.

He got taken away from her when he was ten, after setting fire to her shed.

He never got a chance to tell her that he was trying to save her from her filthy beast of a husband and his collection of disgusting photographs.

He lasted three years in the next house.

An elderly couple whose real children had all flown the nest.

He imagined the old man to be like the old toymaker in *Pinocchio*, looking for a little companion to while away his boredom.

The woman sat glued to the TV all day. Black and white films. Bottle of gin by her side as she stared at the screen with wet eyes.

The old man told him they were building something to make the old woman happy. A wooden cabinet with a tray. Something to lay her books on, her drinks, her plate of Ritz crackers, which he was never allowed to eat.

At first he let the old man cuddle him. It felt nice, the strong, warm arms wrapped around his back. Feeling the old man's heartbeat pressing into his chest, synching with his own.

He didn't even mind when they did it with tops off. It was hot in the workshop. Their clothes stuck to both of their wiry bodies with sweat built up from the wood turning, the planing, the sanding of the wood.

The smell of wood shavings and sticky bodies. The old man's hairy chest tickling his own smooth skin.

It was when the man took off his trousers that he realised it was all wrong.

Sharp, skinny erection pressing hard against baggy white pants.

The boy sliced the man's stomach open with the corner of a chisel before running away. He didn't mean to be bad. But he'd had no choice.

He was lucky in the next house. With the man and the woman and the boy.

But it was already too late for him; his heart had shut down.

His mind only focussed on survival.

If only someone could want him. If only someone could love him.

In the final house, after the woods – the last one before he was on his own – he had hoped to stay quiet, anonymous. Out of the way. But then he heard about the girl across the street, and everything changed.

36

Claire stared at me, her eyes glassy. Could she hear me? When she went like this it reminded me of when she was in hospital. The *bleep bleep* of that machine. I talked to her then, all the time. I told her about anything. I told her everything. But either she didn't hear me or she chose to forget what I'd said. When she disappeared now, I sometimes wondered if she did it on purpose. To escape. There was nothing I could do except keep talking. I'd started now. I had to finish.

'I put a pillow over her face,' I said. 'Barely had to put any pressure on it at all, she was so weak by then. She begged me to do it. Pleaded with me . . .'

Please, Jo . . . kill me now . . .

'She wasn't in pain: the morphine was seeing to that, but it was also loosening her tongue. She couldn't live with the guilt any more, and neither could I, Claire. In that bath in that dump of a flat in Leith, I just couldn't see any way out of it. You were gone, off to your new life . . . Craig was losing interest in me . . . It wasn't her fault . . . I don't think she meant to do it . . .'

Claire's head bobbed slightly, and I was sure that despite her not being able to speak, she could hear me all right. So I continued to blurt it all out.

'She killed someone, Claire. She killed a man who was poaching rabbits on her land. Rabbits, for fuck's sake. As if they were in short supply . . .'

Claire blinked. Swallowed. Licked her lips. She was back.

'She was so ill, Jo. She was going to die anyway. You didn't have to do that . . . You could've talked to me. I would've listened . . .'

I glared at her. 'We're both murderers, Claire. Don't you see? Other people in her situation – they would've called the police. Got someone to come and get him off her land. As for me . . . Well, what excuse do I have? She begged me, but I didn't have to do it. I think on some level I wanted to . . .'

'She was so ill, Jo,' she repeated, as if that somehow made it all right. That was typical of Claire, standing up for me when I didn't deserve it. 'Who do you think she killed, Jo?'

I sighed. I felt calmer now. After my confession, the rest didn't seem so difficult. 'His name was Michael Waters. He had a son. Or maybe it was two. The wife was distraught – thought he'd gone missing. Do you remember? It was big news back then . . . I remember hearing about it at the time. I don't know what happened to the family. There's no one around here with that name now, is there?'

'I'm not sure . . . the surname does ring a bell . . .'

'They never found a body, Claire. No one knows what happened to him. But I do. I know where he is.'

'You're being ridiculous now, Jo—'

'He's buried in an unmarked grave at Black Wood . . . Well, I think it's him anyway. I haven't actually looked. I haven't started digging the place up. I just remember my gran one night, covered in dirt. Her clothes were stuck to her with sweat. I heard her crying in the kitchen. I sat on the top stair and listened to her crying all night . . .'

'Who's Michael Waters, Jo?'

I stood up, opened the door. Suddenly I felt like I was suf-focating. 'I don't know, Claire. I've no idea. But I'm scared ... What if I'm right? What if there's a body buried at Black Wood?'

37

Claire's mouth dropped open. 'Jo . . .' she started. I didn't hear the rest. I had to get away from her now, away from everyone. I ran out of the shop and kept running. I passed through crowds gathered on the street like pigs hanging round a trough. I wanted to be like Richard Ashcroft in that music video where he just barges on. Bats people out of the way like swatting flies. Ignores the shouts of protest. The swearing.

I wanted to do that, but I didn't have the nerve. So I swerved round hand-clasped couples, past fat women with buggies, old men with sticks. I ran past the bakers where Katie Williams' mum worked. I wondered if Katie had already told her what I'd said. OK, maybe I'd been harsh. But those girls had to learn.

Men are not worth it. What good had they ever done me? Barry . . . Craig . . . Scott . . . and all the others in between. They used me, and I used them. It was the only way.

I ran through the alleyway between the hardware shop and the butchers. The sun was like an electric blanket strapped to my back. Sweat trickled down my forehead and into my eyes, the salt making them sting.

I slowed down when I'd skirted past the pub at the end of the Back Street – the one we never went in because apparently it was too rough. I'd been in, though. On my own. Meeting . . . people.

195

Slowing down was a grave mistake. I gulped in air and it felt like I was swallowing grit. My thighs were on fire.

When was the last time I'd run? Done any exercise at all, in fact?

I had no idea.

Something had snapped inside me in the shop. Craig yelling at me – he had every right to – had tipped me over the edge.

I should've called him. Said I needed some time off.

But I didn't. I just did my usual.

I ran away.

Finally, I slowed to a walk, and finally I stopped. I found myself standing outside the brand new glass-fronted library, staring in. A familiar figure sat hunched over a laptop at one of the workstations near the window. He had his back to me, but I knew it was him.

The urge came to me then. Time to act. Time to set my plan into motion. What was I even waiting for? I had to find something I could use. Something I could give to Gray. Evidence. Proof. There had to be something . . . I was so sure Maloney was one of the boys from the woods. No, not just *one* of the boys – the ringleader. The one that hurt Claire. The other one had just hung around, half-heartedly trying to be menacing. Pathetic . . . Surely Maloney must've thought about it since. Was he tormenting those girls up at the Track too, trying to relive his youth? I wondered what else he'd done over the years. I found it hard to believe he hadn't done anything else. He probably had the newspaper cuttings pinned up like some sort of sick trophy . . .

I unzipped the pocket of my hoodie and pulled out the key I'd stolen on Sunday. The single rusty key that was going to find me what it was I needed to put an end to all the crap that was bobbing like a sewer rat in my mind.

I hoped he wasn't planning on leaving the library any time soon. Because I needed enough time to ransack his house.

With the adrenalin buzz still feeding my muscles, I ran up the street onto the main road. I don't know where the energy was coming from, but I knew that when I stopped and let it flood out of me that I'd ache. My jeans felt loose around my waist as my legs propelled me forwards and I realised I'd barely eaten for days. Snatches of things here and there. Caffeine and alcohol feeding my body with empty energy. I knew that when it was all over I would be a wreck.

But I had to unleash the truth. I was sick of being the one that no one believed. The one no one trusted.

I just needed something to prove it.

By the time I reached Rose Cottage, after a twenty-minute run uphill in the baking afternoon heat, my T-shirt was stuck to my body, stretched and translucent over the flatness of my belly. I stopped, bent over with hands on knees, sucking in lungfuls of air.

What I really needed was a drink. My tongue felt like it had been sandpapered.

As I walked round the side of the house I noted the absence of the car, which was good. If he came back early at least the sound of the engine would give me a bit of a warning, buy me a bit of time. I wasn't really sure how I'd get out of the house, if that were to happen, but I'd work something out if I had to. Anyway, I didn't expect to be in there very long.

I was at the back door. The small hedgehog was where I'd left it. I stuck the key into the lock. Then I froze. Something stopped me. I felt a wave of nausea wash up through my stomach and into my throat. I swallowed, and tasted the bitter tang of bile. I pulled the key back out of the lock and ran into the corner of the garden to throw up. I was wiping my mouth on the back of my hand when I heard the crunch of tyres on gravel.

Shit.

I shrunk back against the wall, pulled my knees up to my chest and hoped that the bushes would be enough to keep me hidden. I closed my eyes when I heard the squeak of the gate, his footsteps on the path.

They stopped.

Silence for a moment. Then the footsteps continued. I heard the sounds of the key turning in the lock, then the door being closed behind him. I hugged my knees in tight, and waited.

38

Claire wiped tears from her eyes and tried to work out what to do about Jo.

She'd been increasingly worried since the night in the pub, when Jo had told her about Maloney, saying he was one of the boys from the wood. Claire had felt her stomach lurch then as it did now. She didn't want it all dredged up again.

Her life was hell as it was, without having to relive the past. But no matter what she did, her mind flitted back to it all, now and again. To the people around her back then.

When she'd come out of the coma, the first person she'd seen was Jake, sitting by her bedside.

'Who are you?' She wasn't even sure she'd said it out loud, just in her head – like all the conversations she'd been having for, what, weeks? Months? She had no idea. She'd been able to hear them all talking about her, trying not to lift hopes and in the process killing hers.

'I can hear you,' she yelled, every single day. But the words were only inside.

'I hope you don't mind me being here. I'm Jake. I just moved in across the road from you . . . I heard what had happened and, well, I thought I'd come and visit you. They said they needed as many people as possible to talk to you. Try to bring you round.'

She'd tried to nod, but her head felt too heavy. 'I heard you chatting . . .' She paused, ran a dry tongue around her mouth.

Her throat was on fire. He was pressing a paper cup to her mouth, and she let the warm, slightly chemical liquid leak into her mouth. It tasted like heaven. 'I heard you chatting to Jo . . .'

Jake put a hand on her arm, ran his fingers across the plastic tube that was buried in her hand. 'She's been so worried about you, Claire. She thought you might never wake up. We all did—'

She cut him off with another raspy question. 'Are my parents here?'

He patted her hand. 'They've just gone for a coffee. I told them I'd look after you. It's been a long night. You've been in and out of consciousness for over a day now . . . Can you remember waking up? Do you . . . do you remember what happened to you?'

She blinked. Once. Twice. Remembering the soothing voice from before she could open her eyes. One of the nurses, presumably.

Once for yes, twice for no.

She closed her eyes again after that. Enough for one day. She felt a soft hand stroke the side of her face, wiping away a tear that had tried its hardest not to escape.

Claire blinked again now, back in the present. Back in the office.

She picked up her phone and scrolled down. Her first thought was to call Jake, but after the way that Jo had flatly refused to join them for lunch, she decided against it.

So she called Craig.

'Hey, it's me . . . Listen, I've just seen Jo. What's going on with her – has she spoken to you?'

'I don't know what to do, Claire. I think she's losing it . . . It's like before, when she—'

'Don't talk about that,' Claire interrupted. 'There are things you need to know, Craig. I thought things were going OK at long last . . . but then . . . bloody Scott! I could kill him for this. She's all over the place. She's told me some weird stuff . . . Did she tell you anything about the bloke that came into the shop?'

'I know, I know. Gareth Maloney. I even called Rob, tried to get him to talk to her . . . He came back from his weekend thing specially . . .'

'That was brave of you.'

'I didn't know what else to do. Anyway, she didn't tell him anything.'

'She ran out of here, Craig. I mean, properly *ran* . . . since when does Jo run anywhere . . .'

'She left early today. Again. We had words. She's a nightmare right now, Claire. I'm pissed off, but I'm worried about her too . . . Listen, have you tried calling her?'

'Not yet. She just left. I'm worried about what she's planning on doing . . .'

'Right, well hang up. Call her, then call me back, OK? And try not to worry . . . we'll sort this . . . I was thinking about calling Davie Gray. He's managed to talk to her in the past . . .'

'OK,' Claire said, 'I'll call you back.'

She ended the call, then scrolled through her recent call list to find Jo.

'*The mobile phone you have called may be switched off . . . please leave your message after the tone . . .*'

'Jo, it's me . . . Can you call me when you get this? Please? I'm worried about you . . . Just let me know where you are and I'll come to you. We need to talk about this . . .'

39

Gray was glad to have got the ad in the paper, and had a chance to catch up with Claire. People forgot sometimes, because she always came across as so strong and independent, that she was vulnerable too. It was a shame she'd ended up in a wheelchair. She had a fighting spirit. Gray would've loved to have had her as a sparring partner.

The class had been scheduled for seven, but by half past six there were already a few excited and more than a few reluctant faces peering in through the glass door at the front of the building. Since the news of the second 'attack' had spread, the community was starting to fold in on itself; everyone had an opinion, but no one had any facts. He heard whispering, gossip – but nothing of any use.

He picked up the white jacket of his gi and quickly wrapped it around his naked torso, circling the long black belt round his waist and knotting it in the way that newcomers always struggled with but that he didn't even think about any more. He wiped fresh sweat from his brow with the sleeve.

He'd gone there at six, needing some time to practise some calming katas on his own, the slow, fluid movements of kicks, punches and blocks soothing his mind.

A mind that had been whirring non-stop since he'd spoken to Lydia at the station and thought again about the masks.

He'd got Callum to test out his theory, which had caused

mild hilarity despite the sordid nature of what he was re-enacting.

The balaclava pulled over the sheep mask had led to an interesting effect. From a distance, there was nothing unto-ward. Two bright-blue eyes poking out from the small holes. The rest of the garment obscuring his face and the top of his neck.

Close up, though, it was quite different. Instead of the usual smooth shape of a face, there was a bumpy contour made by the mask, giving the whole thing a slightly distorted look. The effect was unsettling.

Gray had taken photos using Lorna's fancy Nikon that she used when they checked a prisoner into the cells. Close-up headshots, face-on and profile view. He wanted the two girls to look at them, and the jogger, of course, but first he wanted to make sure that the girls of the town were prepared, should they encounter this bastard before he did. He could tell them to avoid the Track. Their parents could tell them too. But he knew there'd still be a fair few who ignored the warning and went up there anyway. Where else were they going to go to drink their bottles of White Lightning or whatever it was that they drank these days? In some ways, the fear and the risk made the place even more attractive.

He also hoped that the creepy bastard might see the advert and decide to give his sick little games a miss. Technically, he hadn't committed a crime. Yet. Unfortunately, being a creepy bastard was not an actual crime. If Gray caught up with him, he'd be sure to let him know that he thought otherwise.

All these thoughts about the Track reminded him of Jo. She had texted him on Tuesday night, just as he'd got home.

I need to talk to you about Gareth Maloney. I know it was him.

He's staying at Rose Cottage. Please, Davie. No one else will listen to me. No one else even wants to talk about it.

He hadn't replied to her yet. He wasn't sure about her theory about this Gareth Maloney and Rose Cottage. But there was no harm in having a word. He planned to speak to Jo again too – about the masks. There was still something niggling him about the whole thing.

By the time he'd made it out to the front door, key in hand, the door had already been opened and a trail of scared-looking teenage girls (and, interestingly, one boy) were filing reluctantly through it.

'Ah, Laura – sorry, I was just about to open it . . .'

'S'OK,' the girl said. She turned to the steadily flowing stream of 'recruits' and said, 'Changing room's in there. Trackies and T-shirt is fine. Bare feet, though, mind. Oh, and Keith – if you're serious about joining in, that's fine too. Boys' changing is down the other end of the hall.'

Gray stepped back and let the boy pass. He recognised him now. Keith Donaldson. A gangly-limbed, nervous lad. Not one of the sporty types. Gray imagined he had his fair share of being pushed around the playground and silently applauded him for his courage in coming to a self-defence night that Gray had – stupidly – aimed at girls only. Who was to say the creepy bastard might not like to frighten vulnerable boys too?

Laura Goldstone reappeared from the changing room, dressed in a white gi like Gray's, same black belt wrapped around her tiny waist, but one tag on the end, compared with Gray's three. At sixteen, she was his second in command at the club and was more than capable of running the place without him. He hoped she wouldn't give it all up when she left school and disappeared to uni or whatever it was she was planning to do. There was a lot she could do with the management skills she'd learned, not to mention the confidence from being fit and strong, and her refusal to be intimidated by men.

'Right,' she said, 'how do you want to do this? I was thinking a basic intro by you, then a bit of a warm-up to get everyone ready, then split into two groups and we can take one each? I take it you're just planning on basic defence stuff? Stuff that'll get you away without getting you on a GBH charge?'

Gray laughed. 'You know my preferences, Laura. Knee to the balls, two stiff fingers in the eyes . . .'

Laura rolled her eyes. 'Well, duh – if you're lucky enough for your attacker to walk out calmly in front of you! What about if he grabs from behind? Or rushes in fast from the front? Do you really think any of this lot are going to have the reaction speed to deal with the two fingers, one knee combo?'

'If you can teach them anything tonight, it's reaction speed. Be on guard. Be ready. Don't be scared to poke someone in the eye . . .'

'How about we just tell them to carry a bottle of hairspray in their bags? A squirt of that buys a bit of time . . .'

Gray took a deep breath, slowly exhaled. Normally he'd say no to this . . . but . . . 'You know what, Laura. That might not be a bad idea at all. As long as it's just hairspray, though. Something you could feasibly be carrying in your bag anyway . . .' He remembered the incident down by the river path from a couple of years back. A frightened pensioner had sprayed multi-purpose cleaner out of her shopping bag in her would-be attacker's face after hearing footsteps close behind her. The stuff with bleach in it. Blinded him in one eye. Worst thing was, he was only running up behind her because he'd seen her purse fall out of her bag and he was trying to return it. Poor woman had ended up with an assault charge on her record. Never mind the poor bloke, scarred for life. Gray wondered what had happened to him. Mark something. Used to work in the council offices. He made a mental note to look him up. After that, Gray had made a point of discouraging such methods of self-defence, tempting though they might be.

Hairspray, though – it'd give you a fright, stop you in your tracks. It wouldn't be very pleasant, but it was unlikely to cause any lasting damage. Unless, of course, you beat someone to a pulp using the can. Gray's imagination tended to turn to the darker side of what humans were capable of, despite living in a town where attacks were few and far between. He'd been brought up on *Taggart*, like pretty much everyone else in Scotland. Banktoun was hardly the mean streets of Glasgow though, thank God. Not that Gray had spent much time in that city. What was the need when he had Edinburgh on his doorstep? What was that old joke – what does Glasgow have that Edinburgh doesn't? A great city forty miles to the east. He chuckled to himself. Must remember to tell that one to Beattie. His colleague had moved from west coast to east when he was twelve and still never heard the end of it. Bit of banter was all it was. Gray was happy enough to take it as well as dish it out. He never got bored of defending his music tastes to Beattie either. The younger man couldn't understand Gray's attraction to The Jam and The Who and 'other old codgers'. Gray had tried and failed to understand why Beattie – or anyone, in fact – could let their ears be subjected to the likes of Dizzee Rascal.

Laura's voice snapped him back to the present.

'Sensei, are we ready?'

Gray took a small bow as he entered the hall, then jogged up the edge towards the front.

'Hello,' he said. 'I'm sure most of you know me as Sergeant Gray' – he paused – 'or Davie . . .' There were a few nods, a couple of shy smiles. 'But tonight I'm not a policeman. I'm not Davie the Mod. I'm not anything else you might call me behind my back. Tonight I'm the sensei of this class – that means I'm in charge, and it means you need to listen to me carefully' – he nodded towards Laura – 'and Laura, who, I'm sure you all know too, is my assistant. My second in command. So you listen to her too, OK?'

There were a few nods, a couple of murmurs. A 'yes, Sensei' from Kevin Donaldson, who was staring at him with saucer-esque eyes.

'Right, so here's what we're going to do . . .'

The class ran for two hours. At the end, Gray was delighted to receive thanks from a sea of red-faced, knackered-looking girls who had a new fire in their eyes that made the whole thing worthwhile. Keith Donaldson had been so excited about it all they'd had to practically scrape him off the ceiling. He hadn't even minded when Sally Stevens, one of the more 'rotund' girls, had accidentally smacked him full-on in the eye during one of the structured sparring sessions.

'Mind and get some ice on that eye, son,' Gray called after him.

'It's fine, Sensei. Never even felt it,' he said.

The lad bounced out of the door, grinning from ear to ear with an instant self-confidence that Gray hoped would become a permanent feature.

He turned to Laura, who'd just come out of the changing rooms in skinny black jeans and a silver T-shirt. Her face was pink and her long blonde hair was dark at the roots with sweat. She was one of those effortlessly good-looking girls that didn't need – or even want – to wear make-up. She reminded Gray of someone he'd known once. Someone who'd once been fresh and carefree until life got in the way and changed it all. He hoped this didn't happen to Laura. She was a nice kid.

'Good work tonight,' Gray said. 'Went well, d'ye think?'

Laura grinned. 'I just hope Track Man doesn't happen to bump into Sally Stevens any time soon. I reckon she'd knock his block off. That right hook of hers was impressive, even if it was a bit . . . uncontrolled.'

He laughed. 'I bloody hope he does – that'll be one simple way to get rid of the dirty b—' He stopped himself. He was sure that Laura was no wee angel, but he wasn't going to be one of those adults who swore in front of kids. He slid his bare feet into unlaced trainers. 'Poor Keith'll have a shiner in the morning, eh?' He picked up his keys. 'Need a lift home?'

She pulled the straps of her backpack over both shoulders. 'Nah, you're all right. It's not dark yet and I'm not going anywhere near the Track. I'll be fine. Have you *seen* the power in these arms, Mr G?' She lifted both arms to the sides, bent them at the elbows and flexed her biceps, which Gray had to admit were impressive. He doubted anyone would get far trying to mess with this lassie; five foot two and lean, but with enough strength to knock a grown man off his feet. He'd found that out the hard way.

'Right then. See you tomorrow night for some proper training then, eh?'

'Night, Mr G.'

'Night, Laura.'

He watched her for a moment, until she reached the cross-roads and turned the corner towards the High Street, then locked the front door and slid the keys into the side pocket of his sports top and zipped them inside.

He opened the storage box on the Lambretta, tossed in his bag and realised it was lucky she hadn't wanted a lift. He'd forgotten to bring the spare helmet.

40

Laura battled silently with herself until she was almost halfway up the High Street.

Sausage supper? Chip roll? Just chips maybe . . .

No. Just walk home, Laura. Have a bowl of Frosties. Cheese on toast maybe.

Have chips! the devil on her shoulder shouted. *You've earned them . . .*

No! The angel shouted back. *You want into those size 6 jeans, don't you? Only another half a centimetre off that belly should do it . . .*

'Fuck's sake, Laura,' she said out loud. 'Get a grip.'

Mad Mary, the tramp that always sat in the bus shelter, grunted something at her as she passed, making Laura flinch. She crossed the road.

Decision made.

There had always been two chippies in the town. It was the smell from the bottom one making her mouth water as she'd passed it that had put the idea in her head. She'd managed to resist, deciding to keep walking straight up the High Street and left up past the park. It was the longest way home, but it was well lit, and even though it wasn't yet dark – the nights could stay light until past ten at this time of year – it was better to be safe than sorry. Laura had never worried about walking home on her own late before, but all this nonsense up at the Track had shaken her up. Even though

210

she'd been doing karate since she was eight. Even though she could floor another member of the club with one perfectly executed punch or kick. Even though she was a black belt . . . Yet she'd never had to use her skills in a real-life combat situation. She often worried that when it came down to it, she would freeze. She'd never told anyone any of this. Everyone thought she was brave and fearless. She doubted anyone would believe her. They'd think she was just playing down her abilities to try to fit in. Like Catherine, who always said she was rubbish at maths, even though she'd got an A in the prelims without even studying. She told everyone she got a C, but Laura had seen the copy of the results sheet when it slipped out of her folder after double physics a couple of weeks ago.

Laura didn't want to be seen as a fake.

She walked up the vennel between the hardware shop and the butchers, coming out directly across from the top chippie, not because it was better – in her opinion, they were both about the same, although she did think the staff in the top one were a bit friendlier – no, it was the top one because it was on the Back Street, the bottom one on the High Street – the High Street being lower than the Back Street, despite the name. Work that one out, if you can. These were things that were just known: to the locals, anyway. She had no idea how newcomers were supposed to find out about these things.

She decided on a chip roll, left open, loads of salt and sauce. The sauce was a runny brown vinegary concoction, the recipe secret and apparently only available on the east coast of Scotland. But as she'd never been to the west coast, let alone to a chippie over there, that was something she couldn't confirm. Maybe this was where the newcomers would come in handy.

She wandered slowly out of the shop, fingers already coated in the slimy brown sauce as she fed the chips from the top of the open roll into her starving mouth.

'You'd think you'd not eaten for a week,' she muttered to herself. Her stomach groaned in response.

Rather than walk back down to the High Street and go the way she'd intended, she decided to take a short cut up behind the library, round the back of the row of houses that lined Tesco's. After that, it was just a short walk home. There was only that one little dark bit that linked the library to the houses: the bit where the trees were too closely packed, blocking out the light. According to the *Banktoun Mail and Post* there were plans to thin these out, but so far nothing had happened because apparently the people who lived in the houses liked the fact that the trees blocked the roof of the Tesco back entrance from their gardens. Laura didn't fully understand this, as all the houses had high fences – but, as was usual in Banktoun, people liked to make a fuss before they agreed to any change.

Christ, she couldn't wait to get away from the place. She'd already started browsing through the UCAS handbook, trying to decide where to go to uni. Her mum and dad wanted her to go to Edinburgh so she could stay at home.

Fat chance!

She was already thinking much further afield; the London campuses looked particularly appealing. There weren't many who were considering London, which suited her fine too. There was nothing *wrong* with her friends, but she had designs on a bit more of a cosmopolitan life. Funny, for a girl who'd never been further than her mum's sister's in Dunfermline, barely across the Forth Bridge.

She walked round behind the library, only vaguely aware

of the light becoming dimmer, the last of the sun disappearing behind the trees.

Once she'd eaten enough of the chips to enable her to sandwich the roll shut, she nibbled round the edges, then rolled the greasy chip paper into a ball.

Maybe it was because she was distracted, daydreaming about her future life at uni, or maybe it was because of the noise of the paper being scrunched and her munching on the chip roll, but she never heard the footsteps until they were right behind her.

But she heard the panting, felt hot breath on the left side of her face as a black-clad arm snaked around her chest, grabbing tightly, almost pulling her off her feet.

It took longer than expected for her fighting instinct to kick in.

The remains of the roll flew from her hand as she bent forwards and to the right in one sharp move, her right elbow shooting back as she shrunk down and away, trying to slide out of her assailant's grip.

He gripped tighter, pushing his weight into her back. Shoved her up against the wall. Hard. Her face scraped across the rough stone as she tried to wriggle free. He tried to pin her there with a knee on her back, a hand against her head.

She moved fast, felt the skin ripping on her cheek as she dropped lower, managing to free her elbow and jab it back into him as hard as she could.

He made a small yelp of pain and only then did she realise that she'd forgotten to scream.

'Help,' she screamed. 'Help! Attack!'

His grip loosened slightly and she felt a burst of adrenalin surging through her body.

She was ten feet tall.

Sliding out of his grip, she spun round and gave him her best uppercut, but he moved just at the point of connection and it ended up glancing off the side of his face, hitting his cheekbone with a sickening crunch.

But it felt wrong. She hadn't hit it hard enough for it to break.

He staggered back from her, a low muffled moan escaping from behind the wool of the balaclava, and she aimed a low kick towards his knee. But he'd found his way again and lunged towards her, and she ended up stumbling forwards as her foot missed its target, knocking her off balance. She ducked back from him and swiped at the side of his face, the bit she thought she'd broken.

Her fist connected again and she realised what the noise was. The crunch.

Plastic. His face was plastic.

She lunged in again, screamed into his face, 'FIRE! Call 999!'

She made a grab for his face, managed a grip of the balaclava before he swatted her off, swaying back on his heels.

Was he dazed?

She didn't wait around long enough to find out. She turned and made to run, fear burning through her veins. Then she was down, her foot hitting something slippery on the asphalt before she fell. *Oh Jesus*, she thought, *floored by a fucking chip roll!* She threw out her arms in front of her, but it was too late. She hit her knee, then her face as she crashed down to the ground.

The air left her lungs in a rapid *whump*.

As she lay, she heard a dog barking, a back gate slamming against the fence. Footsteps running. Two sets. A yell. 'HEY!'

Another voice, quieter: 'Are you OK, hen? Bloody hell . . .
Trisha, phone an ambulance . . .'

Then . . . nothing.

41

Gray slowed the scooter until he was going slowly enough to edge it in through the gate. He dropped his feet onto the floor, turned off the engine.

Apart from the *tick tick tick* as it cooled down, the street was quiet.

He wheeled his pride and joy up to its space under the front window, where he has dispensed with the niceties of a garden to leave space for the bike and his various other bits and pieces around it. Technically, he was supposed to make the single gate into a double space, request that the council come and drop the kerb. At the moment his driveway was unofficial, but he preferred it that way. Less chance of anyone wandering in to have a look at the Lambretta.

He understood the fascination. With the bike, and with him. Some of the town's teenagers didn't quite get his style, his personality when he was off-duty, but he was more than happy to talk to any that did.

He'd been obsessed with the whole Mod culture since he was a boy – his dad had often regaled him with stories of gangs of Mods v Rockers; and Gray would've thought they were tall tales, until he started to buy books on it all. The fashions, the fights, the music. The girls.

The drugs.

That was the only part he didn't embrace. Not because he was a puritan or a party pooper or anything of the like; only because ever since he'd been a kid, he'd wanted to be a copper.

And what could be more Modish than a uniform?

Despite the disappointment he caused for Phil Daniels' Jimmy in the film, Sting's portrayal of Ace Face in *Quadrophenia* was a classic. That Brighton Grand bellhop uniform. Gray would never use the word 'dapper', but he couldn't find a better one. He still scoured eBay, looking for the costume. No doubt it was in the house of one of the legends that were Pete Townshend and Roger Daltrey. In fact, it was Daltrey's look he carried off now – nothing over the top, just that hint of a bygone era. Nothing quite as obvious as the so-called 'Modfather', Paul Weller.

Somehow he couldn't see the Big Ham putting up with that much of a hairstyle, despite purporting not to give a fuck about much at all. He'd been counting down the days to his retirement on one of those red and white desk calendars for months now. Gray had to admit he was looking forward to it just as much, if not more.

The only uncertainty was whether he'd still have a job himself. It seemed more and more likely that the station would be closed down, the town's policing needs served by the county HQ, or whatever it was called now since the forces had merged to create Police Scotland. Gray had bet Callum Beattie that it'd be divided again within two years. A half-baked plan that suited the government's pockets, and nothing more.

After locking up the bike and covering it with a tarpaulin, he headed inside.

The house always felt stuffy, old. He'd barely changed it since his parents had died – both prematurely, heart attack and dementia, respectively, and one of the main reasons that

217

he kept himself as fit and healthy as he could. Apart from the occasional sausage roll, of course.

The grandfather clock in the hall had long since stopped ticking. In fact, he couldn't remember hearing it ticking at all since that night, all those years ago. When his parents had left him home alone and he'd decided to entertain a young woman . . .

Ready to sink into one of his usual melancholy late nights, he flicked on the stereo and 'Ghost Town' by The Specials came on. He could relate.

He'd just switched on the kettle when his phone rang, and he toyed with not answering it. But he couldn't do that. Late-night calls were never someone calling for a chat.

He sighed, clicked the green button. 'Gray,' he said, his tone flat.

'It's me,' replied PC Beattie. 'You'd better get down here. There's been another one.'

THE BOY

He is surprised to hear that the girl from the woods is still alive.

He overhears his latest foster mother talking to the girl's mother on the tiny square of grass at the front that they call the lawn. His bedroom is at the front, which makes a nice change. It gives him a good view of the street.

All the comings and goings.

The girl's house is directly opposite. The parents are always in and out in their little silver car.

Back and forth to the hospital.

'She's improving every day,' the mother says. 'They think she might wake up.'

So she's a fighter, then.

He hadn't expected that. It was the other girl who was the feisty one.

The sexy one.

Still a child, but not for long.

He'd seen something in her eyes. Something hard. Damaged.

Something like himself.

Going to the hospital is a risk.

What if she recognises him? It isn't likely.

But still.

Is it luck or fate or just coincidence that she is there the first time he visits?

He tells the nurse at the front desk that he's a friend from school.

Follows the blue line round endless corridors that smell of bleach and boiled cabbage and death.

Finds her standing outside the room. Face against the glass.

'Hello,' he says, 'how is she?'

The girl turns to face him. Her face pink and tear-streaked. She blinks once, her face screws into a look of confusion, then it passes.

'She's getting better,' she says. 'The nurse said there are signs she might wake up. She's been wiggling her toes. They thought it might just be spasms, you know? Like she couldn't control it. But she's been doing it again today. They're just doing some tests now, then I'm allowed in . . . I wasn't before, but . . . Sorry . . . who are you again?'

The boy grins. 'I've just moved in across the road. I'm so glad she's getting better. I heard all about it and I've been so worried . . .'

'Me too. I still can't believe what happened . . . I . . .'

Two nurses file out of the room. 'You can go in now if you like. Talk to her. There's a good chance that she's able to hear you . . .'

The girl turns back to the boy. 'Are you coming?'

The boy nods and follows her inside.

And so, it begins.

42

Laura was sitting on her granny's couch with a cup of tea and a fat lip. She was glad her mum had said it was OK to take a few days off after the attack. Saved her having to lie and pretend to go to school. Davie Gray had called round in the morning, but she'd refused to get up. She'd heard her mum telling him to pop round to Bridie's to see her later.

Laura had pulled the duvet over her head and groaned.

Why could there not be another policeman come round to question her? Why him? Not only did she feel like a fucking *idiot* for not being prepared, she knew he would be feeling guilty too – for not giving her a lift home.

The attacker was hanging about at the Track. He wasn't supposed to be in the town, in that stupid little lane that she wished she'd never walked up. One thing was for certain, she wouldn't be eating another chip roll in a hurry.

She pulled herself up into a sitting position on the worn velour couch, wincing at the pain. Her right knee was swollen to the size of a tennis ball, but the doctor had said it was just fluid and it would be OK. She picked up the mug of tea her granny had left on the small side table next to the couch.

'Ouch, ah. Jesus.' Her hands were grazed from the asphalt. Raw, red wounds that her mum had taken the tweezers to, to remove the grit. Every time she moved her hands they wept pus, and picking up a hot mug of tea was practically impossible.

She set the tea back down and leant back into the couch. Her hands instinctively going up to touch her face. The scraped skin felt rough, and it looked awful, but the doctor said there shouldn't be any scarring. Her lip hurt, though. It was blown up like a balloon, blackened underneath from where her teeth had cut into it. She was lucky she hadn't smashed them all in. Small mercies.

The thing that hurt most was her pride.

'Stupid. Stupid,' she muttered, punching the back of the couch with her elbows. The only body parts she had that didn't ache.

At least her granny was leaving her alone. She might be an old gossip, but she could see that Laura was in no mood to talk. Maybe Gray would leave her alone too.

The doorbell rang, making her flinch. She sighed. 'Speak of the devil.'

Bridie appeared in the doorway of the living room, her face full of concern. 'Sergeant Gray is here to see you, Laura. Says he'll be as quick as he can.'

Laura fought back the urge to groan. Best to get it over with.

Bridie shuffled off, no doubt to make more tea. Gray appeared in her place.

'OK if I come in?' he said. His expression was pained. He might be a professional, but Laura knew he wore his heart on his sleeve.

She nodded.

He took off his hat and sat down on the chair to her left. Matching green velour. Part of a three-piece set. The other chair was about a metre from the TV, so Bridie could watch without the volume being up at 100, which had caused the neighbours to complain in the past. Not Scott and Jo, of course – their music would drown out any TV. The ones on the other side that Bridie didn't like – apparently because they'd said something to her once, something that Bridie had conveniently forgotten. Laura knew that wasn't the reason, but she reckoned it was too late to start lecturing her granny about racism and bigotry at the age of eighty-one.

Gray coughed, reminding her he was there.

'Want to tell me about it?' The gentleness in his voice hit her hard. She felt hot tears at the corners of her eyes, itching to escape.

'I think I got him in the face. There might be a mark. You should keep an eye out for that. Blokes with shiners. Not Kevin Donaldson, though, you can rule him out.' She tried a laugh, but it was hollow.

'Did you see his face? Can you describe him to me, Laura?'

'It happened so fast. I thought I'd be ready. I thought . . .' She let the tears break free and they burnt little tracks down her cheeks.

Gray leant over and handed her a tissue. 'Laura, you did great. You've nothing to be ashamed of. You got away from him. Someone without your training might not've been so lucky. Just take your time and tell me what happened.'

Laura sniffed, then blew her nose into the tissue. He handed her another and she wiped her eyes.

'He was wearing a balaclava . . . and there was something weird about his face underneath.'

'Weird, how?'

'When I punched him – I was aiming for his nose, but he moved at the last minute and it glanced off, so I only hit the side. There was this strange crunch – not like bone; it wasn't hard enough for that. It was like crunching plastic.'

Gray picked up a carrier bag. She hadn't noticed him

223

bringing it in. He stuck his hand inside. 'Did it sound like this?'

'Yes – that's exactly it. What's in the bag? Can I see?'

Gray pulled out a kids' Halloween mask. A scary-looking black sheep. It was split across the side from where he'd squeezed it.

'If it crunched like that, it might've cut his face . . .'

'I hope so,' Laura said. 'Have you got any ideas who it is?'

'Not yet. But don't worry, I'll find him. I think he might live in the town. I think he spotted you on his way home and decided to take a chance. What else can you tell me, Laura? You can help me catch this b—'

'Bastard,' Bridie Goldstone finished for him. 'Sugar and milk, Sergeant?'

43

I woke to the sound of a car starting up. My muscles ached from the cramped position they'd been forced into. I blinked. The sun was pushing up from behind the roof of the house. Had I really been there all night? I licked my dry lips and tasted the remnants of puke from the day before. I'd blacked out before, but never for as long as this. Wincing at the pain, I pushed myself up off the ground. I took a few tentative steps, until I was close enough to see over the gate to the front drive.

The car was gone.

I had no idea how long he would be gone for. Could be five minutes, could be all day. I had to act fast . . . and I had to get something to drink. My mouth tasted like sawdust and I felt spaced out . . . dizzy.

I walked over to the front door.

The key turned on the first attempt, and I realised I'd been holding my breath. I had thought it might not work, that maybe the locks had been changed. But why would they? No one changes the locks when they buy a new house, do they? They assume the seller has given them all the sets of keys. It'd be a bit paranoid to assume they'd kept a set so they could come back and torment you. It made me think of that film where Julia Roberts keeps finding that someone has lined up all the tins of beans in her kitchen cupboard.

I laughed to myself. No one would think there'd be a key hidden outside the back door, would they?

I wondered where Polly McAllister was now. Wondered if she was still a hippy. Imagined her mum wrapped in a hand-made patchwork quilt in a nuthouse somewhere. I'd always reckoned she was only one step from madness, and since she broke up with Polly's dad, the stride length had halved. Claire would know. Maybe I'd ask her sometime.

After I sorted all this.

A floorboard creaked as I slipped in through the back door. I paused. Waited to absorb the sounds of the place, get my bearings.

The sound of a clock ticking, somewhere nearby. The faint hiss of traffic from the windows that backed onto the road. When I strained my ears I could hear the faint hum of the fridge from the kitchen down the hall.

It felt the same as it had all those years ago. Like it was quietly waiting for something to happen.

The furniture was different. I was pretty sure that Polly's mum would never have allowed a leather couch in there. The walls were drab. Tired. It didn't look like he'd got round to the decorating yet. I stared up at the fancy cornices and saw the sparkly shadows of cobwebs floating in the corners.

In the corner of the sitting room was an old-fashioned bureau that I had to admit was beautiful. A dark, highly polished wood. A shiny brass key sticking out of the closed flap.

I turned the key and gently pulled it open.

Inside were those little shelves on one side, then pigeon-holes on the other. In the space in the middle was a mug saying 'Tea = MC2', a home for a muddle of pens, pencils and a six-inch ruler.

No laptop, of course. He had that with him.

226

Inside each of the pigeonholes was a narrow open file. Maloney was clearly a bit of a neat freak when it came to his home office admin. Each one was labelled, typed onto little pieces of card and slotted into plastic holders. Bills. Banking. Clients. Bids. Household. Misc.

I slid out 'Misc' and turned it round slowly to reveal the contents.

Passport – I flipped it open. Decent photo. Three years left until it expired. I flicked through and saw stamps for places I had no desire to visit. Thailand. India. Cambodia.

A few postcards, disappointingly blank on the back. Souvenirs? One showed the ubiquitous tourist shot of the bench in front of the Taj Mahal.

I rifled through a few other bits, finding nothing of significance. I was about to give up when I pulled out a wad of paper folded up tight, stuffed in behind a little box.

Hidden.

I don't know why, but I knew it was important. The pages were stuck tight, and I had just started to peel them apart when I froze at a familiar sound.

The crunch of tyres on gravel outside.

There was no time to think. I jammed the wad of paper into the back pocket of my jeans, then ducked down beneath the window. The engine was still running, so I risked a quick peek. I was right. It was a Volkswagen. Maloney's car.

Carefully, but quickly, I pushed the other folders back into place and closed the lid of the bureau.

The car door opened; I heard the tinny sound of music from the radio drifting out.

I kept low, crab walked across the floor towards the back door.

Had I touched anything else? I didn't think so.

Luckily, I'd left the door standing open and as I crept out I heard the sound of the car door banging shut, the crunch of feet on gravel.

Coming closer.

I pulled the door shut, but I didn't risk locking it. I scuttled across to the far side of the garden and slipped in behind the overgrown camellia bush just as the side gate squeaked open.

I held my breath.

Froze.

He walked through the gate, whistling along to the tune that'd just been playing in the car. He held a pile of books in one hand, balanced against his chest. In his other hand he was swinging a Tesco's carrier bag and I heard the familiar sound of glass on glass, bottles chinking against each other.

He laid the books on the back step and took a key out of his pocket.

Still, I couldn't breathe. Daren't move.

He pushed the key into the lock, turned it. It caught against the barrel inside.

Metal on metal.

'What the . . . ?' He swung round, his eyes darting back and forth around the garden.

He was going to see me. He had to.

Then he turned back towards the door, turned the handle slowly. Pushed it open.

The door made a quiet creak and I took the time to steal a breath.

'Hello? If you're in there, you better get out quick. I've got a baseball bat behind the door, you know. I'm not afraid to use it . . .'

As he took a step inside, I saw something shiny down by his left foot.

I flung a hand over my mouth to stifle a gasp, and it only confirmed what I already knew. The bloody clasp!

He bent down and picked up my gran's watch, then slowly stood up. His eyes surveyed the garden once more and I had to fight the urge to throw up.

Then he bent once more to pick up the books and the bag, the bottles hitting off each other again. He backed slowly into the house and the door closed behind him with a soft click.

I counted to ten slowly, sure that the door was going to open again and he was going to come out with the bat to find me.

Nothing.

I counted to ten again. Took another breath.

Slowly, I edged out from behind the bush, hugging the fence behind me. Edging slowly, carefully around until I reached the gate.

I unlatched it. Holding my breath again, waiting for the sound of the back door opening.

When I was sure he wasn't coming back outside, I slid through the gate and ran down the path and straight across the road.

Luckily there was nothing coming or I'd have been knocked sky high.

Heart hammering in my chest, I leapt over the low wall and down the dirt path towards the burn.

44

'Popular today, Davie,' Lorna said as he walked back through the doors of the station. 'Pete Brotherstone is here to see you.' She gestured her head towards the interview room. 'He wanted to wait in there.'

'Cheers, Lorna. Bring us a couple of teas, will you?'

This would save him a job. He'd been hoping to get a chance to speak to the lad for a couple of days now, but with the inspector on the case – terrified about upsetting the councillor's reputation – it was proving to be a hard task.

Plus, according to his dad, Petey had nothing more to tell him . . . which was clearly not true.

Gray knew that if he had been playing it by the book, he would have been on the phone to DS Malcolm Reid by now. Called in the detectives – the ones that did all the *detecting*. Gray often wondered what it was he was supposed to do. Apparently, get grief for not playing it by the book.

He often wondered if he should've called them when he found out about Anne's attack, but he'd only found out about it years after the fact – and Ian had begged him not to. Told him to leave it. Told him *Anne* wanted to leave it. Gray had felt an awful churning realisation, just for a moment, that Ian knew more than he was letting on. In the end, Gray looked into it on the fly. But with the only witness refusing to talk about it – whether it was through shame, or guilt or God knows what else – there wasn't a lot he could do. It had changed their relationship. Put a strain on what had once been an easy friendship. Gray wished he'd called in CID anyway and left them to it . . . not that they could've done anything anyway, if she didn't want to make a formal statement.

It wasn't as if the CID lads were a bad lot. Especially not Malkie Reid. They'd trained together in Stirling all those years ago, Reid choosing to push himself through into the detectives as quick as he could. By rights he should've been a DI by now, but something kept holding him back. Gray was never sure if it was just the drink, or if there was more to it, but there were times of extended sick leave that didn't look too good when the annual appraisals came round.

Non-promotion aside, Reid was one of the good guys, and he'd be mightily pissed off when he found out what had been going on . . . Gray just always tried to push things as far as he could. He maintained this was because he liked to have something for them – give them a head start. Truth was, he was desperate to solve something important without them sticking their noses in. He'd got the stubborn streak from his mum.

'Hello, Pete,' Gray said, pulling out a chair.

The lad sat opposite, wringing his hands together like he was washing the dishes. He was wearing a thin beanie hat, pulled down almost as far as his eyebrows, which seemed a bit odd considering the weather, but Gray wasn't going to be the one to question this boy's fashion sense.

'I need to tell you something about the man at the Track,' he blurted. Gray knew from the few times he'd met him that he didn't really understand the concept of introductions and small talk. Sometimes he wished there were more people like that. Better to get straight to the point than wander around in circles all day.

Gray raised a hand, and the lad fell silent. 'OK, Pete. First things first – I just need to get my wee pad out so I can write this down.' He pulled the black notebook from his inside pocket, laid it on the table. Took a pen from the top pocket, clicked it on. 'Right then. Take it easy now. I'm not sure if I can write as fast as you talk, son.' He smiled, trying to elicit a response.

Pete stared back blankly.

Gray nodded. *Come on then.*

'He was outside our garden . . . He dropped something at the cut-through . . .'

Gray felt the hairs on the back of his neck stand up.

'What was it, Pete? What did he drop?'

It was then that he realised that Pete had a bag with him. A small rucksack. He'd had it down by his feet and Gray hadn't registered it was there. He watched now as the boy unzipped the bag, peered inside. He lifted his head up, looked at Gray. An awareness registering.

'I've not touched it. It was just in there. Here, do you want to see?'

He pushed the bag across the table, and without even picking it up, Gray could see what was inside.

A mask.

A black sheep's mask.

45

My lungs wheezed with the exertion, unused to such strain.

Would Maloney call the police? He obviously knew someone had been in there. He had my watch . . . but did he know it was mine?

Shit. I thought back to that morning when I'd met him in Tesco's café.

'Would you like another coffee?'

Then Scott had turned up and ruined it all.

Maloney was there behind me. 'Jo, you dropped this . . .'

He'd picked it up this time too. He'd remember it. An old-fashioned link bracelet watch with a dodgy clasp was something that stuck in your mind. I was sure of it.

The other question was, did he know what I had stolen? I hadn't expected to find anything – I hadn't even been sure what I was looking for. I didn't even know yet what it was that I had found.

Despite everything, I felt safe in the woods. I stopped running, found myself panting hard. As I trampled through the mulchy earth I started to feel the pain in my thighs, my lungs. Everything slowing down. My heartbeat gradually returned to normal and I felt a sudden wave of tiredness, an urge to curl up under one of the heavy, sheltering trees, and sleep.

I was fucked now. I knew it. Going to Maloney's house had been a mistake, but I'd set it all in motion now and it was going to have to come to an end.

I reached the pipe that crossed over the burn, towards the civilisation of Riverview Gardens. Claire's house. I could've gone there. I could've ended this the right way. Called Gray. Told him everything.

But no.

Instead of crossing the pipe, I stayed in the woods. Birds fluttered away as I disturbed their air. A lone crow cawed, warning the wood of the danger.

I reached the edge of the wood and expected the darkness from the canopy of trees to turn to light as I approached the wide-open fields of golden corn, but the light was dull, muted. Fat black clouds hung overhead, ready to burst. The heat was cloying, sticky; thunder was on its way.

As I kept to the trodden path at the edge of the field, I could hear the burn babbling beside me. The sound of a lawnmower buzzed in the distance. The scurrying sounds of small animals in the hedgerow to my left.

I closed my eyes, remembering.

'We'll go away,' I'd said. 'Please.'

I hadn't turned round, but I could hear their footsteps close behind me, getting closer. A murmur of voices, one slightly raised.

Claire had grabbed my hand. 'I'm scared, Jo.'

I'd stopped and looked down at her. Watched her little pudgy face. Eyes filled with tears. Bottom lip quivering.

'I know.' The anger I'd felt earlier had gone. I was scared, just like she was.

I stopped now, recognising the spot. Even now, there was just a hint of a gap in the dense foliage. The taut wire of the fence was still stretched, ever so slightly, from where I'd wrenched it apart and pushed Claire through.

The first drop of rain splashed off the bare skin of my arm, snapping me back the present.

It was time to go back to Black Wood.

By the time I reached Gran's cottage I was soaked through. My sodden jeans and T-shirt clung to my skin. Rain rolled down my forehead, into my eyes. My feet squelched inside wet trainers. I started to shiver, and when I inhaled I could smell that dirty, rainy smell with something chemical underneath, mixed with the stale, damp reek of my own clothes.

I found the key in its usual place. The door opened with a creak, and when safely inside, I let it bang shut behind me. I don't know why, but I didn't lock it.

The cottage was freezing. Luckily, there was a pile of firewood next to the hearth, and although I didn't normally bother, I knew I needed to warm the place up, have a bath.

Work out my next move.

A towel lay draped over one of the kitchen chairs from when I'd left it before.

I peeled off my T-shirt, then my jeans, and as I did, something fell from the back pocket, landing on the tiled floor with a thud.

Maloney's notes. I picked up the pile of folded paper and set it on the table, rubbing my arms to try to get warm. Then I rough dried my hair and my body, and wrapped myself in the towel. I'd never been very good at lighting fires, but this time luck was on my side. A pile of newspapers, rolled into sticks, then some kindling and two of the fattest logs. It took

235

quickly, the whirling wind sucking the flames up the chimney like an angry dragon's roar.

Watching the flames, I remembered what had happened when I'd left the cottage earlier. The strange air. The taps turning off. At the time I'd felt scared, but now, with the fire on and wrapped up warm, it felt like something that had happened to someone else. I was being stupid.

There was nothing here to be afraid of. My mind was playing tricks on me, that was all.

It wouldn't be the first time.

I picked up the wad of folded paper and sat down on the mat in front of the fire – which was now licking the sides of the chimney as if it hadn't had a taste for years. My skin was turning pink at last, losing its blue tinge. Slowly, I unfolded it. There were a couple of sheets, and I had to peel them apart. The top one was a newspaper clipping – which is what had caught my attention in Maloney's bureau. The way it was jammed into the back of the shelf. Something had just drawn me to it. A feeling that it was significant.

I pulled off the top sheet, unfolded it fully.

MISSING LOCAL MAN:
FAMILY FEAR FOR HIS SAFETY

Maloney's missing father. The same piece of paper from Gran's drawer. I knew why she had it. I'd guessed, long ago, that she'd killed that man. Buried him in the woods. It was the next thing I planned to do, next morning when it was light again. I only had a rough idea where the grave was, a vague memory from that night when I'd heard her crying, seen her dirt-crusted hands.

I unfolded the second sheet of paper and laid it on the

floor. It was covered with notes and scribbles. A badly drawn diagram, a jumble of numbers and words.

It didn't make sense.

Wrapping the towel round tighter, I walked over to the drawer beneath the sink, pulled it open slowly. The atmosphere was filled with my short, shallow breaths. The crackle of the fire. The heady scent of the burning logs.

The cutting was crumpled from when I'd jammed it in before. I placed it down on the floor with Maloney's copy and the other piece of paper. As I went to close the drawer, I saw Gran's paring knife, still streaked from the remnants of our picnic on Monday night . . . and a memory hit me.

The rabbit.

I stared at the kitchen table. Felt the spectre of a breeze trickle past my legs, tasted metal in the air.

Somewhere upstairs, a door banged shut.

46

Gray told Lorna to check the mask in as evidence and send Pete home. He would deal with Martin Brotherstone later. If only he'd let Gray talk to Pete right at the start . . . He just hoped that the councillor's loyalty – or was it paranoia? – hadn't led to an attack that could have been prevented. He'd planned to check out Brotherstone's shed for any further evidence, but him not being in had thrown a spanner in the works. It would have to wait. He was swithering about going home for a hot bath and some time to clear his head when the call came in.

'Sarge? Just got this from dispatch . . .' Lorna swivelled the screen so he could see.

Reports of an intruder at Rose Cottage.

'Where's Beattie?'

'Gone out to get a sandwich . . . he'll be back in a minute, he said.'

'Never mind, I'll go myself.' He stepped behind the counter and took the car keys off the hook, then walked out without another word. Beattie was another one he'd have to deal with later.

He pulled up outside the cottage and parked on the street. There was a car in the drive and not much space left behind it. He didn't fancy reversing out onto the main road.

Was it coincidence that the very person he'd been trying to speak to was now calling to ask for his help? Break-ins weren't particularly rife in the town, but there were always chancers.

He paused outside the heavy oak front door, hand over the ornate brass knocker, then stopped. He'd been to this cottage before, years ago.

The previous owners had used the back door as the main entrance.

He walked around the side, lifting the latch on the little gate. He took in the overgrown garden. Heavy bushes. Dark corners. He felt a sudden shiver.

Could someone still be hiding in there?

He was about to wander over and investigate when the back door opened and a man walked out. Gray gave him an instant appraisal. Tall, well built. Sporty type. Neatly styled hair. Clothes that looked freshly ironed. Too clean? He wondered, idly, if the man had recently got changed.

'Hello, I'm Gareth,' the man said, hand outstretched. 'Thanks for coming so quickly.'

Gray took the hand and shook. Firm. Confident.

'Hello,' he said, 'I'm Sergeant Gray. Call me Davie.'

The man nodded and Gray thought he detected a faint shakiness in the too-wide smile.

He didn't meet the description of the man from the Track. Too broad.

But there was something.

Gray had a bit of a sixth sense for it, sometimes.

'Come in,' Maloney said, gesturing inside.

Gray followed.

Maloney stood in the middle of the living room. His shoulders had slumped slightly, and there was a definite hint of awkwardness.

Gray took his notepad out of his pocket. 'So . . . Constable Beattie mentioned something about a break-in. Just wondering why you called the station and not 999?'

Maloney's mouth fell open slightly. 'Oh. Well, I didn't think it was an emergency. I'm pretty sure they've gone. I got the number from the directory . . .'

His eyes flitted towards a dark-brown bureau. A small local directory sat on top, lying open.

It was Gray's turn to be shocked. Even though the things still plopped through his letterbox once a year, he didn't think he'd looked anything up in there in years. Everyone used the Internet these days. Local advertising was dead.

'I can tell what you're thinking, Sergeant. I haven't even seen one of these things for years, never mind looked anything up in one, but, well, I'm new here. I was hoping to find some ads for things to do around here. Ways to meet people, you know? It was instinct that made me pick it up and get the local station number.'

Gray nodded. It sounded fair enough. So why did it just feel a little bit . . . odd?

'Right, so. Is anything missing?' Gray's eyes scanned the room. It looked tidy. Minimal furniture. TV in the corner. Books piled on a coffee table. One of those fancy thin laptops next to the pile. Nothing apparently out of place.

Maloney shook his head. 'That's the thing. I don't *think* so, but . . .' He slapped himself on the head. 'Sorry, I'm so rude. Would you like a coffee? Tea?'

'I'm fine, thanks. Where's the accent from, Mr Maloney? I can't quite place it.'

'Aberdeen – well, just outside. Small place called Laurencekirk. Moved there when I was thirteen and I seem to have picked up the twang . . .' He laughed. 'Not sure if that's a good thing or not.'

Gray smiled, indulging him. Scribbled down the name of the town in his pad. 'Moved there from where?'

'Sorry?' He looked shifty again. Like he'd been caught out.

'You said you moved there when you were thirteen. Where from?'

Maloney swallowed. His eyes flitted to the right, then the left before he spoke. 'Here,' he said.

Gray tried not to register his surprise. 'You lived here until you were thirteen? Can't say I recognise you. Not sure I know any Maloneys at all, actually . . .'

'Well, um. I wasn't around much. I went to school up town. I didn't really hang about with any of the kids from Banktoun, except, well . . .' He shook his head as if trying to dislodge a painful memory. 'And, eh . . . my name wasn't Maloney back then. That's my mum's maiden name. We both changed to it when we left . . . Fresh start, after Dad died and . . .'

Careful, Gray thought. *There's something here. Take it slow.*

He changed tack. 'Right, so you came home, and someone had broken in, you say? If there's nothing missing, what alerted you to it?'

Maloney pointed towards a brown leather sofa in the corner of the room, then walked over and sat down. Gray sat on a matching chair, opposite. Waited for him to continue.

'Well, firstly, the door was unlocked.'

'And you definitely locked it when you went out?'

'Yes. I remember doing it. The lock's a bit stiff, you see, and it'd been a bit of a struggle to turn it. I've got a locksmith coming tomorrow actually. The lock looks ancient . . .'

'Probably a good idea to change it anyway, being new in. Maybe someone had a key . . .'

'Well, yes. Someone definitely had a key. But not from me. Do you know who lived here before? Maybe they came back or . . .'

'I doubt that, Mr Maloney. I do remember the previous owners, and I don't think they were the type to sneak back into their old house.'

Maloney nodded, dropped his head slightly. Thinking.

'The thing is, I'm pretty sure that I disturbed whoever it was when I arrived. I thought I saw a figure through the window, before I got out of the car. I was listening to the radio. Pearl Jam were on. I was waiting for the song to end before I came in.'

'Man? Woman? Can you describe them?'

Maloney shook his head. 'Like I said, just a shadow. I might've imagined it . . .'

'So how did they get out? Did you check that they'd actually left?'

Gray remembered the odd feeling he'd experienced in the garden. Like someone was out there. Or maybe just gone, an imprint left behind.

'I think they hid in the garden until I closed the door. I stood out there, but – well, it could've been anyone. They could've had a weapon . . . I just stood for a few minutes. I thought I heard breathing in the bushes. Rustling.'

'Could've been an animal?'

They looked at each other. They both knew it hadn't been an animal.

'You did the right thing. Could've been a nutter. I don't know if you've heard, but we've had sightings of a man up at the old railway tracks . . .'

'The Track? Yeah, I heard about that. I was working in the library today. I overheard the librarian discussing it with some old woman in there . . .'

Bridie Goldstone, no doubt. By all accounts she'd been quite busy in the town, spreading her insider knowledge.

'Do you mind if I have a look round? Check everything's OK?'

'Be my guest.'

Gray walked slowly around the room. Looked at the windowpanes. Painted shut at the front. He glanced at the directory lying on top of the bureau. It was open at the 'local services' page. The police station number there, as he'd said.

When he'd finished in the living room, he did a quick recce of the other downstairs rooms.

'Have you been upstairs?'

'Yes. Nothing out of place.'

Gray walked into the adjoining kitchenette and opened a couple of cupboards, out of nosiness more than anything else. The first one was full of neatly stacked plates and bowls. The second, a row of cereal boxes that looked like they'd been lined up with a set square and a spirit level.

He fought the urge to push one of them backwards, like the Julia Roberts character escaping from her psychopathic control-freak husband in that old film. *Sleeping with the Enemy*? Something like that. Thankfully, Maloney had mentioned a preference for indie music. The old house was giving him the creeps, and a sudden burst of Berlioz would definitely push him over the edge.

He'd sensed rather than seen Maloney get up from the couch, but when he turned he found the man had flipped open the lid of the bureau. He had one hand inside. Gray walked over and, as he did, Maloney flipped the lid closed again.

'Just checking there was nothing missing from here,' he said. 'I never thought to look before. The key was in, but it was unlocked. I'm sure I locked it.'

'Like the door,' Gray said. He noticed Maloney's hand shaking slightly as he turned the small brass key on the bureau.

'Right,' he said. 'Nothing missing.' His eyes flicked to the left first, this time, and Gray knew he was lying.

He'd read something about the whole 'tell' thing recently, something dismissing it as claptrap. It might not be scientific, but in Gray's experience there was a definite sign when someone was lying.

Something was definitely missing.

He also wondered what it was that Maloney had stuffed *into* the bureau when Gray had turned round . . .

'Look,' Maloney said, 'I'm clearly wasting your time here. Whoever it was is gone. They haven't taken anything . . . I'm getting the locks changed, so . . .'

'Fine. If you notice anything later, or think of anything else . . . you know where to find me.'

Maloney sagged in relief.

Gray turned to leave. Then stopped, turned back.

'Oh . . . just one more thing, Mr Maloney. Sorry if this sounds a bit out of place, but you said your dad died when you were here. Can I ask what happened? Must've been tough for you and your mum. Upping and leaving afterwards . . .'

Maloney looked like Gray had slapped him in the face. 'I . . .'

'Sorry. Sorry.' Gray held up a hand. 'That wasn't necessary. I'm sure it's not relevant . . .'

'I . . . well. Actually, I don't even know if he died. It's just what I tell people. It's easier than trying to explain . . . See, he went out one night . . . and he never came back.'

47

By the time Gray had left, Laura felt calmer, less of an idiot. She knew he wouldn't judge her for her failed defence skills. In fact, he'd reassured her that she'd done everything she could. Her gran had been brilliant too. Bringing her tea. Deriding the man who'd done this to her.

Maybe it was the combination of the numerous cups of tea and the slightly-more-than-recommended dosage of painkillers – some co-codamol that her gran had for her sciatica – but she felt better already. The pain in her knees was barely a dull ache, her skinned, scabbing face merely an inconvenience.

She pulled herself up off the couch with hardly a wince.

'Gran?'

The old woman had disappeared into the kitchen after Gray had left. Laura had heard the sound of the washing machine door being opened. Damp clothes being dropped into the plastic laundry basket. She walked through to the kitchen, limping slightly, but nothing she couldn't handle.

She leant her hands on the sink and stared out the kitchen window to the small garden beyond. Only her gran's legs were visible from her position inside the whirly-gig, where fresh washing was being pegged.

Bob was racing around, yelping happily. Apparently he loved the smell of the fresh laundry and liked to get involved. Laura watched as Bridie shooed the little dog from nipping at the sleeves of a jumper hanging over the edge of the basket. The back door stood open and a warm breeze trickled in. It stung Laura's face slightly, but it wasn't unpleasant.

'Gran? Can I give you a hand with that?'

The woman appeared from behind a curtain of wet washing.

'Laura! Get back on that couch, missy! You're meant to be resting.' She had pegs clipped up one side of her cardigan, presumably to save her having to keep dipping into the small bucketful of pegs that lay on the ground, tipped over by Bob.

'I'm fine . . . and I'm bored. Do you want me to put another load on?' Laura glanced across at the washing basket and saw that it was empty. On the worktop nearby a pile of folded clothes sat, waiting to be put away. 'Or I can take these upstairs for you?' She picked up the pile, then frowned. Shirts? Men's shirts?

'Gran – whose clothes are these?'

They couldn't be hers. Her granddad had died five years ago and she'd gone with her mum when they'd taken all his stuff to the Sue Ryder. All except his favourite shirt, a worn, soft pale-blue one with white pearl buttons. She kept it in a dry-cleaning wrapper, hanging at the end of her wardrobe. She lifted the corner of the pile. It definitely wasn't in there. Why would it be? It's not as if it could ever get dirty again.

Her gran bustled back in to the kitchen, the empty plastic basket in her arms. Bob was jumping up at the hem of her long grey skirt. 'Oh!' she said, taking the pile from Laura's arms. 'These are Scott's. I'll take them back to him the now.'

'Scott's? Scott from next door? How come you're doing his washing all of a sudden?'

'Oh, poor laddie. That Jo's away and left him. I saw her the

247

other day, you know, skulking about up near the top of the toun. She's a strange one, that lassie.'

Laura was confused. 'Jo's left? When?' She liked Jo. She often popped next door to visit when she was at her gran's. She sometimes gave her books, once she'd finished with them. Usually completely random things that she would never have thought of buying. She'd leant her a top once too. Come to think of it, Laura was sure it was still in her top drawer at home. She'd half-hoped that Jo wouldn't ask for it back, and so far she hadn't.

She made a decision. 'I'll take them round if you want?' She wanted to know why Jo had gone. She didn't like to admit it, but Laura had definitely inherited some of her gran's nosey gene.

The old woman screwed up her face. 'You don't need to be doing that, hen. I said I'd take another load too. Might be too heavy for you . . .'

Laura laughed. 'Too heavy for me? What about you? Just wait a minute and I'll put some shoes on.'

Bridie gave her a key and the weird instruction to 'leave the clean washing on the bottom stair, pick up the stuff from the basket in the kitchen, and don't go disturbing him if he's asleep'.

Why would he be asleep? It was the middle of the day, and as far as Laura was aware, Scott worked in an office. He'd hardly be in there snoozing in the middle of the day. She wondered if her gran was going a bit doolally. She'd heard her mum and dad whispering about it one day, saying she'd forgotten to pick up her pension and that was hardly like her,

248

seeing as she was tighter than a pair of support stockings. It'd been her dad had said that. Her mum wouldn't have dared, even if she'd thought it.

The first thing that Laura noticed when she let herself into Scott's house was the darkness.

Then the smell.

None of the curtains had been opened, and apart from a chink of light leaking out from above the rail in the living room where one of the curtains had come off some of its loops, she could barely see. It looked like someone had yanked the curtain too hard, then not bothered to fix it.

Everything looked different in the muted light; everything had changed colour with the effect of the sunlight against the covered windows.

The smell was something else. A mixture of sweat, greasy food and stale alcohol, all melded together to create a cloying, fetid reek. When was the last time anyone had opened a window?

Laura felt a trickle of fear run down her back. Became aware of her aches again, as if the painkillers had chosen this exact moment to wear off, reminding her that she was injured, vulnerable.

When had she become such a scaredy-cat? It was the same house. She'd been in there plenty of times before. She shook her head, trying to clear the feeling of unease.

She was about to pull the door closed behind her, then thought better of it. The small blast of air would do the place good.

She placed the pile of clean washing on the bottom stair and walked through towards the living room. The layout was the exact opposite of Bridie's house: a mirror image. The décor was different too. While Bridie's was all floral wallpaper and puffy furniture, this place was leather and Ikea wooden units. It was really nice, usually.

She walked further into the living room and identified part of the cause of the smell. Pizza boxes lay strewn like rubbish washed up on a beach. Polystyrene chip cartons, beer cans lying on their sides. Spilling out of everything were the contents of the containers. Pizza crusts, wrinkled chips, dark spots on the carpet from the spilled lager. Cheap supermarket own-brand stuff it was too.

What had Jo done to him? More importantly, where was he?

She got the answer to that via the creak of a floorboard upstairs.

Her heart leapt up her throat, sticking in there like a giant gobstopper.

'Whoosair?' The voice came from the upstairs hall and slithered down the stairs.

Laura took a deep breath, let it out. 'It's just me. Laura. From next door.' She paused, and the floorboard creaked again. Was he coming down? She really hoped he wasn't coming down. From the sound of his voice, he was drunk. She didn't really want to talk to him in that state.

Another creak. She glanced up and saw him peering down at her from the top of the stairs. A frown on his face. Something dark under his eye. Blood?

Laura swallowed. 'I'm just collecting your washing. There's some clean stuff on the bottom stair. You might need it. Shirts and stuff . . . for work.'

'Aye,' he muttered, lurching off, trailing a hacking cough. That was the other smell in the house. Stale fags. Oddly enough, their reek had been masked by the overpowering stench of the rest of the crap that was lying around. She thought of how his bed sheets must smell, and shuddered.

'I'll leave you to it then, doll. I'm off today. Feeling a bit . . . under the weather.' Another wracking cough. Another creak. She stood still for a moment, then heard the sound of water in the pipes above her head. The toilet flushing.

She swallowed. Thank God for that.

She turned and walked into the small kitchen, spotted the laundry basket.

The pain in her body was back with a vengeance now. It hadn't been her best idea. She wondered if the adrenalin that had kicked in had caused the painkillers to become ineffective. When she got back next door, she was taking two more and going to bed. End of.

She started to pull the clothes out of the laundry basket and stuff them into the giant Co-op bag for life she'd brought with her. There wasn't that much in there. Why would there be? It was clear he hadn't been going to work. She pulled out jeans, then a small top that looked like Jo's. She hesitated, then stuffed it into the bag. Maybe she could drop it off at the bookshop. Or maybe she might keep it.

A dark fleece jacket had been balled up and jammed tight into the bottom of the basket, so she pulled it out and shook it flat before dropping it into her bag. As she shook, something fell out from inside and slid across the floor. Pair of boxers, it looked like. It was hard to tell in the weird ochre light.

She pulled out the remaining items, then set the bag down. She was sure she felt her knees creaking as she bent them. Suddenly she felt a hundred years old. She wouldn't be back at karate for a while, that was for sure.

That bastard.

She walked towards the back door, to where the boxers had slid across the lino and, wrinkling her nose, bent down again to pick them up. The pain in her knees screamed.

She lifted up the boxers, and a flash of static bounced off her fingers. She dropped them like they'd burned her. 'What the . . . ?'

These weren't boxers. Who wore thick nylon boxers? Ignoring the pain, she bent down again, picking up the 'thing' at one corner, trying to flick it back into shape.

It took her a moment to work out that she was holding a black balaclava.

48

Gray was just pulling up outside the station when his phone rang again. He'd never had so much happening in so few days. He looked at the display: *Laura*.

'Hey there, you – how you feeling?'

'Davie . . .' Her voice was breathless; he picked up her fear.

'What is it, Laura? Calm down . . . where are you?'

'It's . . . I'm still at Gran's. Can you come round? I need to show you something. Please . . .'

What was this now? 'Of course, I'll be right there.'

He parked outside Bridie Goldstone's house. Noticed that the curtains were still closed in the house next door. So Scott still hadn't surfaced. He made a mental note to pop in on him when he got a chance. Make sure everything was OK.

Laura greeted him on the doorstep. Her face was pale, except for two pink patches on her cheeks. She was jiggling from side to side, the weight on her damaged knee clearly bothering her.

'Aren't you meant to be resting?'

Her eyes flicked from side to side, checking the path that ran down the middle of the two houses. She took a step back, letting him into the house. 'Did he see you?' she hissed.

'Who? Are you OK, Laura? What's happened? Where's your gran?'

'She popped out to get something. I dunno. Listen . . . she sent me next door . . .'

Gray stepped fully into the hallway, pushed the door closed behind him.

'Next door . . . ?'

'Yes! To Scott's . . . she had a pile of washing. I said I'd take it in and get the next load. She's clucking about over him like he's some damaged wee bird, but . . .'

'I thought you were in agony? How did you manage to do all that?

She backed in through the open door of the living room. Her eyes were wide, gleaming.

'She gave me co-codamol . . . Think I took one too many . . . Gave me a bit of a buzz, but it's wearing off now . . . Anyway . . .'

'Laura, can you sit down? Tell me what's happened?'

Her eyes were still darting about, and he couldn't tell if it was an effect of the drugs or her heightened excitement. He felt his own heart rate begin to speed up.

She turned away from him, bent down to take something off the couch. Her blanket lay in a heap at the bottom. An empty bottle of Lucozade was on its side on the floor nearby.

'Look,' she said. '*Look* . . .'

He reached out to take what she was offering him in her outstretched hand. Something black. He couldn't work out what it was, at first. But then he unfurled the crumpled fabric and realised what it was he was holding.

A balaclava.

He reached into his pocket for one of his plastic 'evidence' bags.

'Where did you get this, Laura?'

She had her hands on her hips now. The high colour in her cheeks seemed to be glowing. She radiated excitement . . . fear . . .

'Laura?'

'I found it in Scott's laundry basket . . .'

Gray felt his mouth go dry.

'. . . and there's something else,' she said, smirking now, despite her pain. 'He's got a black eye . . .'

49

I was nine when I first skinned a rabbit.

We'd come from a balmy summer's evening, but the atmosphere in the kitchen was a different kind of warm. It hung. Heavy, like velvet curtains. I could taste metal in my mouth.

Gran's shotgun stood propped up against the fireplace.

I stared at the kitchen table and felt my shopping bags dropping out of my arms. It was covered with newspaper, already soaked with dark, congealing blood.

They were laid out in a neat row along the centre of the table.

Four fresh rabbits.

Three skinned and ready for the pot; one left for me.

'Well?' she said. 'What do you think? You ready?'

I walked over to the table and leant in for a closer look. The skinned rabbits were pink and smooth. Almost like skinny chickens.

'Where are their heads?'

'They're outside in a bucket. Got the innards in there too. Need to take them into the woods later. Leave them out for the foxes.'

A feeling of nausea swept through me and I stepped away from the table. I didn't like the idea of the rabbit heads lying out there in the woods. The foxes scavenging them.

Gran picked up my bags and I heard her footsteps clunking up the stairs. 'There's an apron there for you,' she shouted down. 'Gloves too. If you want them.'

I stared at my rabbit. Imagined the feel of its insides on my bare hands. I pulled the apron over my head and crossed the strings around my waist and back to the front, where I tied them in a neat bow.

Lying next to my rabbit was a small paring knife with a wooden handle. It was my gran's special knife. The one that my granddad used to use. I'd seen her sharpening it on a stone. I picked it up and pressed the tip into my palm and a small bubble of blood squeezed out of my skin.

'What're you doing?' I hadn't heard her come back down. She'd taken her boots off.

I jumped and dropped the knife on the table. 'Oh! I was just checking it was sharp.'

She frowned. 'You know how sharp it is, JoJo. You've seen me sharpening it. You can't muck around if you want to do this. You need to be careful.'

I looked up at her and felt my bottom lip start to tremble.

'Oh, come on now, you silly sausage.' She grabbed me and hugged me tight and I flung my arms around her, trying to make them reach each other at the back. She was a big woman, but she felt strong and safe. Eventually, she let me go. 'Right. Are you wearing gloves?'

'No. I don't want to.'

'OK, but you know you'll be scraping blood out of your fingernails for a week.' She handed me the knife. 'You need to turn it onto its back, then spread the hind legs and hold them flat. See? Like this.'

She pressed the rabbit's legs onto the table, her other hand resting gently on its stomach. She moved to the side to let me take over.

The fur felt soft but rough. When I pressed on the stomach it still felt slightly warm. She must've shot them not long before I arrived. The others would've been skinned and made ready in minutes. She was an expert at this.

She gently adjusted the position of my hand on the legs. 'Now you need to make little nicks all the way up the middle of its belly. Imagine you're unbuttoning a winter coat.'

As I got closer to the neck, the coat came apart naturally, exposing its grey stomach. I remembered the next bit from when I'd watched her before. I turned the rabbit round so its head was at my belly, and I carefully slid the knife all the way up through the thin grey skin. It was more like unzipping than unbuttoning now. Like sliding scissors up a sheet of wrapping paper.

I tipped it onto its side and the pile of pink guts slid out effortlessly. Then I lifted it up by the legs and poked about in the cavity until I disconnected the blobs and strings from whatever they were attached to inside. The innards plopped onto the table and Gran scooped them up and dropped them into a plastic bag. The rabbit felt light and hollow in my hands. I flipped it onto its front.

This was the bit I liked best. I made a small slit across its back, then held the two pieces of fur and pulled them apart. The coat opened wide across its back. Pulling it off the legs was a bit trickier. It reminded me of trying to pull off long socks that were sodden and stuck fast from playing outside in the snow. I pulled the fur over its head as if I was removing a woolly jumper.

I stopped to survey my efforts and turned to face Gran. 'Am I doing OK?'

Gran smiled at me. 'You're a natural, hen. Want me to cut off its head?' She was holding another knife now. Much bigger. I supposed you could use the small knife for that part too, but it'd take much longer and probably make a lot of mess. I stood back and she sliced through the neck with the carving knife, and there was a small crack as the knife sliced cleanly through. She tossed the head into the bag.

'Wait,' I said. 'Can we bury it?'

'Bury it?' She laughed. It rumbled from somewhere deep in her chest. 'You're a daft one, sometimes.'

'Please?'

She frowned, then took the head back out of the bag. She pulled down the fur that was covering its face, like a jumper stuck on its head, and it was a rabbit again. My rabbit. Its lovely rabbit face, fully intact. Only the glassy eyes hid the fact that it wasn't living. That and the fact that it didn't have a body.

'I'm calling her Jessie,' I said. 'I'm going to make her a cross for her grave.'

In my head, I heard Jessie's screams.

I gave up on the rest of the rabbit's body. Gran cut off the feet and the tail and sheared off the fat from around its belly. She put all four rabbits into a giant pot of cold water and salt, soaking them before she portioned them up for stew. I made a cross from two twigs, wound them together with string. We buried the rabbit's head and Gran bowed her head and said a solemn little prayer.

I wondered if the little cross was still there. I could picture it . . . but it was so long ago, it'd be weathered and broken from the years.

But I knew now.

If I found Jessie, I would find other remains too . . .

259

50

Claire knew she had to talk to Craig properly. Face to face. She checked her phone. It was 4.30 now. Almost twenty-four hours since she'd spoken to Jo. No phone calls. No texts. She couldn't handle this on her own.

She locked up the office, wheeled herself down the street and through to the High Street, which was deserted, most of the shops getting ready to close. There was little reason to hang about the High Street in the evenings; nothing stayed open late except that one pub down the bottom that she'd never dared go into.

When she arrived at the bookshop, she glanced through the window and was pleased to find Craig on his own. She had no real issue with his assistant, Sharon, but she felt like the girl was a bit of a leech, trying to befriend them all. Then again, it's not as if she had so many friends to choose from herself. She was feeling lonely. Anxious. Jake had texted her last night saying he was working late, which was pretty common during the summer months – so much stuff to be serviced and ready for the harvest. So many overworked industrial-sized grasscutters. Without him, she'd had another night on her own, too much time to dwell.

'Hey,' Craig said, pulling the door open and letting her wheel herself through. 'I was just about to call you – ask if you'd heard anything?'

'Nope. Nothing.' She scanned the room. 'Where's your sidekick?'

'Sharon? She just popped out to get something from next door. She'll be back in a minute. I'm leaving her to close up tonight.'

Claire turned back towards the street and peered out of the window. Bridie Goldstone was waddling her way down towards the newsagents too. If Sharon bumped into her, she'd be lucky to make it back before closing time.

'Any idea where Jo might've gone then?'

Craig shrugged. 'She wouldn't go back to Scott's, I'm pretty sure about that. Something's going on, though. I saw him outside the other day. Looked like a right state . . .'

'Could she be up at Black Wood? I mean, does that place even have water, electrics, all that?'

'I went up last night. No sign of her. Doesn't mean she's not there now, though. I think she's been going up there for years, Claire. Think about it. All the times she's gone missing before . . . plus, it's where she went that time . . . after . . .'

Claire squeezed her eyes shut, trying to stop the memory from resurfacing. She hadn't been there. Hadn't seen it. But the image had stuck with her regardless. The drip of a tap into a pool of pink water. Jo's pale skin. The deep cuts on her wrists that she took pains to keep hidden.

'Don't. Don't say it, Craig. I can't bear to think of her up there alone like that. Spooked. Scared. She needs help. I think she might've stopped taking her medication . . . It was working too. She seemed so calm recently. Until she got this notion about Gareth Maloney . . . I mean, it can't be him – how could it be? How can she be so sure now, when at the time she said she never saw their faces?'

261

Craig sighed. 'To be honest, Claire, I'm getting sick of the whole thing. We've carried her for years. You have, even after everything that's happened . . . I know she feels like it's all her fault, what happened to you in the woods that day . . . Maybe this focus on Maloney is to try and get rid of her own guilt? I don't know . . .'

The bell above the door chimed, giving them both a start.

Claire spun round in her chair.

'Hi . . .'

Speak of the devil, Claire thought.

'Oh hello! Gareth, isn't it? What can I do for you?' If Craig was surprised to see him, he was hiding it well.

'I'm looking for Jo, actually,' Gareth said. He stuck a hand in his pocket and pulled out a watch. Held it out towards them both. 'Any idea where I can find her?'

Craig's eyes widened. Claire gasped. She'd recognised it straight away.

'What're you doing with Jo's watch?' she said.

Gareth's lip curled at the edge and Claire couldn't decide if it was a nasty smirk or just confusion. 'She dropped it in Tesco's café . . .'

Craig shot Claire a glance, and Claire shook her head, ever so slightly. *No,* she was saying to him, hoping he picked her up. *Don't do this.*

'I'm afraid Jo's not here at the moment,' Craig said. Trying to sound confident. Trying to act like nothing was wrong. Claire willed him to shut up. Gave him a hard stare. He looked away.

'Maybe you could give me her number . . .' Gareth said. 'I can text her, tell her I found it . . .'

No, Claire pleaded with her eyes. This would tip Jo over the edge. She knew that Jo was convinced that this was the man who'd done them both wrong, and despite not really believing her, she wasn't about to put Jo's theory to the test. If Maloney was one of the boys from the woods, then wasn't he dangerous? Putting him in touch with Jo could be a recipe for disaster . . . On the other hand, maybe it was time for Jo to have it out with him, once and for all . . .

'I could always call Sergeant Gray,' Gareth continued, changing tack. 'I mean, I think he already suspects that she was the one who broke into my house earlier, but . . .'

Claire felt a scared fluttering in her chest. Jo had broken into his house? What the hell was she playing at?

'OK, OK,' Craig said. He wouldn't look at Claire. 'Here.' He scribbled numbers down onto a piece of paper, ripped it off the memo pad, handed it to him. 'Be careful, though, please? She's not well . . .'

What the hell was Craig doing?

Gareth looked down at the paper. Pulled his phone out of his pocket and started keying in the numbers.

He shrugged. 'I just want to give her the watch back.'

Claire tried to catch his eye, but he kept his gaze fixed on the phone as he typed. *I don't like this*, she thought. *I don't like this at all.*

51

The pile of sketchbooks sat on the kitchen table, taunting me. I'd brought them down from the bedroom earlier, trying not to think too much about them. At some point, Gran had taken them from my bedroom and put them away in her wardrobe. Clearly she'd thought I didn't want them any more, or maybe it was just because she was hoping she might find something in there that would help her . . . with what, I don't know. I'd drawn inside those books for as long as I could remember. Only at the cottage, though; I never took them home. I don't think my mum even knew they existed. They were like a diary of sorts. Snapshots in time: me trying to make sense of everything that had gone on in my life.

I was scared of what I was going to find.

Sitting at the kitchen table, I picked the one on the top of the pile, flipped it open.

Me and my mum sitting under a tree covered with bright-green leaves and red, perfectly round apples. We're grinning; Mum's holding a book. In the background is a dark figure, mouth set in a straight line, eyebrows jagged like the sharp chevrons on a blind bend.

I shuddered, snapping the book shut. I remembered drawing it. A fantasy image of a happy time with my mum . . . overshadowed by the dark, scowling face of my dad as he watched on. I opened the book again and flicked through. It was full of variations on the same theme. Me and Mum in the kitchen baking cakes, Dad throwing us daggers from by the fire; me and Mum in the car, singing – the sounds depicted by my little shaky scribbles of musical notes – Dad in the back seat, hands over his ears, eyes clamped shut, drowning us out. When I flicked to the final pages, all of the drawings had been scribbled over in thick black marker pen, obscuring what was once there: the thoughts I'd had as a child.

I remembered doing that too, after it happened. Trying to hide the evidence of my bad thoughts that I was so sure had got my mum killed.

It was the summer after Claire had finally come out of hospital. The police turned up while we were eating our tea – rabbit stew, freshly prepared from the day's catch. I'd been allowed to shoot one of them myself, and my arm still ached from the recoil of the gun. I'd opened the door to the tall man in uniform and immediately been sent upstairs to my room. I hadn't gone there, though – I sat at the top of the stairs, just out of sight, as the policeman spoke to my gran in a low, sad voice. Silent tears streamed down my face.

'I'm sorry to have to tell you this, Mrs Thompson, but your daughter and son-in-law have been fatally injured in an accident . . .'

'How did it happen? Was he drunk?' My gran's voice sounded harsh and I imagined the policeman looking at his colleague, raising his eyebrows.

'We don't know that yet, I'm afraid. All we know is that your son-in-law appears to have lost control of the car on a sharp bend, colliding with a tree—'

'Did she have her seatbelt on?'

'Mrs Thompson . . .'

'Did she? Just tell me, officer. I'm not a child. I'm not about to pass out from the shock. That man . . . I've been expecting something like this to happen . . .' She slammed a fist on the table and I felt myself flinch. 'That poor bloody child.'

'We'll send someone round to see you in the morning, Mrs Thompson. We'll need a formal identification, but it can wait . . . Maybe you can tell us more about your son-in-law then, when it's sunk in a bit . . .'

She started crying once they'd gone, and I'd tiptoed along the hall to my room, trying hard not to make a sound. I heard my mum's voice as I drifted off to sleep . . . *I'll always love you, Jo . . . Remember that . . . whatever happens.*

I only went back home once after that, to pack up the rest of my clothes and my paltry collection of books and games. Gran had arranged for someone to go in and sort out all of Mum and Dad's stuff, which I was glad about. I didn't want to see it. It hurt my chest when I thought about them too much. They were a lot of things, but they were still my parents.

I took another book from the pile, opening it at a random page.

Gran in a filthy dress, arms streaked with mud. In the background are dark trees, their branches seeming to reach for her. A bright yellow moon shines down on a small mound of earth behind her – and in the distance, a small stick-like figure of a boy.

Fear trickled over me like ice, and suddenly it all made sense. The conversation with Maloney . . . The vision I'd had when I'd first come back to the cottage. The piece of paper I'd taken from Maloney's bureau, full of seemingly random numbers and letters.

They weren't random at all. It was a set of directions to the grave.

52

Claire watched Gareth as he disappeared out onto the High Street. He was soon out of sight. She felt sick.

'Why the hell did you give him Jo's number?'

The colour slid from Craig's face, leaving just two angry pink spots on his cheeks. 'We need to put an end to this, Claire. Sounds to me like he does know her. Maybe it's about time she found a new friend.'

'Why, though? Craig – it doesn't make sense. She's so sure it's him. You only met him a few days ago. You don't even know who he is. What if she's right? What if he's dangerous?'

Craig started typing numbers into his phone. 'Don't be so dramatic, Claire. That's Jo's job. Anyway, I do know who he is. I recognised him when he came in the second time. It didn't click at first, what with the name he uses now. It threw me . . . He lived here years ago. Moved away when we were barely teenagers. He's that boy whose dad went missing. That bloke who worked up at the farm-machinery place . . .'

'The place where Jake works?'

'Yeah, that's it . . .' Craig let the sentence trail off, scratched his head. 'You know what, Claire? Jake knows him. Christ, it's coming back to me now . . . You should ask him about—'

Claire cut him off. 'Oh God, Craig . . . Jo told me something awful about that man who went missing. I thought she was making it up. Michael Waters. That was his name. She said he had a son. Maybe two. You don't think that this

Maloney . . .' She let her sentence tail off. Her head was spinning. She took her phone out of her bag. Her hands were shaking so much she could barely hit the keys. She hit Jake's speed dial and it went straight to voicemail.

'Oh shit,' Craig muttered, as if trying not to react to her panic, 'I'm going to call Gray. Tell him what's happened. Tell him to go and find her. She might not have been there last night, but where else could she go? She needs help. She must be heading to Black Wood. I'll get Gray to go up there and get her. Maybe by then she'll have had a message from Maloney . . . He can give her the watch. Get her to explain what the fuck she was doing in his house . . . If it *was* her. Leave Gray to sort it all out, eh? He seemed OK. It's not like he's going to hurt her or anything . . .'

Claire shook her head. She couldn't believe what was happening. 'Have you lost your bloody mind?'

'I'm sorry, Claire. I am. I just wanted to get her out of my hair. But what you said about Michael Waters . . . I'm worried now.'

He was about to hit 'call' when the door opened again. Neither of them had noticed Sharon passing the window.

'*Jeeesus*. I had to duck up round the Back Street to avoid Bridie. She was waiting for me outside the paper shop. Did you know her granddaughter got attacked last night?'

Claire and Craig exchanged glances. 'Really?' Claire said, trying to hide her panic. 'What happened?'

'Stupid cow decided to take a short cut on her way back from karate . . . he jumped her round the back of Tesco's. She fought him off, but she's in a bad way.'

Claire thought back to the advert. If Gray hadn't arranged that last-minute self-defence class, she wouldn't have been out on her own . . . but then . . . wasn't this nutter meant to be hanging out up at the Track? The previous two had been in broad daylight, and he hadn't actually *done* anything . . .

She made a decision. 'Craig, can we go please? We can make that call on the way . . .'

Craig nodded. 'Is someone coming to meet you, Sharon? I don't want you walking home on your own tonight. I can come back if you like? Or maybe we should just close now . . .'

'Don't be daft,' Sharon said. 'Another half an hour's not going to make any difference. It's still daylight. Besides, I'm not a stupid wee schoolgirl, am I? I'll be fine. You two go wherever it is you're going. Have fun.'

'Right, OK. But if you change your mind, call me – OK?'

'Bye,' Claire muttered. She was worried sick about Jo. *Have fun?* How could Sharon be so oblivious to her and Craig's distress?

Craig pushed her out of the shop, and as soon as they were out of Sharon's earshot, she said, 'Please. Call Davie. Before it's too late.'

Craig took out his phone, called up the last number he'd typed in, hit the call button.

It went straight to answerphone.

'Sergeant Gray? It's Craig. I'm here with Claire. Listen – we're worried about Jo. We know she's been up at Gareth Maloney's house, and now . . .' He paused, raised his eyebrows at Claire, who nodded back at him. '. . . we think she might be at Black Wood. She's not answering her phone. I don't know if you're still at the station or what, but . . . we need to speak to you urgently, OK? If you get this, please call me back. Otherwise we'll see you soon. We're on our way to the station right now.'

Claire had turned her head to look up at him as he spoke

269

into the phone. His voice was wavering. He was scared too. She watched him slide the phone back into his pocket.

'Right, tell you what. Let me call Rob. He'll be able to fit your chair in his car. We'll tell him to meet us at the station, then get him to drive us up to Black Wood, OK?'

'OK,' Claire said. Things had started to swarm inside her head. Too much going on. This was what usually caused the blackouts – the last thing she needed right now. 'OK . . . but hurry!'

53

Gray sat and looked at the man in front of him, confused about what he was seeing. Only a week ago, he'd seen Scott jogging along the river path when he'd been out there for a Sunday morning stroll. The younger man had looked fresh, pink-cheeked and sweaty. He'd panted out a hello to Gray as he'd passed. Gray had admired his efforts. It was a hot, clammy morning and a walk was as much exercise as Gray could bear under those conditions.

The man in front of him now was like an artist's impression of himself. Aged by twenty years and dressed in clothing befitting a tramp.

If you'd asked him a week ago, Gray would've placed Scott and Jo on the 'potential summer wedding, nothing too fancy' list. Now Jo was AWOL and her bloke looked like he'd spent a week living in the cellar of the Rowan Tree with nothing but the clothes on his back and a few kegs for company.

Even his eyes were pink and watery, as if he'd barely seen daylight. The right one was florid with purple bruising, a small red cut underneath.

'Right, son. Let's get this over with.' Gray nodded at Beattie, who switched on the tape recorder. 'Scott Philips, thanks for agreeing to be interviewed. Before we start I must remind you that you're not under arrest, you are entitled to free legal advice and a solicitor can be called for you, and that you're free to leave at any time. You don't have to say anything, but it may harm your defence if you don't mention when questioned something you later rely on in court. Anything you do say may be taken down and used in evidence. Do you understand the caution?'

'Yes . . . and I don't need a lawyer.' Scott's voice was thick, as if he'd stuffed a scarf down his throat. His eyes were directed towards the wooden table where his elbows rested.

Gray and Beattie looked at each other. Beattie raised his eyebrows and Gray shrugged back. 'Present at this interview are Sergeant Davie Gray and PC Callum Beattie. Time is 17.05. In order for us to verify your statement, this interview is being recorded. OK?'

Scott's shoulders flinched.

'Is that a yes, Scott?'

'Yes.'

'Right,' Gray started, 'you know why you're here, don't you?'

'It's not mine.'

'Are you referring to the balaclava? For the benefit of the tape, this is a black, nylon-mix balaclava, recovered from the suspect's laundry basket by a Miss Laura Goldstone, who was staying with her grandmother, Mrs Bridie Goldstone, in the property next door to the suspect, at the time.'

Scott eventually lifted his head. He glared at Gray, and Gray felt disappointed.

'It's. Not. Mine,' he repeated.

Beattie shifted in his seat. Gray changed tack.

'You know that Laura was attacked, don't you? Someone gave her quite a fright. Lucky she was able to fight him off. Managed a swift punch to the side of his face, by all accounts. Want to tell us how you got that cut below your eye?'

Beattie cut in: 'For the benefit of the tape, suspect has a three-centimetre gash just below his right eye. The injury looks fresh, and has not been professionally cleaned and dressed.'

Similar to its owner, Gray thought, a bit nastily. It was unusual to see Scott dressed in tracksuit bottoms and a stained T-shirt when he was usually in a suit. Maybe a cheap Topman suit, but a suit nonetheless.

Scott sighed, looked away. 'I told you. I can't remember.'

'You've a cut like that and you don't know how you got it? Looks tender. There must've been a time when you didn't have a cut, a moment you realised you had it – can you not work out what happened in the time between?'

'I was drunk, all right? I've been drinking for . . . a few days now.'

Gray nodded, lowered his voice. 'I can see that, Scott. Maybe you'd like to tell us what it is that's troubling you?'

Scott looked at him. Blinked. Opened his mouth. Closed it again. 'Nothing. It's nothing. Look, I was a bit worse for wear last night. I was in the pub. I think I might've tripped or something.'

'Which pub?'

'The Rowan Tree.'

'Can anyone vouch for you? Anyone see you leave? What time?'

Scott nodded. 'The barman, he'll remember. I was pissed. He told someone to walk me home.'

Gray and Beattie exchanged a look.

'Who was that then, Scott?'

Scott frowned, fidgeted his hands in front of him. 'Claire's boyfriend,' he said. 'Jake. He took me home. I think he must've given me more drink, though, cos I woke up on the

273

kitchen floor, sick all over myself. I'd only just cleaned it and gone upstairs when Laura came in to get the washing.'

'Where did you put the dirty clothes? In the wash basket? Laura didn't mention that anything smelled of puke.'

'No. I put them straight in the machine. They'll still be there. Reeking, no doubt. Thinking about it, I don't think I've put anything in the laundry basket for days.'

'So the black fleece that Laura pulled out . . . the balaclava . . . are you saying you didn't put them there?'

'Aye. That's exactly what I'm saying.'

Gray leant back in his chair. 'Right. That'll do for now. Interview suspended at 17.25. You can go home now, son. But don't go anywhere else, OK? We might need to speak to you again.'

Scott nodded. 'So you'll be talking to Jake then?'

'Oh yes,' Gray said, 'we'll be talking to him all right.'

54

Sharon locked up the shop ten minutes late. A couple had come in just as she was about to close, and she hadn't had the heart to turn them away. It wasn't like she had anywhere she needed to be. She started to wander home. She was in no great hurry. She wasn't meeting anyone after work, which was unusual, but with the week she'd had, she was just too knackered. A bath, an early night . . . then tomorrow she would talk to Craig.

She was starting to regret taking the job in the bookshop over her other offer, the clothes shop up town that sold all the Goth stuff she liked. She'd started reading the Tarot recently, and there were plenty people she knew who were interested in her readings. She had good intuition.

It had been fun at first. Craig was always funny, in a dark, twisted kind of way. Dry. That was it. She'd really liked Jo at first too. Her cutting comments were always right on the money. She'd thought that Jo had liked her too, despite being quite a few years older. She'd seemed interested in Sharon's lifestyle, her music. What she read. OK, she did hate it when she called her 'Shaz', but she knew it was affectionate. Well, at least she'd thought it was. At the moment, it just felt like she was taking the piss.

Walking out and leaving her in the shop – how many times in a week? Three, four? It wasn't on. She'd ruined her weekend, then when she'd bumped into her in Tesco, she'd been a total bitch to Ben, her latest admirer – who, to be fair, was a bit of a wimp.

But still.

She'd heard all the rumours, of course. Who hadn't? You can't live in a small town and expect to get away with much. Jo's parents had died when she was young, and she'd been brought up by her grandmother in a weird old cottage – apparently. People liked to say that Jo's gran was a witch, and Sharon would've loved that to be true. She'd also heard that Jo still owned the cottage. God, that place would have a few tales to tell within its walls. She'd really hoped to get to know Jo a bit better. Ask her about it. But it didn't sound like she'd be getting an invite up there anytime soon.

She wondered if Jo was living back there now, now that she'd split up with her frankly 'too boyband' boyfriend. Nice enough as he was, she'd expected Jo to go for someone with a bit more bite.

Then there was her friend Claire . . . that poor cow in the wheelchair that worked at the paper. That was a weird friendship, no doubt at all. Apparently Jo had been there when Claire had had the accident that severed her spinal cord, all those years ago.

Sharon would've loved to know more about that, too. But for some reason Claire hadn't really taken to her. Maybe it was because of the way she couldn't help staring at her ridiculously sexy boyfriend, Jake. Now, *he* was the kind of man she'd have expected Jo to be with.

He worked at the firm on the edge of town where they made the lawnmowers and the farm machinery and stuff like that. Or maybe they didn't make it, but they fixed it and whatever, because plenty of times she'd seen him walking back into town from there, head to toe in thick black grease. That permanent scowl on his face.

What the hell was he doing with prim, prissy Claire?

They were an odd bunch, truth be told, but she felt special hanging out with them – them being just those few years older.

She was almost home when she realised she'd left her bag in the shop.

'Damn it,' she muttered, stopping, rooting about inside her thin cotton jacket, hoping she at least had her phone. The rest she could pick up in the morning. It wasn't like she was going anywhere, and her dad would be home by now to let her in.

She'd just turned off the main road and into the narrow alleyway that led to the back of her house when she heard panting somewhere close behind. Footsteps. Running.

She turned and, expecting to see a jogger, pressed herself back against the wall to let him pass.

He stopped right in front of her, his breath coming out in rasps.

'Jesus Christ, it's you,' she said. 'You gave me a right fright!' Her heart started to beat just a little bit faster then. Something felt off. He looked strange . . . He looked angry, pumped up . . . riled . . . 'What is is, Jake? Are you all right?'

She noticed a cut on the side of his face as he stared into her eyes. She felt herself start to shake, and his face seemed to crumple in on itself then, like an empty crisp bag. A sudden thought hit her and she felt like she might be sick.

'Jake? Has something happened to Claire?'

He sniffed, rubbed a hand across his face. 'It wasn't meant to happen like this, Sharon. No one was supposed to get hurt . . . It's Jo. I need to see her . . .' He shook his head and started to pace back and forth in front of her. He muttered something that she didn't quite catch. Woods? Did he say that Jo was in the woods?

She stared back, open-mouthed. *Say something, Sharon!*

He cocked his head, scrutinising her. Terror had closed her throat. But he didn't say anything else, made no move to touch her, just gave her a sad half-smile and marched off – his pace picking up into a run just before he disappeared round the corner, out of sight. She felt about inside her jacket, hoping to find her phone, but it wasn't there.

Shit, shit, shit! She tried to control her panic. Took a deep breath. With her legs still threatening to give way, she about turned and walked out of the alley the way that she came, and headed for the police station – hoping that she wasn't too late. Hoping that someone would still be there.

55

I unfolded the piece of paper and looked at it again. It made sense now.

14L . . . 25SO . . .

Fourteen left, twenty-five straight on . . . I had to follow the trail, see for myself. My stomach was churning. When had I last had anything to eat?

I wasn't even dressed.

Remembering I'd left the front door unlocked, I quickly bolted it and ran upstairs. I glanced into Gran's room as I passed. The wardrobe doors were open, as I'd left them. Stuff still strewn across the floor.

The door to my old room was closed. I never went in there when I came back here. Too many memories.

I pushed the door open, and it squeaked as it swung into the small room.

Nothing had changed. Single bed pressed against the far wall. Small, dirty window with sad-looking yellow curtains.

I blinked, shoving the memories away.

In the small wardrobe I found a white cotton sundress that I'd forgotten all about. I'd bought it a few years ago, after seeing it in the sale in one of the hippy shops in Cockburn Street up town. It reminded me of the dresses I'd worn as a child, two deep pockets at the sides. I'd wanted it. It hung there, unworn. The tag still attached to the neck label.

I dropped the towel at my feet and slipped the dress over my head. It felt soft on my skin; I didn't bother with underwear.

Then I leant into the back of the wardrobe and pulled out the thing I'd hidden in there years ago, wrapped in an old sheet.

Gran's shotgun.

I'd put it there that day, before the ambulance came and took her away. Something in me knew that I might need it again sometime.

I released the catch and cracked it apart. It was loaded. I had no intention of firing it, but I wanted it beside me.

Just in case.

I walked back downstairs, laid the shotgun on a chair, picked up the map and was about to head outside when my phone buzzed. A text message flashed on the screen.

Jo, it's Gareth Maloney. I have something of yours. We need to talk. Can we meet?

A sudden euphoria enveloped me. All the events of the last few days started to make sense. It was fate that Scott had thrown me out. It was fate that Maloney had walked into the shop. I was meant to be here for this. At Black Wood. Whatever it was that was happening had started here. Things were about to come full circle.

I typed back. *Come to Black Wood.*

I closed the inbox down, was about to drop the phone onto the table, when I noticed that the message envelope was still flashing in the corner of the screen. Another message? I hadn't heard the phone buzz again.

I opened it.

I need to see you. Everything has gone to shit.

It'd been sent an hour earlier – when I was walking up

through the woods. The reception was patchy there, which explained why I'd missed it.

Fuck.

Not now.

I was about to respond, say: 'I'm not here.' Lie. Anything.

Panic danced in my chest.

He couldn't come here. Not now.

Bang bang bang.

Too late.

56

The shotgun lay on the chair where I'd left it, in full view. Trying not to panic, I pulled an old tablecloth out of one of the cupboards and shook off years of trapped air; newly released dust motes puffed around the room. I threw it over the table and pulled at each side until it was even, concealing the gun underneath.

Perfect.

Bang bang bang.

His insistence scared me. How could Maloney have got here so quickly? Had he followed me to the cottage? I knew we needed to talk, but he'd been hanging around the town for at least a week, acting like butter wouldn't melt. Pretending that we had once been friends, instead of . . . instead of what he was. Instead of admitting what he'd done. So why the urgency now? I was starting to regret coming up to the cottage on my own.

Maybe he was coming to apologise?

Was he suffering regret? Remorse? I could forgive that.

Somehow I didn't think that was the way things were going to go.

Bang bang bang.

On the way to the door, I passed the drawer that I'd pulled out earlier. The paring knife lay inside. I didn't think; I just dropped it into the right-hand pocket of my dress, then picked up the drawer and slid it back into place. Like the gun, I had no intention of using it. But the unease that I had felt earlier was turning quickly into full-scale panic. I'd thought I wanted this: a confrontation. But now that it was happening, I realised the danger I was putting myself in.

What was I thinking, telling him to come here?

I took a deep breath, trying to slow the frantic beating of my heart, which seemed ready to burst through my ribs. I glanced round, steadying myself.

Everything was fine. The kitchen looked normal. The fire was still burning gently in the hearth. The slight breeze that inhabited the cottage was keeping it alive.

Bang bang bang.

I flinched.

Standing behind the door, my hand shook gently as I laid it on the bolt, ready to slide it free.

This was it. No going back.

After twenty-three years, I was finally going to get some answers.

I slid back the bolt, and before I could take a step back, the handle turned and the door was shoved hard inwards. I stumbled backwards, catching my hip on the side of the table.

'Hey, what the . . .'

He barged past, started pacing back and forth in front of the fire. His hands grabbed at his hair, rubbed at his face. Finally he stopped and leant his hands on the mantelpiece. He let out a long, slow breath.

'Jo . . . you need to help me . . .'

My shoulders sagged in relief. Thank God he'd texted me. I'd thought the timing was awful at first, but in the kitchen alone, awaiting my fate, suddenly I was delighted to have someone there with me. But something was wrong, and I felt my relief turning to fear.

'What's happened, Jake? What've you done?'

I backed myself around the table. The pain in my hip sung, but I ignored it. This wasn't right. This wasn't how it was meant to be. I'd never seen him like this. He was always so calm, so assured. The little game he played when Claire was there, pretending he hated my guts: that was all it was – a game. I backed further away from him, shivered, like someone had dropped icy-cold water down my back. Thinking about it, he had been angry recently too. The other night, when I'd mentioned Maloney . . .

'What's happened to your face?' I said. My breath was coming out in short bursts. Panic kicking in. I didn't know why, but I knew I had to get rid of him before Maloney arrived. I was missing something here, and I needed him to just go away and leave me to deal with Maloney alone. I knew that now.

He turned to me, a confused look on his face, took a few steps towards me. 'I banged into a beam at work. Please, Jo, I've done something really stupid. Something bad . . . but I swear, I never meant to hurt anyone. I just wanted to watch them. See their faces . . .'

'What are you talking about, Jake? Hurt who? What have you done?'

He closed the gap between us, placed his hands on my shoulders. He smelled of sweat and fags and the Dove soap that he always used. I closed my eyes, breathing it in.

This was all wrong. I couldn't deal with this. 'Maybe you should talk to Claire . . . Maybe it's time we stopped all this . . .'

'No, Jo . . . You don't understand . . .'

'Someone's coming,' I blurted. 'They'll be here in a minute. You should go.'

He shook his head slowly. He didn't believe me. 'Who's coming, Jo?'

I stared at him.

I was about to tell him when I heard the familiar sound of a car coming up the drive, crunching and popping over the potholes.

He turned round to face the open door and I took the opportunity to reach into my pocket. I held the knife tight in my hand.

He turned back towards me, eyes wide with fear. His hand reached up to my throat before I could react. He squeezed. Tight. 'You stupid bitch,' he spat, 'what have you done?'

Then, just as quickly, his hand was off me again, and I dropped to my knees, gulping in air.

He was gone.

Outside, I could just make out the corner of a silver car.

Footsteps.

'Knock knock,' a voice said into the open doorway. 'Is everything all right?'

57

I stood up slowly, trying to let my breathing return to normal.

'Hi. Sorry, yeah. Come in.'

Gareth Maloney walked into the cottage. He looked calm. Relaxed. I was still shaking, cold suddenly, wishing I'd worn something warmer. His eyes took me in. Flitted downwards. Realising that my nipples were probably visible though the thin fabric of my dress, I crossed my arms across my chest.

He smiled, then gently pushed the door shut behind him. He turned back to me and his hand reached into the front pocket of his jeans as if he was about to take something out. Then he seemed to change his mind. Crossed his arms across his chest.

Mirroring me.

'Who was that?' He cocked his head towards the front of the house, where he must've seen Jake only moments earlier. I wondered where he'd gone. Felt scared about what he was going to do.

Wished he would come back.

'No one. Nothing. Don't worry.' I'd regained my composure, but I felt the fluttering of nerves in my stomach. 'Can I get you a drink? Tea . . .' I let the sentence trail off. I wasn't sure there was any tea. The last food and drink I'd had was from the other night, and that was already in the bin outside. I couldn't remember the last time I'd drunk tea in the cottage.

He shook his head. Glanced around the kitchen. 'Nice place. Yours?'

'My grandmother's. I lived here for a bit. Not recently, though. I'm trying to decide whether I should move back in properly . . .'

He nodded, his eyes still flitting around the room. Distracted. 'I, um . . .' He put his hand in his pocket again. He had something clutched in his fist.

I took a deep breath.

'I've got something that belongs to you . . .' He held the hand out, still a fist.

I took a step towards him. Felt my heart start to speed up again. I held out my hand. He took my wrist, turned my hand palm up. Dropped something into it. I knew what it was. I knew the weight of it. The cold feel of the metal.

'You should think about getting that clasp fixed.'

I closed my hand over Gran's watch, slipped it into the left-hand pocket of my dress. Stared into his eyes, but couldn't read him.

'Why didn't you give it to the police? I assume you *did* call them.'

He nodded, pulled out a chair from under the kitchen table.

I took his cue and pulled out another. My eyes flicked to the chair at the back. The one where the shotgun sat. Waiting. Just in case. I slid my hand into the pocket of my dress and squeezed the knife.

My phone sat on the far side of the table, just out of reach.

The tension hung heavy, like a dark fog.

'I spoke to your Sergeant Gray, yes.' His eyes kept darting about the room. What was he looking for? 'He wasn't very helpful, to be honest. Anyway, I only did it to scare you.'

287

'What?'

'I saw you in the garden.'

I clutched the knife tighter. I was clutching the blade. I could feel it cutting into my skin.

It's sharp, JoJo . . . be careful.

I fiddled with it. Tried to flip it upside down so I had a hold of the handle.

'Why didn't you come for me? Drag me out?'

He shrugged. 'I knew what you were doing . . . luring me here . . .'

A hard lump formed in my throat. 'How did you know where to come? How to find the cottage? Have you been here before?'

He blinked twice, rubbed a hand across his face.

'Of course not. What makes you say that?'

He was lying. Why?

'Let's cut the bullshit, Jo. What do you say?'

My head started to spin.

'We need to talk about what you did to Claire . . .'

He smirked, a small burst of laughter escaping his lips. 'You sure you want to do that, Jo? It was a long time ago.'

I felt a sudden rush of anger. Blood gushed through my veins.

'Twenty-three years,' I spat. 'Have you fucking *seen* Claire? Have you *seen* what you did to her?'

The smile slid off his face. 'Not me, Jo. I didn't do anything. Anyway – I've been away, haven't I? Been up north. Me and Mum. She never got over us losing Dad. Dragged us off to stay with her sister. We left before the new school term started. I never even got a chance to say goodbye to any of my mates. She knew, Mum did. She knew he wasn't coming back . . .'

I stood up, my thighs colliding with the table. It slid across the floor slightly, knocked into him where he sat. He pulled his chair back and stood to face me.

I shook my head. What the fuck was he talking about? 'I fucking *saw* you,' I was shouting now. Acidic sparks flew out of my mouth. 'Your fucking mask *slipped* . . . I *saw* you . . .'

He took a step towards me. 'But what did you see, Jo? You saw my face, yes. Clearly you've never forgotten it. I've never forgotten yours either. How could I? I saw—'

'I SAW THE ROCK IN YOUR HAND! I SAW *YOU*!'

He took a step away from me just as the door flew open, banging hard against the sink behind. An angry figure burst inside, stopping abruptly at the scene before him.

'I saw you too, Gar.'

58

Gareth spun round towards the door and I shrank back against the wall. What the hell was he talking about? My eyes flicked to my phone. Could I make a grab for it while they were distracted?

'Well, well. Look what the cat dragged in . . .' Gareth said. 'Hello, Jake.'

Jake stepped into the room. He turned to face me, his eyes dark, wild, then he turned back towards Gareth.

My mouth fell open. They knew each other? How could they know each other? What did Jake mean when he said he'd seen Gareth too? I inched towards the shotgun as I tried to process this information.

The two men stared at each other.

'Jesus Christ. I feel like I've seen a ghost. I *thought* it was you earlier . . .' Gareth continued. 'What were you doing running off into the woods, eh? Up to your old tricks again?'

Jake smiled sadly. 'How come you never came to see me, Gar? You've been back for a week now . . .'

I heard the hurt in Jake's voice. I was missing something, but I couldn't work out what.

Gareth laughed. 'What the fuck would I come and see *you* for? You ruined everything. You and your bloody hunting . . .'

'You liked it too, I seem to recall. You had your eye on

something bigger than the odd rabbit, though, didn't you, Gareth? Why don't you tell Jo all about it, eh? About that day in the woods . . . about what you wanted to do to her . . .'

'Shut the fuck up, Jake.'

'She was only a kid, you sick bastard.'

'I *said*, shut the fuck up . . .'

I could barely breathe. Jake had been in the woods. Jake had seen what had happened. He'd known all along, but he never said a thing . . .

'I tried to make it right, Jo,' Jake said, as if reading my mind. 'I tried to look after both of you. I tried to give you *both* what you needed. But I had to keep it separate . . . I was too scared . . . scared you'd work it out and you'd both hate me . . .'

'Boo fucking hoo, Jakey. You always were pathetic . . .'

They were close to each other now, and I felt myself trying to back away, putting as much distance between me and them as I could.

'I loved you, Gar. I loved all of you. I wanted to be your brother. Why couldn't you just let me? They wanted both of us, not just you . . .'

'Bloody do-gooders, fostering a brat like you. I never understood why. I never understood why I wasn't enough . . . Why the fuck did he take *you* out hunting with him, eh?'

Jake shook his head. 'He said you didn't like it . . .'

Gareth laughed. 'He was scared of me, more like. I made some crack once about shooting someone . . . It was just a joke . . . Prick! It was all his own fault . . .'

'What was his own fault?'

'Getting himself shot, you fuckwit. What do you think I meant?'

Jake took a step back, his mouth open wide. He turned to face me, his eyes searching for answers.

I cleared my throat, tried to stop my voice wavering as I spoke. 'How did you know he got shot, Gareth?'

I'd never told anyone about my suspicions – not until I'd told Claire earlier yesterday, and I was absolutely certain that she wouldn't have breathed a word.

Gareth let out another angry burst of laughter. 'The two of you are as thick as each other, aren't you?' He turned to me, said, 'Haven't you worked it out yet?' Then back to Jake: 'I followed him that night. That night when you decided not to go . . . He waited for you, didn't he? Then you didn't bother to turn up. I knew where he kept the gun bag. He had three in there, you know. Not two. I sneaked one out of the bag when he was in the bath. Hid it under that fat magnolia bush at the bottom of the garden. He never checked the bag before he left. Why would he?'

I watched Jake watching Gareth. His face never left his. His hands by his sides slowly clenching and unclenching as he listened to the story. I was as rapt as he was – I'd thought I had it all worked out . . . Gran had killed the man after she'd caught him poaching one too many times . . . buried him in the woods and tried to forget all about it. The only thing that surprised me was that the police hadn't dug the place up and found him.

Gareth continued: 'I waited until he'd had his first kill. A fox. I watched his grinning face under the moonlight, happy with himself . . . happy to have a new thing for your creepy collection. I knew he was thinking about you then, not me. Not his *real* son. So I decided – if I couldn't have him, no one could . . .'

'What did you do, Gareth?' Jake's voice was wary.

'I shot him, of course. Lifted him clean off his feet. I was crouching over him, listening to his ragged, pleading breaths, when *she* came out . . .'

He turned to face me and I felt my blood turn to ice in my veins.

'Jo?' Jake said, his face a picture of confusion.

Gareth sneered. 'No, fuck's sake. Not *her*. Her gran. She'd seen the whole thing. I'd started to panic by then, but she calmed me down. He was dead then. Heart must've given out from the shock. "I'll fix this, son," she said to me. Stupid old cow . . . She thought she was protecting me from ruining my life. She even wrote a note and told me to leave it with his things, make it look like he'd run away . . . Cops bought it, too. A grown man can do whatever he likes, they said. They had a quick scout around the woods, but they didn't find anything. Bit lax they were back then. Sounds like they haven't changed much, either . . .'

I was crying now, trying to make sense of what Gareth had said. My gran had helped him cover it all up . . . she hadn't killed him herself. Somehow that didn't make me feel much better.

There was an awful noise then, like a tortured animal. Jake lunged at Gareth and the two of them fell to the floor. Jake tried to pin Gareth down while he punched and kicked at him, while Gareth tried to grab hold of his arms, wrestling him away.

I used the commotion as a diversion, sliding across the back wall towards the other end of the table, where my phone lay. My hand reached for it, and just as I tried to pick it up, the two men crashed into the leg of the table, sending my phone skittering off the other end, followed by a loud crash as something heavy fell to the floor from a height.

No . . .

Gareth had managed to slide away from beneath Jake, and the two of us dived beneath the table at the same time. The shotgun lay on the floor, spinning gently before coming to an eventual stop.

We stared at each other, and time seemed to freeze as we both worked out what we were going to do next. I hesitated too long, and we both moved at the same time, grabbing for the gun, but Gareth somehow managed to spin round and kick out at me, knocking the gun away from my grasping fingers just as he managed to grip it with his own.

I heard shuffling as Jake tried to get up and away before Gareth reappeared, and I slid myself away and upwards, fast, cracking my head on the underside of the table.

Lights flashed in front of my eyes.

My body lurched, and I watched the cold stone tiles as the floor came up to meet me. I was only vaguely aware of a deafening bang before everything went black.

59

Craig shouldered open the door of the police station and wheeled Claire in, bumping her up the ramp and into the waiting area.

'Is Sergeant Gray here?' he said. Claire could hear the panic in his voice, and she forced herself to take a few deep breaths, trying to stay calm.

'He's in an interview. Can I help?'

Claire noticed that the woman behind the desk already had her jacket on, ready to make a sharp exit. No surprise that her nickname was 'Lazy Lorna'. It had just gone five, and Claire was surprised there was an interview going on at this time of day. She wondered who it was, and felt prickle of something run down her spine.

Jo? Had Gray already found out about her breaking into Maloney's house? No . . . he couldn't have.

'Right. Well. We'll wait then.'

Craig turned her chair around and flicked the wheel brake with one foot, then he sat down on one of the plastic chairs and put his head in his hands.

'You OK there?' Lorna said. 'Can I get you a tea or something? I'm sure it won't be long. Him and PC Beattie are just having a quick chat with Scott—'

'Scott Philips? Jo's boyfriend?' Claire cut in. Craig's head snapped up. Lorna's face went beetroot.

'Sorry,' she said, 'I can't tell you anything else. I'll get that tea, OK?'

She disappeared into an office somewhere behind the desk, and Claire turned her head to look at Craig.

'What the—' he started.

'Oh my God . . .'

They both spoke at the same time.

'What's Scott doing here?' Claire said, leaning down to flick off the wheel brake and spin herself back around to face Craig.

Craig stood. 'Where's the interview room? Do you know?'

He didn't wait for an answer and disappeared down the corridor. Claire went after him. 'Craig . . .'

'It's all right,' he said. 'Just go back through.' He'd walked to the end and was on his way back up. The station was small. There were only a couple of rooms off either side of the corridor, and one down the bottom with a triple set of locks – which Claire assumed led to their holding cells. Evidently, Craig had decided not to make a complete fool of himself by hammering on any of the doors.

Claire took a deep breath and spun back round.

At the desk, Lorna was waiting for them, silently. Two plain white mugs with steam billowing from them were sitting on the counter.

Craig took one, handed the other to Claire.

No one spoke.

After what seemed like an age, Claire heard the sound of a door opening. Voices she recognised as Gray's and Scott's.

'Thanks for coming in, Scott. We'll be in touch. Beattie, sign Scott out, will you, please?'

As the voices drew nearer, Claire moved back until she was close to where Craig sat on the chairs beside the counter. She saw Scott first, and avoided his gaze.

'Scott,' Craig said. It was a statement. Scott nodded back an acknowledgement, then passed behind Claire's chair. She couldn't help wrinkling her nose at his scent.

Sergeant Gray paused, taking them in.

'Hello,' he said. His eyes flitted from Craig to Claire and back again. 'To what do I owe this pleasure?'

His smile dropped as soon as he heard Craig's tone.

'Did you get my message? I left you a message. It's Jo—'

'I've been busy,' Gray said, a frown settling on his face. 'What's happened? Where is she?'

'That's just it,' Claire said, her voice thick. 'We don't know, Davie . . .'

Claire caught a glimpse of a cloud passing over Gray's face. 'You better come through.' He nodded towards Lorna, who was fidgeting behind the counter as if she would rather be anywhere but there. 'You get off now, Lorna. See you tomorrow. Beattie can mind the desk for the last wee while.'

Beattie looked annoyed, but Gray ignored him. Lorna bolted from behind the desk as if she'd been released from a trap. Scott skulked out behind her and the door swung shut. Gray gestured for them to enter the room on the left, the door still open. Clearly this was where they'd just interviewed Scott.

Claire felt uneasy as she allowed Craig to push her into the room.

'Is Scott—'

Gray held up a hand to silence her. 'Never mind that. What's going on?'

Craig and Claire looked at each other.

Craig spoke, his voice calm. 'Gareth Maloney came into the shop. He had Jo's watch . . .'

'And we don't know where she's been for at least a day, Davie,' Claire blurted, 'and she told me that something happened to that man who went missing all those years ago . . . Michael Waters? He's Maloney's dad, and—'

'And Jake is Maloney's foster brother,' Craig cut in. 'At least we think he is, but Claire's tried phoning him too, and there's no answer . . .'

'Wait. What? Your Jake, Claire? Your Jake knows this Maloney?' He paused, rubbed his hands across his face. 'You know what, I knew there was something. I went to see Maloney. Something was off about him. Something he wasn't telling me . . .'

He was about to say more when there was a sharp rap at the door. The door opened and Beattie's head appeared in the gap.

'Sergeant Gray, sorry to interrupt, but there's someone else here who needs to talk to you, it seems.' The door opened wider, revealing Sharon, her eyes rimmed with blurred black eyeliner, which had streaked down her cheeks.

'I saw Jake,' she said, quietly. 'He was going nuts . . . I don't know what's going on, Sergeant Gray, but he scared me. He mentioned Jo—'

'Jo?' Claire said. 'Does Jake know where Jo is?'

Sharon blinked, and a dirty tear slid down her face. 'He said something about the woods—'

Claire gasped. 'Black Wood?'

'I don't know,' Sharon said. 'I think so. You better get up

298

there, Sergeant Gray. I've got a horrible, horrible feeling . . .
It's something *bad*. I think something really bad is happening
up there . . .'

60

Slowly, I came to. My head throbbed from where I'd whacked it on the table, and I touched it gingerly, expecting to find a huge egg, but I hadn't expected blood. It felt warm and sticky on my fingers and I realised that some had spilled down my face, leaving an uncomfortable trail on my skin. I wiped my hand on my dress, and my stomach turned at the sight of it.

There was no sound except for a rasping, heavy breathing. Finally, I looked out from beneath a corner of the tablecloth and saw Jake slumped against the fireplace.

Oh Jesus, Gareth . . . What have you done?

'Jake?' I whispered, not sure where Gareth was and reluctant to remind him of my presence. 'Jake, where's Gareth?'

A groan.

I sucked in a breath, relieved to get a response. Then I slowly pulled myself out from under the table and crept towards Jake.

He was half-sitting, half-lying like an old rag doll. His arms were by his sides, and in the centre of his T-shirt a dark-red stain was blooming like a flower recorded on time-lapse photography.

'Jake, can you hear me?'

Jake's head hung forwards onto his chest. At close range, the shotgun pellets had acted like a rifle bullet, not dispersing at all but hitting his chest with such impact that it had sent his body into shock.

'Jake? Don't try to talk, OK . . . I'm going to call for help. It'll be OK. Just try and let me know – did Gareth go upstairs?'

Nothing.

I tried again. 'Did he go outside, Jake?'

Another groan.

Ignoring the pain in my skull and the itchiness of the blood congealing on my face, I tried to think fast. *Bolt the door . . . Call an ambulance . . . Stop the bleeding . . .* I felt panic rising in my chest then, not knowing which one to do first. I grabbed a towel from the back of a chair, wrapped it awkwardly around his chest, pulled it tight behind his back. I lifted his hands and tried to get him to press onto the wound in his chest, but as soon as I let go, his useless arms dropped back to his sides.

'Jake, please? Please try . . .'

I lifted his arms onto his chest again, and this time they stayed put. His breathing was coming out in sharp rasps, and the effort of keeping his hands in place seemed to make the breaths more ragged.

Don't die, Jake, I begged, silently.

I stuck a hand into my pocket. Where the fuck was my phone? Then I remembered it being knocked off the table. I turned, leant down and lifted the tablecloth, and found it lying smashed to pieces on the stone floor.

Stupid mistake.

I felt his presence before I heard his footsteps. I turned slowly and found Gareth blocking the door, a horrible smirk on his face.

'Lost something?'

I didn't respond.

301

'I took back what you stole from me, by the way. My little map. Good, eh? Have you worked it out yet? I was half expecting you to be knee-deep in mud when I arrived. You disappointed me, Jo. Hanging round with my stupid ex-foster brother hasn't done you much good, has it?'

Jake's breathing had turned quieter and I felt sick at the thought that I might lose him. Gareth had ruined my life once before. I wasn't letting him do it again.

'What were you planning to do, Gareth?' I said, walking slowly towards him. I watched the confusion in his eyes, a brief flash, then the anger returned as he waited for me to continue. 'Dig him up and take him home? What's your mum going to think about that?'

He laughed. 'She'll be delighted. She's spent twenty-three years convinced that my old man didn't love her. I can't wait to be the hero. Tell her the truth. Tell her that little runt she fostered killed the love of her life . . .'

Jake groaned. 'You fucking liar . . .'

'Still with us, eh, Jakey? Not for much longer I hope . . .' He took a step towards him, swung his leg back and kicked Jake hard in the head. He toppled over, still clutching the bloodied towel.

'*Nooooooooo!*' I screamed. I threw myself at Maloney, catching him off guard and knocking him into the open doorway. He fell flat on his back and I fell on top of him, hard. I think he hit his head on the doorstep, because there was a dull thud and a growl of pain, but it only dazed him momentarily.

He tried to shake me off, swiping at my head, missing, trying again. I was too quick for him.

I pressed down harder, trying to keep him there with my full bodyweight, while I slid my hand into my pocket and toyed with the knife. Turning it slowly inside the palm of my hand.

Maloney had stopped swatting at me. He didn't seem to be moving at all; his eyes were closed and his breathing was very slow, barely making a sound. I squeezed him with my thighs.

Nothing.

I shifted my weight slightly, easing backwards. Was he dying? Had the bang on the head caused a bleed? I felt my heart hammering in my chest and I slowly stood up, bending over him slightly, trying to look at his face.

Still nothing.

I stood up fully, then took a step over him, out onto the doorstep. I moved slowly, carefully, still terrified that he was going to wake up.

Maybe if I had moved a little quicker I might've got away.

My right foot was hovering over his shoulder, a split second from passing over him, when he grabbed onto my ankle and pulled me hard. I cried out as I landed half on the step, half on the gravel of the drive as he twisted himself round, dragging me towards him.

I screamed, and immediately his hand was clamped over my mouth, the weight of his body crushing my legs as he pulled me further into him.

'I missed my chance that day in the woods, but I'm not going to miss it again now,' he spat. 'You little slut!'

Pinning me down with a hand on my face and a knee on my chest, he took his other hand off the step to try to unbuckle his belt, and taking the only chance I would ever get, I shoved my hand back into my pocket and pulled out the knife.

'Oi . . .' he started.

But the hand holding the knife shot out of my pocket of its own accord. It lunged into the soft flesh of his stomach, and it twisted, lifted upwards. Opening up his stomach. I'd expected it to be harder on a large animal, but really it was no more difficult than gutting a rabbit.

His legs collapsed from under him, the hand that was clamped over my mouth slid off and he fell over to one side with a thump, like a felled deer.

I lifted my hands to my face and watched as the dark, viscous liquid dripped slowly onto the ground beneath me, then I stood and walked back into the cottage just as the faint sound of sirens drifted in on the breeze.

'Jo . . .' Jake groaned.

I crouched down beside him, pressing my hands on the towel, trying to push his blood back inside of him.

The fire flickered and, eventually, went black.

61

Gray recognised the body of Gareth Maloney lying sprawled across the doorstep. Taking a pulse was a formality, considering most of the man's innards were lying in a heap beside him. The stench was eye-watering.

Inside the cottage wasn't much better. Jake was slumped in front of the fireplace. Blood seeping out from beneath him, a bloodied towel wrapped around him like an apron. A small-bore shotgun lay abandoned on the kitchen floor. The room was filled with the coppery tang of blood and a hanging cloud of gunsmoke.

Jesus . . .

Beattie stepped into the room behind him and immediately started to gag, throwing his hands up over his mouth. 'What the f—'

'Get back outside. Get the paramedics over here right now, then call CID. We need to do this right now, PC Beattie. Set up a cordon. No one comes in or out, except for me and the paramedics. Got it?'

Beattie stumbled back into the driveway and Gray could hear him retching as he staggered across towards the ambulance. Thank Christ the three of them had turned up at the station. Telling him about Maloney. About Jake. Everything had somehow slotted into place.

Jo.

It was all about Jo.

He'd hoped he would make it up here before it all kicked off, but by the looks of things he was about five minutes too late.

'Jo? Can you hear me?'

He edged towards the girl, who was sitting pressed against the back wall. Her arms were linked around her knees, her eyes tightly shut. She was rocking, ever so slightly. Back and forth. Back and forth.

'Jo? Are you hurt?'

Her hands were dark and sticky with congealing blood. Her once white dress looked like it had been tie-dyed. He crouched down in front of her and put his hands over hers, gently prising her fingers apart. Retrieving the knife. She gave it up without protest.

Behind him he heard the voices of the paramedics, assessing the situation. He shuffled over until he was in line with Jo, and sat beside her. She still hadn't opened her eyes.

Oh, Jo . . . I promised your mother I'd look after you . . . Why did I not see this coming?

When he was sitting beside her, able to see her out of the corner of his eye while also able to observe the paramedics, he extended a hand – trying to get her to hold on to it. The rocking had stopped now, and she stayed with her arms locked tight.

Eyes blocking everything out.

He spoke to the paramedics. 'Can you wait until the CID boys get here before we call the forensics, or do you need me to do it now?'

The blonde female of the two turned to face him. 'First things first,' she said. 'This one's still alive . . .'

Gray turned towards Jo and her eyes pinged open, her gaze

fixed straight ahead. Vacant. Like one of those creepy blinking dolls.

*

I couldn't help it. My eyes sprang open when the paramedic spoke. She was looking back towards me, her face neutral. Her partner, an older bloke with a perfect circular bald patch, was manoeuvring Jake towards a stretcher that was laid out on the floor. To my left, Davie Gray sat – his knees pulled up to his chest, mirroring my position. I could see him from the corner of my eye, but I didn't move.

'Jo,' he said, 'can you hear me? Can you tell me what happened?' His voice was gentle, encouraging me to speak. I didn't think I could if I tried. My throat felt thick, like something was wedged deep inside it. My lips felt like they'd been stuck together with glue. My head still throbbed from where I'd hit it and I had to clench my hands into tight fists to stop them from shaking.

Gray got the message. Didn't speak again. We sat together and watched as the two paramedics hoisted Jake onto the stretcher, the female making soothing platitudes: 'You're going to be fine . . . We've got you now . . . Try to breathe normally . . .'

They'd placed an oxygen mask over his nose and mouth. The older bloke had stuck some huge dressing across his chest like a giant plaster. Placed his hands back on top and urged him to 'press as hard as you can, son . . .'

Outside was the crackle and hum of radios, voices. Footsteps crunching on gravel. The sound of another car bouncing over the potholes. The air in the room seemed to have been sucked outside.

I closed my eyes again. Felt myself drift away. I felt calm, finally. The presence I'd felt since that day at Gran's grave seemed to have left me alone at last. The house felt still, at peace. As if balance had been restored.

Gray took my elbow and helped me to stand, and I followed without protest. I wondered, vaguely, if I'd have to step over Maloney or if he'd already been taken away.

62

'How is she?'

Gray looked up from his notes, and frowned. 'She still hasn't said a word. She's refused water, tea, a sandwich and everything else she's been offered. She won't even wash the blood off her hands.'

'Christ. Is she catatonic?'

'Of course not!' Gray snapped. 'She's in shock. I've had the on-call doctor take a look at her and he wants to give her something to relax her, but she won't open her mouth. He's checked her over and dressed the wound on her head. He said it's better to leave her be. She'll have to talk eventually.'

Rob laughed. 'I'm not so sure. I had a client once who refused to speak for three months. She had to be sectioned for her own good. She lasted three days in the Royal Ed before she broke her own neck with a twisted bed sheet and the metal bars from the headboard . . .'

'For Christ's sake, man. What do you want me to do? I've pulled Lorna back in, got her on constant monitoring duty, peering in through that bloody hatch. She's got nothing in there to harm herself with . . . She just needs some space. I wanted to take her to the hospital, but the powers that be vetoed that.'

Rob waved a hand dismissively. 'Fine, fine. Look, there are things we need to put in place. I know you want her questioned as soon as possible, but until she's been properly assessed, she's no good to you . . . and she's no good here. I can call in a Section 2 and get her taken to the hospital?'

'Not yet. I want to try again first. Then you can have a go . . .'

'I'm not even sure she'll want me to help . . .'

'How did you even know she was here?'

'Craig phoned me after he left the station. He said you were heading up to Black Wood Cottage. He wanted to see for himself. I told him to leave it alone. I said we could call you later, find out what happened – if anything. But he wouldn't back down. He had Claire and Sharon with him too. Practically hysterical, the lot of them. So I drove us up there. Saw the place surrounded by police and ambulance. I've never had much time for the girl, but she's Craig's friend and . . . and, well, she needs help.'

'She does need help, Rob. But I'm not so sure it's psychiatric help she needs.'

'Are you kidding? She's killed one man and put another one in a critical condition . . .'

'We don't know that yet. At the moment, she's our only conscious witness, and until she speaks to me, I'm keeping her here under lock and key, OK?'

Rob rolled his eyes and sat down on one of the blue plastic chairs in the reception area.

Gray watched as he pulled his phone out of his pocket and started texting rapidly. Half of him was glad that the man had shown up, but on the other hand, everyone had heard the rumours about Jo and Craig. He was worried that Rob had an ulterior motive. Getting Jo locked up in a psychiatric hospital would definitely keep her away from his boyfriend. It was a small town; things spread like a disease, no matter how hard you tried to prevent them.

310

He left the solicitor sitting in the reception and walked back through to the cells. 'I'll take over for a bit, Lorna. Go an' see if there's any update from the hospital, eh? I want to know if DS Reid has managed to talk to Jake yet.'

Lorna gave him a sad smile and stepped back from the door. 'If there's anything you need, give us a shout, eh, Davie?' She handed him the keys. 'Oh, and . . . go easy on her, Sarge. I'm not sure she's ready to take it all in.'

Gray took the keys and unlocked the cell door. Jo was down the far end of the narrow bed, arms wrapped round her knees, just like at the cottage. Gray wanted to throw his arms round her. Tell her everything was going to be OK. It wasn't going to be, though. No matter what happened next, none of their lives would be the same again.

'Jo?' he said, sitting down on the edge of the bed. 'Are you ready to talk yet?'

Jo lifted her head, stared into his eyes. He stared back, noticed the way the golden flecks shone in the light creeping in through the barred window. The irises were a deep brown, but the halos of amber speckles were what gave it away. She had her mother's eyes, that was for sure.

He rubbed his hands over his chin, and the rough hair bristled beneath. He dropped his head towards his chest.

'Did you love her?'

Gray's head snapped up. He felt a chill run down his spine. 'Who?'

'You know who,' Jo said. 'She loved you, you know. My gran knew. She knew everything. She told me, just before she died . . .'

'Told you what?'

'About my dad. He saw you together, you know. That's why he took her away. That's why he . . . killed her . . .'

311

63

Gray had been barely sixteen. Already over six feet tall, shoulders as broad as those of the man he would become. They'd met in the Station Inn. She was sitting on a bar stool, all short skirt and long legs and dirty laughter echoing out from behind shining lip-glossed lips. She was holding a straight glass full of clear, fizzing liquid. Ice and lemon chinking as her hand shook – her whole body seemed to vibrate with laughter. The man she was talking to was old – too old – but, Gray knew, with very deep pockets.

How could he compete with that?

He'd seen her before, of course. Hundreds of times. She'd left school now, got a job in Cairn's the bakers on the Back Street. He remembered her from school: always in a crowd, always laughing, swearing, smoking with the cool kids and hanging out in the park on Friday nights.

Gray had been too shy to approach her. What would a blossoming seventeen-year-old want with a scrawny kid like him? It was different now. She was what, twenty? Maybe twenty-one. Five years apart seemed like nothing now.

Now that he'd grown up.

He'd walked up to the bar with a confidence he hadn't felt. Ordered a pint of lager, laid a fiver on the bar – right in the gap between her and the old man, who was trying his best to get a hand on her bare knee.

The man had taken a step back. 'Oi, watch yourself there, son . . .'

Miranda had giggled. 'Oh, leave him alone, Jim. The laddie's just wanting a drink.'

'A drink of you, mair like.'

They hadn't been together then, but Jim still acted like she was one of his possessions, one of his shiny trinkets to be kept safe in a locked velvet box.

She laughed again, and the sound reminded him of small tinkling bells.

He took his pint and his change, sat on one of the padded bench seats facing the bar. His pint sat in front of him, untouched. Trickles of condensation running down the sides.

He watched her. Ignored the voices around him. The other punters jostling for space around the bar, laughing, backslapping. The heels of heavy pint tumblers thudding off the bar. The clanging bells on the bandit, coins spattering into the tray below.

Eventually, she joined him, leaving Jim at the bar with his cronies.

She stared into his eyes, and he felt his insides fluttering like sheets drying in the wind. 'Aren't you going to drink that? It'll be warm by now . . .'

He kept his eyes locked on hers as he lifted the pint glass, knocking the contents back in one. The warm, bitter liquid hitting the back of his throat. Flowing deep inside him, pooling in his stomach. Hitting his veins. Firing inside his head. Fuzzy, soft. Ready. *What is she playing at?*

She giggled again. Those tinkling bells.

In the background, the jukebox was playing 'The Bitterest Pill' by The Jam. Weller's voice gruff and sensual. Full of regret and longing. Someone won the jackpot and the bandit emptied its contents with a never-ending clatter of metal.

'Do you fancy coming back to mine?' Gray said, eventually.

She leant down to pick up her handbag. Her eyes never left his. 'You've got the most beautiful eyes,' she said. 'That blue's so deep and dark I feel like I could swim in it . . .'

He chuckled. 'That's one hell of a line.'

They stood up together, eyes still locked. A moment in time.

He took her hand, and she let him. As it cupped round his, it felt small and delicate, like he was carrying a tiny bird.

'Won't your parents mind?'

'They're away. They won't be back tonight. Don't worry about it.' He tried to sound confident, but he could hear the quivering in his own voice. The longing.

'How old are you, anyway?' she said.

Gray said nothing at first. They walked slowly. Him savouring the feel of her hand in his. Listening to the gentle clip-clop of her heels on the pavement.

'Old enough,' he said, as they reached the front door of the cream-fronted terraced cottage. He dropped her hand, fumbling with the keys in his pocket.

She ducked under his arm as his quaking hand fiddled with the lock, spun round until she was facing him, pressed herself up against his chest. Her head only came up to his shoulders, and she tipped her head back, exposing the soft pale skin of her neck, offering up lips plumped with blood.

He lifted her in his arms, carried her inside. Kicked the door closed behind him. The house was silent but for the ticking of the old grandfather clock in the hallway and their breaths, mingling together in short, desperate puffs.

She pulled away. 'Hang on a sec.' She turned towards the clock, turned back to him with a frown. 'I haven't got long . . . Jim'll be expecting me back before last orders. He likes to walk me home, he—'

'I'm sorry, Miranda,' he said. It took all of his strength to push her away. He wanted her so badly. But he knew she would never stay. What would she want with a kid like him? What was he supposed to offer her?

She looked confused, then angry. 'You bloody tease. What am I meant to do now, eh?'

She wrapped her coat around herself, calling him more names under her breath. Banging the door hard as she left.

Gray always wondered if she'd started the paternity rumour herself, to try to get his attention. She'd come back to him several times over the years, fuelling the fire, then letting it go cold. But Gray knew she'd never leave Jim.

And, sadly, he knew that Jim was never going to let anyone have her but him.

One day he'd tell Jo how much he'd loved her mum, and how he'd had to let her be.

One day he'd tell her about the reports of the accident, where neither of them had been wearing a seatbelt, and Jim had wedged a triangle of wood under the brake pedal so that he couldn't change his mind.

But not today.

64

I don't know how long I'd been sitting there, hunched up on the uncomfortable hard bed in the cell. The policewoman – Lorna – had tried to make me drink water, drink tea, eat a fucking ham sandwich. And she just kept talking . . . talking . . . *yack yack yack*.

I couldn't move. I felt like my muscles had fused into my bones. My flesh was stiff and inflexible, like the horrible plastic piss-cover on the too-thin mattress I was sitting on.

She'd told me about Scott – and the balaclava belonging to Jake. I had no idea what was going on there. Had Jake panicked? Had he really done that to Laura? I tried, but I couldn't make myself believe it.

I sat there and watched Davie Gray torturing himself with the memories of my mother. The silly cow. I knew the rumours about him being my dad were a load of rubbish, but Polly and Claire's goading that day had pushed a button. If only I'd kept my temper in check. Hadn't made Claire go over the pipe that she was so scared of. If only, if only, if only.

*

Gray pushed the memories to the back of his mind. He turned to face Jo once again. This time, he wasn't letting her away with saying nothing.

'What happened, Jo? You need to tell me. The CID lads

316

will be back soon, and they'll want answers. You've a solicitor sitting outside, waiting to help you . . . will you talk to us? Please?' He leant over and placed a hand on Jo's bare foot. It was freezing.

'OK,' she said, 'I'll talk to you.' She uncurled herself and slid off the bed.

As he walked her through to the interview room, he heard a commotion in the reception. Raised voices. Something making a clatter. Chairs being scraped across the floor.

'Jo? Can you hear me? It's me, Claire . . . I'm here. I need to talk to you . . .'

'Please, Claire, you can't see her at the moment, she's—' Lorna's voice cut off by more yelling from Claire. The clattering, apparently her wheelchair, as she tried to manoeuvre too fast along the narrow corridor. Rob's voice trying to calm her down. Lorna's. Craig's. Christ, they were all in there.

Where the hell was Beattie? He couldn't still be at the hospital.

He shoved Jo gently into the interview room and closed the door. The lock clicked into place; it only opened from the outside.

He marched down the corridor and into the fray.

*

When I heard the door snick shut I knew it was locked, and I panicked. I started rattling the door handle, but it wouldn't budge. Funny how I'd been in that cell for hours and hadn't felt scared at all, yet in this small carpeted room with its cheap table and chairs, I felt trapped. Claustrophobic.

I stopped rattling the door. Stepped back, trying to get my breathing to return to normal. Let my heart rate slow back

317

down. I could hear the raised voices coming from the front of the station.

I was still reeling about Jake . . . being Maloney's foster brother, being the other boy in the woods . . . There was so much I needed to hear from him. Why? Why the hunting? Why the girls at the Track?

All I knew for sure was that Jake had been there the whole time.

Manipulating me. Manipulating Claire.

*

'Claire, you need to calm down.' Gray took the handles of her chair and pulled her back into the centre of the room. She was ranting, screaming.

'I need to talk to her,' she shouted, directing her voice down the corridor towards Jo, locked in the interview room. 'Jo, *please* . . . tell me you didn't hurt him?'

'Claire, that's enough.' Craig spun her round to face him. 'You need to calm down, you're going to make yourself sick . . . Claire? Claire?'

Gray pushed Claire out of the way and crouched down until they were at eye level. Claire's face had gone slack, her eyes lolling back into her head. He turned back to Craig, a shocked Rob standing by his side. Lorna was behind the counter, her face drained of colour. 'Call a bloody ambulance,' Gray shouted at her. 'Now!'

At that, the front door swung open and PC Beattie burst into the station, panting with the exertion. 'Sarge, it's Jake. He's awake . . . and he's talking.'

318

65

The air was heavy with the echoes of muffled voices, the rattling metal of squeaky-wheeled trolleys. That familiar smell of antiseptic and over-boiled veg.

I stared at Jake in the bed, hooked up to the beeping monitors, and I remembered Claire. Small and scared, oblivious to the fact that the boy who had come to visit had been partly responsible for her being there.

He must've sensed me, because his eyes opened as I approached the bed.

'Hello,' he croaked.

'Hi . . . How do you feel?'

'Sore. You?'

'Sad.'

He closed his eyes again.

'Do you want me to go?' I said.

'Don't be stupid. It's just the lights in here. Too bright.' He raised a hand, and I took it and squeezed it and he opened his eyes again briefly as he said, 'Ouch.'

'We can't do this any more, Jake,' I said. I sat down on the chair next to his bed. 'It's not fair on Claire.'

'I always thought she knew, Jo. I didn't think we'd hidden it very well . . . the whole *enemies* thing . . .'

I nodded. 'She's no idea. I'm sure of it. She's too trusting. She'd never believe we'd do that to her. Or maybe she's in

319

denial – just like with everything else. She must remember something about what happened in the woods that day.'

'Doesn't matter now anyway,' he said. 'Once the police question me and I have to tell them about the stupid fucking *shit* that I've been up to, I doubt she'll still want me anyway.'

'Oh, so I get to keep you, do I? The booby prize . . .'

He laughed quietly. 'That's not what I meant. Anyway, it's time for a fresh start, I think. Sort myself out. They want me to speak to a shrink in here, find out how messed up I am . . . Any tips?'

I picked up his hand again and nipped the flesh. 'Don't joke. They'll help you. In fact, I think it's about time I spoke to one myself. It's been too long. I don't think my meds are working any more. I haven't been myself lately. What Scott did . . . it threw me. I should never have got involved with the whole Maloney thing . . .'

'Are you being charged?'

I frowned. 'I expect so, although your evidence that it was self-defence will help. I killed him, though. I have to live with that forever, no matter how much of a bastard he was. Not to mention a murderer himself. Anyway, they're keeping a close eye on me. Gray's managed to get me on house arrest at his until I go to court on Monday. He was supposed to be going out for a curry tonight – first time in months, apparently. He's well pissed off that he's got to babysit me.'

'I bet he's delighted, Jo. He's always had a soft spot for you . . .' He paused, waiting for me to respond. When I didn't, he continued: 'Listen, I'm pretty tired now. Do you mind if I go to sleep?'

'Course not, don't be daft.' I leant down and kissed him on the cheek. 'Oh, er . . . Claire says she's coming in to see you tomorrow. Hope that's OK?'

'Jesus . . . Of course it is. I really didn't think she'd want anything to do with me after all this.'

'Must be that charm, eh. What's happening about you and the police, by the way? Are they charging you with assault?'

Jake opened his eyes wide, tried to shake his head, despite the pain. 'I didn't assault anyone, Jo. I told you that. I told them that too, although I don't think they believed me . . .' He paused. A dark shadow seemed to distort his features, just for a moment. Then it was gone. 'Yes, I admit – I frightened those two girls up at the Track,' he continued. 'I got a kick out of it – their scared faces . . . It was like when I used to shoot rabbits and watch their startled eyes . . . When Gareth came back, something snapped inside me. I can't explain it. We used to go hunting together, when we were kids . . . but he was, I don't know. He was weird, Jo. He scared me—'

A thought struck me then. Christ, I'd been so stupid. 'It was you, wasn't it? The other night in the woods. Lurking there. Trying to freak me out. You scared me, Jake. I thought it was Maloney. What was all that about, eh?'

Jake put his hands to his temples, squeezed as if he was trying to crush his own skull. 'I just wanted to know what it was like to be him. I thought . . . I thought when he came back, he'd come to find me. I thought I was still his brother.' He started to cry then, an angry sob. 'I'm just so fucking tired, Jo.'

I leant in and took his hand. 'It's OK, Jake. It's going to be OK. Listen, I've got to go. Feel better soon . . . I'll come and visit again. When I can.'

'Jo, wait . . .'

I turned back. 'What is it, Jake? I have to go . . .'

'Don't you want to know about the masks? The sheep masks? Don't you want to understand?'

I shook my head sadly. 'It doesn't matter now, Jake. It's over.'

He fell back into the pillows and I left him there, staring at the ceiling.

He was the black sheep. Just like me.

Gray was waiting for me outside, an expectant look on his face.

'Well?' he said.

I shook my head. 'He didn't hurt Laura, Davie. I know he didn't. He's a bit of a prick sometimes, but he wouldn't hurt a fly . . .'

Gray frowned. 'Well, if it wasn't him, Jo, then who the hell was it? There's no one else in the frame. He planted that balaclava on Scott . . . There'll be forensics linking him to those shoe prints at the Track, I know it. Who's he trying to protect? Anyway, it's out of my hands now. CID are all over it. They're looking into Jake . . . as well as you. And Maloney, of course. You know they'll be searching Black Wood. Digging the place up . . .'

I shrugged. 'I don't care about any of that. I just don't want Jake getting the blame for attacking Laura. He's damaged, Davie, but he's never hurt me. He's never hurt Claire. Well, not physically anyway. Jesus, me and her have got a lot of talking to do.'

Gray said nothing and I continued babbling. 'Will I go to prison, Davie? For what I did to Maloney? He would've killed me, you know . . . after he'd—'

He cut me off. 'I know, Jo. You don't have to tell me again. Jake's backed up your story too. They'll be able to tell that it was Maloney who fired the gun. What you did to him . . . well, it was bad, Jo. Really bad. But you've got a good solicitor there. We'll do everything we can. In the meantime, though, you're staying with me until your hearing on Monday. I'm hoping you'll get bail, but you know I can't guarantee anything.'

I nodded. 'I appreciate you looking out for me, Davie. I know my mum would've wanted it.'

Gray blinked, and I was sure I saw a tear at the corner of his eye.

'You're spot on about that, Jo. There's so much I need to tell you about your mum. She wasn't bad. You know that, don't you? Your dad had a hold on her from the minute they met. Anyway, like I said . . . not now. Right now, we're going back to mine. Someone needs to look after you . . .'

I opened my mouth to protest and he raised a hand to silence me.

'It's non-negotiable, Jo.'

He turned to leave, and I glanced back at Jake before following him out.

As he walked across the potholed tarmac towards the car, I took my phone out of my pocket. Scrolled through my contacts until I found the one I wanted. Hit *dial*. As I waited for it to connect, I ran a finger across my eyebrow. Felt the tiny bristles of hair that were already pushing their way through the skin.

'Jo? Where are you? Are you OK? Is Jake OK? Did—'

Her voice sounded strained. I could tell she'd had one of her episodes again. She was going to have to see someone about those. I'd make her.

'Get Rob to give you and Craig a lift, Claire. Come round to Davie's. We need to talk. A lot.' I hung up.

I caught Gray's eye as he climbed into his car. He gave me a small, sad smile.

There were things I needed to say to him too.

66

Pete took his time walking home. He was in no rush. He wanted to savour the time on his own. He walked round the side of the house, opened the back gate and tiptoed into the garden. He tried hard not to make a sound. The lights were off, the house bathed in darkness. This meant that his dad was still out, and if he was out on one of his nights out where he drank too many whiskies, he wouldn't be back until late. This was good for Pete, because even though his dad never came down to the shed, he was worried about having the light on tonight.

Because tonight was a special night.

Pete closed the gate quietly, stopping briefly to listen for sounds coming from the neighbours' gardens, or anyone out at the Track. He knew that people had been avoiding it at night, since the thing that happened to the girls.

He knew he'd been good. He'd done the right thing, taking the masks down to the police station. He had to punish Jake, for shouting at him and not acting like his friend.

Because Jake *was* his friend. They'd met three hundred and twenty-three days ago – all thanks to his dad. Sometimes his dad *did* do nice things. It made up for all the times he just shouted and screamed and told him he was a useless *excuse* for a son. Pete didn't really understand why he would be an excuse for son. He *was* a son. Sometimes his dad said things that didn't make sense.

Pete had gone to a school in Edinburgh that was full of kids who didn't get on very well at the usual schools, like the one in Banktoun. Some of the kids were in wheelchairs, or they spoke in funny strangled voices, or some were just like Pete – which was normal, but *not normal* (as his mum used to say, before she gave him a big squeezy hug). He'd never really understood what that meant either.

When he left school, Pete told his dad he wanted to be a bus conductor so that he could check the tickets and because he knew all the bus routes in the whole of Scotland off by heart. His dad had laughed at this and told him that buses didn't even have conductors any more, but that didn't make sense because then who checked that people had the right tickets and knew where to go?

Anyway, his dad had got him an even better job than being a bus conductor, and because of that he got to do loads of really cool things – *and* he got to meet Jake, who was his best friend in the whole world.

One time he'd thought that Anne was his best friend, but he realised he'd made a mistake with that. Because she was his dad's friend, wasn't she? His special friend. He'd seen them together that night. Heard them laughing together, although Anne's laugh had sounded funny and not the usual one she did when she was with him, and she'd been saying, 'Don't be daft, Martin, you know I don't want this . . .' and Pete didn't understand what it was that she didn't want. That was why he had followed her.

He followed her to the park. He wanted to know what she didn't want, and he wanted her to be his special friend. Not his dad's! His dad had loads of friends. Anne was supposed to be his! So he had grabbed her and cuddled her, but she hadn't liked it and she'd run away from him and she fell, and that was when he got a bit scared and ran back home.

He never told anyone what had happened.

That was in their old house, though, when they lived near the park. He was sad that Anne had never come round to look after him in the new house. He'd asked his mum about it and she'd told him he didn't need a babysitter any more, and she was right because after that his mum and his dad never went out at the same time, and then not long after that his mum had got ill and then she had died. He missed her. He missed Anne too. He was just glad he was still allowed to go and see her in the shop.

He'd loved going to his job. He still didn't know why his dad had told him he wasn't allowed to go any more, since that day the policeman had come to the house.

He remembered the day he started. He replayed it over and over in his mind, like watching a really good film like *Star Wars* or *The Empire Strikes Back*.

When the car pulled up outside the gates, Pete had started to feel all sick in his stomach. It had started at home in the morning. A strange squirmy feeling like wriggling worms.

'I don't think I can go in, Dad, I'm not feeling well. I'm scared I might be sick . . .'

Being sick scared him. He remembered the horrible scratchy pain in his throat from after it happened one time when his dad had made him eat prawns for dinner. He hadn't wanted the prawns because they were pink, but his dad said that when they were in the tomato sauce they'd be red and that they'd look just like baked beans . . . and they sort of did, but they'd tasted really different from baked beans and just before he went to bed that night he started to feel dizzy like the room was spinning round and round and then he was sick. He'd been so scared of the sick when it came out, yellow and hot, and his dad had promised him he wouldn't ever have to eat prawns again, so Pete thought that meant he wouldn't be sick again. But he'd felt sick again, sitting in the passenger seat of the car outside the gates to his new job at the big yellow factory where they made lawnmowers and things for all the farms, like baling machines and even tractors. Or so his dad said.

'Don't be daft, Petey – it's just butterflies . . . You'll be fine when you get in there. Think about all the things you'll be able to do . . . You know they have to count out hundreds of nuts and bolts and all sorts of stuff like that to make those machines? I've got you a job as the chief counter – they'll all be coming to you for the bits they need. Give it a go, eh, son?'

Pete had been confused about the butterflies. He hadn't eaten any butterflies, so he knew it wasn't that making him feel sick, but before he could think any more about it a man had come out and knocked on the car window, making him jump right out of his seat.

His dad had pressed the button and the window slid down inside the door and he spoke to the man and said, 'Ah, Jake, here's your man. Can I trust you to show him the ropes?'

The man called Jake had leant into the car. He smelled like soap and the oil from car engines. His breath warm with the fresh smell of cigarettes. He wore a green overall that looked a bit like he was in the army, and Pete suddenly felt the sickness go away and he knew – he just knew – that this was going to be OK.

Pete climbed out of the car, taking his bag with his cheese sandwiches and his can of cola and his plain crisps and followed the man to the factory. When they went inside, Pete had felt wobbly with the sounds of screeching metal and the

328

hot air that smelled of fire. He'd tried to back out, but the man called Jake had taken him by the elbow and leant down and spoken into his ear and said, 'Don't you worry, Pete – I'll look after you now.'

And Pete had smiled and said back, 'Where are the ropes?'

'What ropes?'

'My dad asked you to show me the ropes. Can I see them?'

Jake laughed and shook his head. 'Let's get you some over-alls first, eh? Then I'll show you the ropes.'

'Promise?'

'I promise.'

But Jake had broken that promise. He had never, ever on any days he'd been there, shown him any ropes.

And he'd broken his promise again tonight, because he said he was coming to see him and that they would work on the Collection and that everything was going to be OK.

Pete stepped into the shed and flicked on the light. Everything was just as he'd left it. The shelves along the back wall were filled with neat little cardboard boxes, tied with string. Each one was labelled with what was inside.

Rabbit. Vole. Sparrow. Mouse. Rat. Badger.

(These ones were the big boxes for the whole animals.)

Fox tails. Rabbit feet. Claws (assorted). Small bird heads.

(These were for multiple animal parts.)

Each box was dated, and the approximate location marked, like Jake's favourite one: *Badger, Black Wood, April 1988.*

Pete lifted the badger box down and untied the string. The animal inside was just bones now. Pete and Jake had cleaned it carefully, pulling off the last of the rotted flesh and fur, wiping the bones with bleach until they shone. Then they'd rearranged them back so it looked almost like it was joined together again.

Jake had told Pete that he was 'very honoured' that he was to be the 'custodian' of the Collection. He said he'd been looking for a good place for it for years and years, and as soon as he'd seen Pete, he knew that he was the best man for the job. Jake told him that a custodian was a very, very important person and that they could only do the job if they didn't tell anyone else about the job ever, ever. Not even his dad.

Pete put the badger back in the box and placed it back on the shelf. He looked at his watch – a big square-faced one with chunky numbers that his dad had got him for his six-teenth birthday – and wondered again where Jake was. He was scared that he wasn't going to come, even though he had promised.

Jake had been really angry after Pete had tried to play the Game with the girl in the town. He didn't even care that she had cut Pete's face when she'd hit him as she'd struggled to escape. Jake's face had been bright red when he'd shouted at him, saying, 'What have you done? What have you done?' and then Pete had felt a bit sad that Jake shouted at him so he had tried to get him in trouble – just a little bit – so he took the masks to the police station and pretended that he'd seen someone drop them at the cut-through. He wanted Jake to get in trouble now, just for a little while. So he might know what it was like when someone was bright red and shouting in your face and making you feel horrible and sad.

Jake should've been happy! Pete had done it as a surprise for Jake – he wanted to show him that *he* could play the Game, not just watch it. Jake had been really, really happy

330

when Pete had watched him play the Game with the two girls at the Track – when he watched it all on the telescope. Jake said that maybe next time they could record it on a video, so it would be like a film and they could watch it over and over again.

Together, like best friends do.

Jake had never told him that he couldn't play the Game too.

Pete knew that he would have to tell someone about the Game one day. He wouldn't be able to keep it a secret forever. It would spin around his head until it finally burst out.

Maybe he'd tell Anne about it, next time he was in the shop. Or maybe that policeman, because he'd been nice to him when he went to the station and hadn't shouted at him or shaken him like his dad did.

Not tonight, though.

He smiled as he looked over the Collection one last time, then he turned off the light and closed the door of the shed.

THE WOODS

The field is longer than he thought, and by the time he and the other boy have made it out of the woods, the girls are blurred spots in the distance.

He starts to run.

His heart is hammering in his chest. He didn't plan this. Doesn't know how it's going to end. He knows that the other boy is following at a distance, knows he doesn't want to get involved.

That's OK.

This works better as a one-on-one. He has no interest in the plump, snivelling little girl in the dungarees.

The girls are sticking to the edge of the field, where there is a well-trodden path of hard-packed mud. People walk their dogs down this way. There is a stile at the end of the field that takes you out onto the main road. He assumes that's where the girls are headed. On their left is a barbed-wire fence that holds in the small trees and bracken that line the burn.

The girls stop.

He slows down and listens to the gentle burbling of the water as it mixes in with the ragged sounds of his breath.

He is right behind them.

'Oi,' he says, directing it at the girl in the red skirt. 'Where d'you think you're going?'

She whirls round and, for the first time, he can see panic in her big brown eyes.

332

The other girl is whimpering like an injured puppy.

'I've got a knife,' he says. His hand is in his pocket. He's holding onto nothing, but they don't know that.

'*Please*,' she says. 'We'll go away.'

He considers this.

Behind him, he hears the footsteps and ragged breaths of the other boy as he struggles to catch up. 'Just leave it . . .' he shouts.

He frowns. Ignores him. Addresses the girls again.

'OK. I'm going to let you away. This time. But you'd better go away. And you'd better not come back. Or else . . .' His threat trails off into the ether.

He watches as the girl in the red skirt prises apart two strands of the barbed wire to let her friend crawl through. They're not walking to the end of the field. They're going to cross the burn. Here? There's nowhere to cross here. They'll get wet. They'll get a telling-off when they get home.

They're gone.

Stuck on a knot of barbed wire, fluttering softly in the breeze, is a little ragged square of fabric, from a torn red skirt.

He can hear their voices drifting up from the burn. They're arguing. The little girl won't walk across. He walks over to the fence and hunkers down near the section where they squeezed through.

He can see them through a gap in the bushes.

The little girl is standing on a flat rock in the centre of the burn. The water is almost up to the top of her wellingtons, but another big step and she'll be across on the other bank. She won't get wet.

'Oh *come on*!' The taller girl's voice is exasperated, pleading. 'Just take a step. You don't even have to jump! I'm the one who's going to get soaked here.'

'I can't!' the little girl shouts back at her. Her voice is thick with snot and fear. 'I'll fall in!'

The other girl shakes her head. 'I'll catch you. OK? Just take a bloody step . . .'

The little girl starts crying again. Big, angry sobs. 'Stop shouting at me. This is all your fault. I told you I didn't want to go in the woods. I *told* you I just wanted to go home . . . I—'

He's sick of her whining. He picks up a stone, raises his hand. But before he can let go, a rock breaks free from the packed mud at the edge of the field, tumbles from the bank, splashes into the water below.

The girl in the red skirt sees the rock hurtling towards them both and she jumps back, her foot sinking into the burn. She stumbles, rights herself. She screams, 'Bloody hell, this is all *your* fault!'

She shoves the other girl.

Hard.

The little girl slips backwards on the flat rock and lands awkwardly and her voice is cut off by the sound of a splash, a sickening *crack*.

Then there is nothing but the sound of the water burbling round the rocks.

He slaps a hand over his mouth, stifling a gasp, but it's too late.

She turns to face him, squints up at him, and he realises that he is still holding his hand high, the stone gripped tight in his fist.

He pulls back.

But he's already seen the flowering puffs of red swirling in the water around her feet. The little girl lies flat out on the rock. She's not moving.

She turns away, and he watches as she slowly looks up and down the path to see if anyone else has heard, or seen.

He hears heavy breaths behind him, turns around. The other boy is there.

'Your mask,' he whispers.

The boy leans towards him and pulls on the elastic strap. He must've snagged it on the barbed wire, exposing his face. Did she see his face? Doesn't matter now. He lets the boy adjust his mask. Stares into his glistening eyes. They communicate without words.

What have we done?

Nothing. We weren't here.

They edge backwards.

An ear-splitting scream.

'Help! Someone . . . please. Help! It's my friend . . . she's hurt . . .'

The boy clenches his entire body, sucks in a deep breath. Feels that prickle. Pushes away his excitement as he slowly exhales.

Not now, he thinks . . . *later*.

He grabs the other boy's arm and they run off down the side of the field, out onto the main road. Hearts thumping. Chests bursting. Panting.

We need to get away . . .

Away from the thing that he wants.

The red-skirted devil.

ACKNOWLEDGEMENTS

Thank you RJ Barker. I meant it when I said I would never have got anywhere with this book if you hadn't read those opening chapters and told me it was worth finishing. Thank you Eva Dolan, Fergus McNeill and Luca Veste for the early feedback that turned the book into what it became, and an extra thank you to Luca for introducing me to the best agent in the world, Phil Patterson, who believed in me from the start. Thanks to all at Marjacq, who I am proud to be represented by, and to Keshini Naidoo, whose fresh pair of eyes helped me push it over the line. Thank you to everyone at Black and White Publishing for showing such enthusiasm for this book from the start: Campbell for signing my very first author contract, Janne for keeping me on track with *everything*, Ali for the fantastic cover, Laura for the great publicity planning and to Karyn, my fantastic editor, whose insight helped me polish this book to a shine – thank you for making my first experience of being edited so painless.

I've met so many readers, writers and bloggers via social media and various crime-writing festivals and events, many of whom have gone on to become friends in real life and without whom I couldn't imagine continuing this journey: thank you, all of you. And a special thanks to Lisa Gray for my first newspaper feature and for lending her surname to my much loved Sergeant.

To my husband and self-appointed manager, JLOH, thank you for riding the never-ending rollercoaster of book publishing with me, for keeping me in tea and toast, and for the enthusiastic distribution of my business cards. If there's *anyone* in the UK who hasn't received one, I want to know why. And finally, to my family, and to all of my friends, old and new – thank you for supporting me through this madness, for always believing in me: I love you all.

Other fiction titles from Black & White Publishing

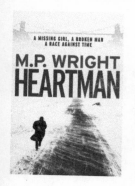

Heartman
M.P Wright
RRP £7.99 – 978 1 84502 775 9
Also available in ebook

Bristol, 1965. In the dead of winter, a young deaf and dumb woman goes missing without a trace. But the police just don't care about a West Indian immigrant who is nowhere to be found.

Enter Joseph Tremaine 'JT' Ellington: a Barbadian ex-cop not long off the boat, a man with a tragic past and a broken heart. When local mogul Earl Linney hires him to track down the missing girl, JT soon finds himself adrift in a murky world of prostitution and kidnapping where each clue reveals yet more mysteries. What is Linney's connection to the girl? Have more women gone missing? And what exactly is the Erotica Negro Club?

Facing hostility and prejudice as well as the demons he left home to escape, JT must unravel a deadly conspiracy in a dangerous and unfamiliar world.

Heartman is an atmospheric, confident debut: Devil in a Blue Dress meets Chinatown set in the rough world of Bristol nightlife, in the pubs, shebeens and nightclubs that are the haunts of prostitutes and criminals.

www.blackandwhitepublishing.com